Taming His Wicked Duchess

SADIE BOSQUE

To my mother, who loved telling me and my sister the detailed, graphic stories about her giving birth to us. She scared the hell out of me. So now I am scarred for life and you get to read about it.

Contents

Acknowledgement

My dear beta reader, Nicole Yost,

Thank you for spending your precious vacation time reading my novel, then rereading it and reading it again. Without your input, the book would be a total mess.

My dear friends, Fenna Edgewood and Cara Maxwell,

Thank you for lifting my spirits when I thought my book was a complete mess—and let's be honest, it was. But you made it manageable.

And my dear friend and editor, Tracy Liebchen,

You make my book readable. And without you, I would never meet a single deadline. That's just a fact.

Author's note

This work of fiction contains adult content, strong language, violence, death, bullying, pregnancy, child birth and other content that might be triggering to some.

Chapter 1

December 1741

D ane ran panting into the winding, narrow alley. Sweat trickled down his forehead, his clothes clung to his body, and his cuts stung. His left knee radiated sharp pain, and he was certain his shoulder was dislocated, but he couldn't afford to stop. He had to keep running.

This was not how he imagined his evening ending. Not even close.

He was supposed to be at Lord Norfolk's musicale, drinking wine and having boring, trifling conversations, while listening to Norfolk's young sisters perform.

At the time, it seemed like torture. Now? He would rather be bored.

The alley narrowed even further, and he had to twist sideways to fit through. A few more steps and he'd be out.

Perhaps he could summon his trusty mount, Midnight, and gallop away into the misty night toward freedom.

The moment Dane poked his head out, he reared back. No, not freedom. Everywhere he looked, redcoats—the King's personal militia—were scouring the area, spread out, looking for him. *Damn.*

He was definitely not going to make it to the end of the musicale. He had left his wife sitting and whispering with her friends, without even saying a word.

Normally, his wife wouldn't have noticed his absence, he was certain. They had a deal, after all. They arrived at social functions together and then went their separate ways. Except, at the end of the night, they were always supposed to leave together. And if he failed to return by the end of the musicale, he was certain there would be hell to pay.

He looked down at his torn, dirty, bloody clothing. He could not show up anywhere in his Shadows uniform and especially, not in a state like this.

His evening attire waited for him under the seat of his carriage that still stood by Lord Norfolk's townhouse, but in order to change into it, he'd need to soak in a bath for an hour or two, not to mention bandaging his injuries.

He turned back and tiptoed his way into an adjoining alley. He needed to think.

There was no way he was trapped. He knew these streets like the back of his hand. But so did his pursuers. And there were more of them.

He had been following a group of bandits who were operating slave ships for quite some time now. Bandits, who had mistakenly abducted the Earl of Payne, thinking that he was one of the Shadows. In doing so, they had declared war between themselves and the Shadows.

Recently, Dane found out that one of the men behind the abduction was part of an elite secret Society, the Brotherhood of the Crimson Fist.

Ever since finding this out, he had been looking for a connection between the Brotherhood and these thugs and was hoping to uncover the leaders behind these atrocious groups.

So when he had received a note from his trusted source that the bandits had arranged a meeting with one of the Brotherhood's members by the docks, he immediately ran to follow them.

He planned to gather the information and maybe follow them back to their leader. Where had it all gone wrong?

He wiped his forehead with his sleeve and continued down another path. The voices sounded fainter. Perhaps he had finally left them behind. He couldn't be certain, though. So he didn't slow his steps.

It wasn't the time to lower his guard. It was never the time to lower his guard.

Out on the streets, he was vulnerable. What he needed to do was hide out somewhere until dawn. Dane knew the area and recalled an old, abandoned factory nearby. If he could just get there, he'd be able to find shelter for the night. In the light of dawn, perhaps he would manage to escape.

He poked his head out of another alley.

No. Not safe either. The bandits were out there, laughing loudly, their daggers bared. No doubt in anticipation of catching him.

He looked around the dirty alley, then reached his hand out and groped at the wall. It was made of bricks. *Scalable.* He tried to hook the toe of his boot on the brick. *Yes!* He could definitely scale this wall. He tried to raise his right hand and flinched. Perhaps not with a dislocated shoulder. But what choice did he really have?

He looked down at the scroll peeking out from his leather satchel tied to his waist.

In hindsight, *this* was when things went wrong.

Everything was going fine and according to plan, until the thug Dane had been following was handed a scroll—the scroll that, according to another man, contained all the names of people on the Brotherhood's roster.

That's when Dane became too eager. The thought of bringing down the criminal society like this had him too excited. He had waited for the bandits to part ways, but in his haste, he hadn't noticed that the man with the scroll was being watched.

He should have known this sounded too good to be true.

It was a setup.

The moment he showed himself, three more thugs jumped out, accosting him, and when he ran, he got surrounded by King's men. It was a miracle he even managed to slip away, and with the scroll, no less!

So, here he was, in a dirty alley, with a dislocated shoulder, wounded knee, and a scroll peeking out of his leather satchel about to scale the wall up to the roof.

Well, if he was going to survive, he needed another miracle or two.

Dane shook the thought from his head. He untied the leather satchel from his waist, brought it to his lips, and bit on the strap. He didn't want to lose the satchel halfway up, nor risk discovery with an involuntary scream of pain. A satchel between his teeth would prevent both. The bitter taste of leather touched his tongue, and he grimaced. He would have to endure it, nonetheless. With his right arm close to his body, he raised his left arm, gripped one of the bricks with his fingers, and started scaling the wall.

His feet rested comfortably on the footholds, easily supporting his weight, although his knee burned. His left arm was strong enough to lift him, even if his right arm was useless in his endeavor. He crushed his body closer to the wall, gritted his teeth, and ground them against the leather strap.

No, he wouldn't scream, and he wouldn't fall.

Right foot up, left foot, then up went the arm. With his body pressed against the wall, he reached for a stone above his head and then straightened. Right foot up, left one, then up he went again, repeating the motions. So far, so good.

Dane ground his teeth deeper into the strap of the satchel as he made his final leap onto the roof of the building. He bore his weight on his left arm and plopped torso-first onto the roof. His legs followed.

He rolled onto the roof and then straightened and dusted his clothing. Taking the satchel into his hand, he looked around.

Here, on the roof, it was safer. His pursuers rarely looked up.

Still, he crouched as he made his way toward the abandoned mill, jumping from roof to roof. He reached the factory in a few minutes without being discovered.

It was slightly taller than the building Dane was currently on, and the gap between the buildings was wider than he was used to.

Damn it.

Dane approached the end of the building farthest from the

factory to create momentum for his jump.

If I die, I suppose this is as good a place as any.

Dane ran with all his might before pushing off with his feet and jumping as high and far as he could. He hit the roof of the factory and rolled a few times as the momentum carried him farther.

Dane finally plopped onto the roof, lying on his back, watching the dark sky.

His left hand immediately went to cradle his right shoulder, and he bit his lower lip to keep himself from screaming. The pain was terrible.

At least I am still alive.

But he was in for a good deal of agony on the morrow. Once the thrill of the chase wore off and he was back in his bed, he would feel the entire might of this night's injuries. And that's before the confrontation with his wife, who was certain to berate him for leaving her alone at dinner.

He grimaced and spat onto the roof. "I should have stayed at the bloody musicale."

Dane sat up with a groan and looked out onto the street. Everything seemed quiet, except for the light wind carrying the leaves and litter. However, quiet didn't mean that it was safe to leave. People were still out there, searching for him.

Dane crouched on top of the roof as he looked for the trapdoor he knew was there. It was difficult to see in the dark, and to make matters worse, droplets of mild rain started drumming against his head and shoulders.

Great. All he needed was to get soaked and die of pneumonia. As if his troubles weren't dire enough.

Aha! The trapdoor!

Dane unlocked the door and slowly made his way down. At

least he'd be sheltered from the rain.

He landed on the floor with a loud oomph. His feet hitting the floor made a hollow sound, and the disturbed air surrounded him with a circle of dry dust. Dane coughed into his sleeve.

The factory looked empty. He could definitely hide here until dawn. Then he would be likely to make it home without being followed, although not unnoticed.

Or he could call for Midnight. He'd left her not far from the factory. Close enough that she might hear his call and take him away from this ghastly place.

Unless the thugs got to her first.

Dane's heart constricted from the painful thought. No, Midnight was a clever girl. She wouldn't give up without a fight. But staying all night at this place was no longer an option. He needed to get to his mare.

Dane slowly made his way toward the exit. He stepped into a large hallway and froze in place. Something was wrong. It seemed like the air itself stilled, unmoving, waiting for something to happen. He felt as though someone was watching him. A feeling that he'd had for the past few weeks every time he went outside, maybe months.

Dane suddenly understood how the stags might feel when they heard the rustle in the leaves and their ears perked up, their hair standing on end in anticipation of the attack. Now he was the one being hunted.

Dane looked around the sparse room. It was empty save for the rubble lying on the floor and half a dozen columns propping up the ceiling. The columns were wide enough to hide a full-grown man. Which meant there were half a dozen places an enemy could have hidden. That, plus the dark corners of the vast room, left Dane feeling completely unprotected.

Who would have hidden in a place like this? Did they anticipate his arrival or did they follow him on the ground as he was leaping from roof to roof?

Dane reached for his baldric, more out of habit than out of practicality, because he knew there was nothing there. He'd lost his sword and dagger a few miles from here. He had one more dagger in his boot, but at the moment, he was reluctant to crouch before the unseen enemy.

So he did the only thing he could do and took a few steps forward. Let the enemy think he didn't anticipate an attack. Let the enemy show themselves first.

He'd passed one column when a movement caught his eye from the left. He turned and ducked just in time before the blow could reach his face.

He deflected one heavy blow after another from the tall and broad assailant, at least a head taller than himself, and at least a few stones heavier. Dane's strength was depleted, his muscles ached, and his bones hurt but the attacker kept pounding on.

This is it. This is the end. The dark thoughts crossed his mind unwelcome.

"What do you want from me?" Dane gritted as the assailant thrust him against the column, his forearm on his throat.

"From you? Nofin!" The man laughed loudly, his voice booming in the empty building. "But your head will get me a nice sum from the king."

"The king?" Dane croaked. There was a buzzing in his ears and clouding in his eyes.

The attacker sounded far away when he spoke next. "Two

8

thousand pounds for a traitor's head."

Traitor?

The word had no meaning. Dane's strength had left him and the thoughts were making no sense to him when something glinted in the dark.

Then a force propelled Dane's attacker against him before letting go.

What the devil?

The thug was suddenly on the floor, rolling around with something dark, akin to a demon or a shadow.

A shadow?

Dane's eyes lit up with relief. Not just a shadow.

One of the Shadows!

The Shadow had disengaged from the thug at that moment and jumped up onto his feet. He threw a glance toward Dane as if to make certain he was still alive.

Well, he was. Although he was frozen in shock and in relief.

A fellow Shadow!

Who would have thought anyone would be out tonight? The Shadows were under distinct orders from their unseen leader, Erebus, to stay inactive. And although Dane had understood the precautions before, now he realized the severity of Erebus's orders.

There was a price on Shadows' heads from the king!

And yet, someone else was out there besides him. Someone else had disobeyed the orders and was now fighting to save him.

The Shadow and the thug were locked in a deathly fight a few feet away. Dane didn't want to intervene. Not yet. He needed to gather his strength and only attack once he had a perfect chance. He didn't want to interfere prematurely and cause more harm than good.

Besides, the Shadow was fighting skillfully and lithely. He was shorter than Dane and more agile.

Was it St. John? He fit the general build of the Shadow, and he was a few years younger than Dane, thus more light-footed. And if that was him indeed, then Dane didn't mind leaving the fight to him. That man owed Dane a favor or two. Not that St. John knew.

The thug threw the Shadow against the column and went in to strangle him, much like he'd done with Dane moments before. Only the Shadow was quicker, and he slipped away from the thug's grip at the last moment, sliding to the floor.

The moment the thug turned, Dane pounced on him with a punch to the face. Blood streamed out of the thug's nose as he gagged helplessly. He raised his hand to cover his bleeding nose, only to realize he was still holding on to something.

Dane squinted at the object in the thug's hands. He was holding the Shadow's mask!

Dane punched the thug again, and as he slid down the column, his eyes glassy, Dane turned sharply and met the Shadow's eyes. The mask was off, and the handkerchief was pulled down, tucked under his chin.

No… not his. *Hers.*

Dane's eyes widened in recognition and shock. The Shadow was not St. John at all. He wasn't even a man.

She was a lady!

And not just any lady. A lady Dane knew. A lady he'd wed. *His wife.*

Five months earlier...

"For the first time, please welcome, His Grace the Duke of Kensington and Her Grace the Duchess of Kensington to the dancefloor," the majordomo's voice boomed around the silent ballroom.

Lady Caroline—now the Duchess of Kensington—placed her dainty hand in the crook of Dane's arm as they descended the staircase and onto the ballroom floor. She didn't press her hand against his arm; she didn't lean on him. Her fingers floated just above the fabric of his jacket as if a mere touch would taint her.

They reached the center of the dancefloor and turned to face each other. He performed a deep bow, and she a graceful curtsy. Then the music started playing, and they were swept up by the rhythm of a dance.

Her eyes were cold, glassy even, as she stared at some point beyond his shoulder, not meeting his gaze. But Dane's attention was consumed by his duchess. For the first time since their betrothal, hell, for the first time *ever*, he was

11

determined to learn her features.

She was his duchess.

No matter how conniving, lying, and scheming of a lady she was, from this point on, she was his.

"It's impolite to stare, rather brazenly, as you're doing now," she said without ever meeting his gaze.

"Is it polite to speak without looking at one's partner?" Dane raised his brow.

She finally turned toward him. "As a gentleman, it is your duty to start the conversation. Before the conversation has been initiated, a lady should not look at the gentleman."

"Ah, so the first faux pas was yours. You initiated the conversation," he noted.

"You stared," she countered.

"You are my wife now," Dane said, narrowing his gaze. The word 'wife' exited his mouth with a foul kind of distaste in his voice, and she'd heard it. "I can do whatever the hell I want."

"Swearing in front of a lady—"

"Is what? Impolite?" Dane bit out.

"So is interrupting her."

She was as cold as marble, and her facial features hadn't moved this entire time. What had Dane gotten himself into? Truthfully, many people thought him cold and unfeeling. But many people also believed theirs to be the perfect match.

And perhaps it was.

"I have a few stipulations regarding our marriage," she spoke again.

"You are not in any position to make stipulations."

"Yes, I am. As your duchess, I can make your life quite miserable if I want to."

Dane raised his brow. First, her uncle blackmailed him into

marrying her. Now she was blackmailing him? He shouldn't have been surprised.

"Please, I'd like to hear your terms," Dane said with a smirk. "Not that I plan to agree to any of them. As your husband, I can make your life quite miserable too. Perhaps more miserable than you can."

She instantly stiffened, her entire body tensed as if prepared for flight. Then she smiled and twirled, just as the dance dictated.

"First, there will be no heirs. You are not to enter my bedchamber under any circumstances. Ever."

Dane threw his head back and laughed. The crowd probably thought they were having nice, newlywed banter. However, these words did seem sweet to his ears coming from her. He didn't want to bed her, just as he hadn't wanted to marry her in the first place. "I wouldn't touch you even if you begged me," he said.

Surprise showed in her eyes, and then something akin to confusion. Did she think herself so desirable? True, many considered her quite the beauty, with her dark mahogany locks, milky white skin, plump, cherry red lips, and willowy figure—

Dane grimaced in disgust. Not him. He never had a problem filling his bed, and he wouldn't have that problem now that he was married. As for his title, it was secure with his two young half-brothers.

"Second," the duchess continued once she caught her breath, "I don't want any rumors about our estrangement."

Ah, so she wanted him to keep quiet about his mistresses. He could arrange that… or he could humiliate her.

"On one condition," he said.

13

She blinked at him. Again, as if she did not anticipate his reaction. "Yes?"

"You shall be the perfect duchess, looking out for my servants, running the household, orchestrating the balls and soirees. Everything to a tiny little detail. And if I find something lacking, I shall renege on our deal."

She lifted her chin. "Fine. But you agree that we are to present a unified front, yes? We arrive at the social functions together and we leave together."

"Next thing you will be telling me to dance with you at every function."

She stiffened again. "That will not be necessary. In fact, I would prefer it if we didn't dance at all."

"You set many rules for someone so eager to marry me."

She raised her head, her eyes blazing with fire. Finally. He was afraid she wasn't capable of passionate emotions. Although he didn't know why he cared. "I never wanted to marry you," she said and stepped away from him as the dance came to a stop. "I just didn't want anyone else to do it, either."

Chapter 2

Caroline stared at the person before her. He was dressed in the Shadows' attire, although it was ripped and bloody in places. The handkerchief was still tied around his mouth and nose; the mask was still in place, although it was askew. But Caroline knew that it was Kensington.

Her husband.

After all, she had followed him out here. Just like she had followed him every night since they returned to London.

Usually, he was too elusive, and she had always lost him halfway through the night. Tonight, she had feared that she'd lost him, too. But then all hell broke loose, and the hunt for her husband had begun, leading her right to him.

But why? What was he doing here? What had he done to deserve the pursuers' wrath? There weren't just common bandits after him, either. Redcoats were sweeping the streets, and if she wasn't mistaken, this thug, lying unconscious at his feet, was not a common criminal. He was one of

Hades' men—the man who struck fear into the hearts of all of London.

If anybody could anger all these different groups at the same time, she was not surprised it was her husband.

After all, she did suspect him to be the criminal mastermind audacious enough to blackmail the peers and peeresses of the realm for God knew what personal gain. And at the same time, he wore the uniform of the secret society sworn to protect the common folk.

No wonder everybody was out for his blood.

Yet here he was, standing before her, bloody, swaying weakly. At her mercy.

But he had caught her, too. Or rather, he had caught her first. Even now, he was looking at her unmasked face in utter disbelief.

"Duchess?" he croaked. Then his eyes glazed over and he fell, helpless, to the ground.

Caroline blinked, stunned for a moment, uncertain of what had just transpired. Then she carefully walked toward him, fully aware that this could be one of his ploys. To do what?

He was too weak to fight her fairly. If she came closer, he could attack her and suffocate her with his weight. Nevertheless, she needed to be sure whether this was a trick. She slowly crouched before him and placed her fingers on his throat.

His skin was warm to the touch, although lined with sweat. His pulse beat steadily against her fingers, but he didn't react to her touch at all.

He was unconscious but alive.

Bastard.

For a moment, Caroline contemplated leaving him there.

Someone would find him eventually. Be it the thugs, the redcoats, or the thief-takers. Lying here, injured, covered with blood, wearing the Shadows' attire, he was doomed. And this was what she wanted, wasn't it? For him to answer for his sins.

She grimaced. No, she couldn't leave him here just as much as she couldn't kill him.

Although it would've been easy.

Nobody would know it was her. There were dozens of thugs outside, and nobody knew that Caroline was even there. In one split second, she could become a widow. She could be free of the shackles of her captor, and she could avenge her uncle's death.

But even in a moment of rage, calm and collected reason nagged at the back of her mind.

You need more proof, Caroline. You need to find it and then you can hang him with it.

Caroline squared her jaw, her fingers curling tightly into fists. Her gaze fell to his side. A satchel hung from his shoulder. He still clutched it between his fingers. Could it be something of worth?

She carefully lifted it away from him, then tied it to her baldric. Taking a deep breath, she slowly reached out and took the mask and handkerchief off Kensington's face.

She let out a breath as she uncovered her husband's features. For, of course, she was right. It was him.

His mouth, usually pressed into a thin line, was now relaxed. His lips were full, almost as if he were pouting. His thick, dark lashes threw shadows on his cheeks. He looked calm, almost innocent.

But he wasn't innocent, was he? That was the entire reason

they were here.

Caroline forced herself to feel hatred for this man. He was the reason her uncle was dead—her poor uncle, who had loved her and cared for her his entire life, had been blackmailed and threatened by this beast until he descended into madness and finally took his own life.

He'd forced her into an unwanted marriage for God only knew what reason.

He was the reason for all her troubles.

But for some reason, Caroline could not summon enough loathing for him. She felt curiously empty.

No. She would not be able to kill a man in cold blood. No matter who he was. No matter if it promised revenge and would let her out of the cold, calculated marriage he'd trapped her in. But neither could she leave him to the thugs outside or the thief-takers.

Whatever they'd do to him, it would not be justice enough.

No. She would be the one doling out justice.

She patted his body, noting that he was bleeding from a few different places. How badly was he hurt?

What caused him to collapse?

She bent over him, took him by his waist, and turned him to the side, hoping that would make it easier to throw his arm over her shoulders and lift him up. He was a heavy fellow. She had trouble keeping him on his side, much less hoisting him over her shoulder.

"I am cutting out bread from your diet from now on, Kensington," she muttered as she hauled him into a sitting position. She had to dig in her heels and push with her leg muscles to keep him upright. "And potatoes."

Caroline wasn't small, by any means. For a lady, one might

even call her tall. She was also fit. She had been training since she was in leading strings, so she'd never considered herself to be weak. But dragging her husband's huge body was no simple task.

"You're too heavy," she continued her one-sided conversation with an unconscious man. "That's why that thug overpowered you and not me. It makes you slow."

She took his right arm and moved it up in an attempt to throw it over her shoulders, only for him to groan and move, fighting her off him.

Caroline jumped away from him as he caught his shoulder in a tight grip and growled in agony.

"If we get caught, it'll be your fault," she told him angrily, although she wasn't certain he'd heard her over his groans.

"My shoulder is dislocated," he gritted between his teeth.

Caroline stifled a smile. He was in a great deal of pain then. *Good*.

He propped himself on his left arm and threw her a glance under his furrowed brows. "What the devil has just happened? And why are you wearing… that?"

That was what bothered him? Caroline raised a brow. "Why are you?"

He puffed a frustrated breath and tipped his head toward his shoulder. "Help me, would you?"

Caroline blinked, surprised at his reaction. Instead of being angry at her and demanding an explanation, he just… asked for her help. She carefully walked toward him. This could all be an act.

"I assume you know what to do," he said, watching her carefully.

Caroline didn't answer. She grabbed his meaty, enormous

shoulder with her hands, which looked dainty on his body, pressed her knee against his other shoulder, and pulled hard.

Kensington roared before falling back, left hand on his injured shoulder.

Perhaps that was why the thug had managed to best him in their confrontation. He was in pain.

"Get up. We need to leave," she said as she righted her clothing.

He nodded and rolled onto his side. "Help me up," he growled after one unsuccessful attempt to sit up.

"Why would I do that?" she asked with furrowed brows, stepping away suspiciously.

"I need to get you out of here," he gritted. "Didn't you see the redcoats outside?"

What?

"And thugs." He made another attempt to sit, this one successful, although he still looked quite dizzy. He pushed onto his feet, swaying lightly. Caroline took an unconscious step toward him, her arms outstretched. The next moment, his left arm was around her shoulders, his weight making her knees bend.

"Lud, you are heavy," she gritted, then huffed a wayward strand of hair out of her face.

He threw her a suspicious look before saying, "Apparently we—and by we, I mean all Shadows—have a price on our heads. The king himself wants us dead."

That made a bit of sense. That's why every night dweller in London was chasing after him!

"My horse is a few streets over," Kensington continued. "I can get us out of here."

Caroline threw him a side-eyed glance. Was he trying to

save her? Without acknowledging the fact that she had just saved him!

He was a dead man before she showed up.

Yes, she had been contemplating killing him just a few minutes ago, but he couldn't have known that.

"Do you know what is happening?" she asked cautiously.

Kensington shook his head. "No. I mean, I have an inkling." He glanced at her clothing before grimacing from the pain. "But I don't care. I need to get you out of peril first and foremost. Then we can discuss your attire."

"My attire?" She scoffed, then threw him a side-eyed glance. "How about thanking me?"

"For what?" he grumbled.

Caroline gritted her teeth. "I saved you."

He shifted, taking some weight off her and bearing more of it on his own. "I don't think so."

"You fainted!"

"I most certainly did not. Gentlemen don't faint," he said between his teeth.

She let out a laugh. "Then you, sir, are not a gentleman."

* * *

Dane's wife was definitely not who he thought she was. Not who he'd expected.

When he had been blackmailed into marrying her, he thought she was a shrewd opportunist. When she'd refused him her bed, he'd thought her cold and rather disagreeable. And when she'd proceeded to avoid him while carrying on her duties as a duchess perfectly, he'd found her predictable and boring.

Well, turned out he was wrong.

There was nothing predictable about the woman who was letting him lean his weight upon her as she tried to get them to safety.

She was trying to save *him*.

Isn't that my job?

Dane glanced down at his wife's clothing once more.

She was a Shadow.

How did that happen?

Dane knew all the people on the roster. Or at least he'd assumed he did. He had been part of the Shadows society since his birth. He'd been initiated when he turned twelve. And he became a lieutenant—one of Erebus's few trusted men—at fifteen. He thought he knew all of the Shadows' secrets save for one—Erebus's identity.

Apparently, he was wrong about that, too.

The more he thought about this entire situation, the more questions he had. She was not surprised that he was one of the Shadows. His hand went straight to his face. Yes, the mask was off, and so was the handkerchief.

How long had she known? Was it possible that she'd known all along?

He had been blackmailed into marrying her. Blackmailed under the threat of giving him up as a Shadow. And Erebus was the only person in a position to have all the evidence against him. Could it be? Was it her?

She was a perfect duchess, able to take care of his estates without blinking an eye. Nobody would suspect *her*, the perfect lady.

He took a deep breath, his mind clearing and his headache letting go. He would have to solve the riddle that was his wife later. For now, they needed to leave. She was still his wife, and he was still responsible for her survival.

"Wait," he said as he attempted to bear his weight on his own. He swayed, and his wife caught him against her once more.

"You are wasting time," she gritted out.

Dane squinted down at her. She was so tiny. How had she managed to hold him for so long? Although taller than most women, she barely reached his chin. Her dainty hands on his body burned through his clothing, causing his heart to beat faster. Her warmth comforted him, although her tone of voice wasn't inviting—his eyes traveled up to meet her gaze—and neither was her expression.

"I am well. My wounds are not deep. I can walk now."

"If you fall again, I am not carrying you," she muttered, slowly stepping away.

"Not that you'll be able to. Especially not onto the horse," he said and rubbed his swollen head. There was a bump on the side. "Did you hit me with something? Because I definitely wouldn't just faint."

She looked at him, exasperation evident on her face. Dane didn't think he'd ever seen her exhibit as much emotion in the past five months of their marriage as she'd exhibited in the last five minutes. She was freer here under the guise of the Shadows. And he was curiously drawn to that freedom.

"If we don't leave now, the thugs will be upon us. And then there would be no escaping for you."

Interesting choice of words. "What about you?"

She didn't answer. Instead, she walked toward the side door and peeked out. "Where did you leave your horse?"

Dane pushed her gently aside and stepped out of the old

mill. "Not far."

He looked around the quiet street before putting his fingers to his lips and letting out a low whistle.

"What are you doing?" the duchess muttered behind him, but her voice got drowned by the loud sounds of horse's hooves before a gleaming black mount appeared from the mist, like a mystical beast. The horse whinnied and shook its mane, huffing and puffing in frustration.

Surely Midnight had gotten bored standing all by herself on the dark street corner when all she wanted to do was gallop and run amok. *Soon*, Dane promised silently.

"Let's hope those thugs didn't hear us, Midnight, my dear," he whispered as he patted his mount. "Now, down."

The horse lowered obediently. Dane waved his hand, gesturing for his wife to precede him.

"That was unnecessary," she said quietly, before fluidly mounting the saddle. She rubbed Midnight on the side. "But she is a very well-behaved animal. Aren't you, darling?"

Her voice was soft and soothing. Dane had to shake himself from the unusual sight. He'd never seen his wife act so gently.

He rarely saw his wife at all, so this shouldn't have been surprising.

Dane carefully mounted behind her, sliding her down the saddle. His thighs made contact with her hips, his groin pressing against her soft bottom.

Dane smirked. This was probably the closest he would ever be to his wife. Not that he wanted more. Although at this moment, her warm buttocks pressing against his thighs did make his cock twitch in reaction. She had an athletic figure, his wife—and a tiny waist. He reached around her to grab the reins and kicked the horse gently to a start.

Chapter 2

Midnight rose majestically and trotted away from the narrow streets.

The duchess sat straighter, so her back wouldn't touch his chest.

Dane leaned forward, his lips behind her ear, her scent—of orange blossoms, her salty skin, and the outdoors—wafting to his nose. "Relax and hold on," he whispered before snaking his arm around her and pulling her close to his chest.

She made a noise in protest, but he urged the mount to a gallop, so whatever words she had on her lips got lost in the sounds of horse hooves beating against the pavement and the loud wind howling in their ears.

Chapter 3

⟡

Caroline's entire body tensed as her husband rushed the horse into a gallop and leaned in close, his chest flat against her back. To say she was uncomfortable was to say nothing at all. And it wasn't just because they were sharing a mare, although the last time she had doubled on a horse she had been five, and her uncle was teaching her to ride. But the thought of a man she loathed—the man she suspected of being a murderer and blackmailer—sitting so close to her that she could feel his breath on her ear made her shiver unpleasantly. She could not relax, and that made the ride even more uncomfortable than it already was.

As a result, it seemed to take them forever to reach the Kensington residence. The duke stopped the mare at the side of their townhouse and dismounted in one quick motion. He held up his left hand for Caroline, but she swiftly jumped off the horse without his aid. Kensington raised his eyes heavenward for one split second before patting the mare on the rear, and the horse cantered away, presumably toward the stables.

Smart girl.

Then he tipped his head at the wall, and said courteously, "After you."

Caroline raised her head. They were standing just below the duke's bedchamber windows. Normally, she would have argued. She had her own way of getting into the house undetected by servants while wearing the Shadows' attire. But not only did she not want the duke to know her hideouts, but she also didn't want to let him out of her sight. So she threw him an irritated glance and started climbing the trellis that led into his bedroom.

She quickly made her way up, climbed into the room, and immediately rushed to the adjoining room door. She dashed to the servants' bell, calling for her lady's maid. Then she quickly hid the satchel inside the boards of her floor and walked back to Kensington's room.

But the moment she crossed the threshold, she was thrown bodily against the wall. She only managed to raise her hands in defense when a heavy body pinned her to the wall, successfully trapping her hands between their chests. She felt a cool blade at her throat and swallowed involuntarily, but managed to raise her eyes to meet her husband's furious, gray ones.

"Who the devil are you?" he growled between his teeth, his eyes wild, like a cornered animal.

"I think you know the answer to that question," she said calmly.

"Do you mean my wife the liar, or a Shadow and a traitor?"

Caroline hardened her gaze. "You weren't exactly forthcoming about your identity and your pastime either."

"Firstly, how about you tell me why you're wearing the Shadows' attire while as far as anyone is concerned, you are not, in fact, one of the Shadows."

"How would you even know?" she protested. "No one knows who is the part of Shadows." This was a lie, of course. A few people knew. Caroline knew that Kensington was one of those few. But she enjoyed rattling him. Especially when he sought to intimidate her.

"You're either daft or you're pretending to be daft. Either way, it's not a pretty sight for a duchess. Not my duchess."

"I am not your anything," Caroline spat, baring her teeth like a wolf. Just being associated with Kensington made her blood boil.

His eyes glided down her body. "Where's the satchel?"

She tossed her head defiantly. "What satchel?"

"The one you took off my body," he growled again, his breath making the wisps of her hair move at the sides of her face.

She didn't reply. Just looked at him silently.

"Don't. Even. Try it," he hissed between his teeth, still looking directly at Caroline, "or your mistress is dead."

Caroline raised her brow and then craned her neck to see Rea, her lady's maid, creeping up behind them, a dagger in hand. Caroline's lips twitched in a smile. Rea probably came to her room and when she didn't find her mistress there, moved toward the sounds of Kensington's growling. She would never have used that dagger on anyone, of course. Kensington didn't know that, however. And Caroline was proud of her timid lady's maid for even picking it up once she heard the sounds of distress.

"It's fine, Rea," Caroline assured. And it was. She could

easily overpower the wounded duke if she wanted to. A light pressure against his shoulder and he would be easily incapacitated. But she rather not use force against the wounded, frightened beast. "Please prepare me a bath. That's what I called you for. You can leave the dagger in my room."

"No," Kensington growled. "Leave the dagger at my feet before you go."

Rea raised her questioning eyes to Caroline. Only once she smiled and nodded did the lady's maid leave the room with an apprehensive look on her face.

"You can let go of me now," Caroline said, returning her gaze to her husband. "I won't hurt you. If I wanted to do that, I would have done it back at the factory."

Kensington gave her a sardonic look. "The satchel, please."

"I hid it. You're not laying your hands on it."

"You seem to be under some kind of a mistaken impression that I am the one under suspicion, when in fact, it is I who should be suspicious of you."

Caroline didn't even know how to respond to that. "Why is that?"

"You are wearing Shadows' attire, although as far as anyone is concerned, you are not a part of the society. You accosted me in the factory—"

"I saved you!"

"—and stole the scroll I got beaten and hunted for. And, oh, yes, I can't forget the most important detail, can I? You forced me to marry you."

Bitter laughter escaped Caroline before she could form any other reply. "This is preposterous! Have you hit your head so hard that you mixed up all the facts?"

"I did not hit my head. I am pretty certain you were

responsible for my insensible state. It took me a few moments to get my wits back, but I can see it all clearly now."

"Somehow, I doubt you see anything," Caroline retorted. "Now take your blade off me before you hurt yourself."

Kensington smirked before lowering his dagger. "I don't trust you."

She smiled slightly. At least he wasn't daft. "Can't trust anybody."

Kensington took a step back, then stumbled and hissed.

He was in pain. Aside from his dislocated shoulder, Caroline had noticed a few bloodstains on him, but there was no telling how badly he was injured. Something had caused him to faint earlier. And although he seemed to have regained his wits, he was clearly still suffering greatly.

Good. One part of Caroline was glad for his pain. Another part of her pitied him. No, she could not be a cold-blooded killer. No matter how much she wished she could. "You're injured."

He let out a bitter chuckle. "You don't say. Did you think I'd need your assistance otherwise?"

Caroline curbed the urge to roll her eyes. He was a conceited scoundrel, and she could not trust him. But what now? They couldn't very well stand like this, frozen in this tableau of animosity forever. One of them had to move. She needed to know what was on that scroll he'd been carrying. But she also couldn't let him out of her sight. She couldn't let him get away and report to his accomplices about her identity.

"Then let me help you," Caroline forced out between her teeth.

Kensington threw her a suspicious gaze. "I have my valet for that. For now, you can go to your room. But I will have footmen watching your chamber from every angle. Now that I know what you're capable of, I am not going to let you out of this house."

Caroline let out a laugh. "Why would I leave, Your Grace? Everything I've been looking for is right under this roof."

"Listen here, Duchess." Kensington stepped toward her and swayed lightly. He must have been in a worse condition than she'd thought. Yet, he didn't hesitate to threaten her. "You think you have a choice? If you don't do what I say, I can make your life a living nightmare."

"So can I. And the fact that you're showing your mistrust so aggressively does not free you of my mistrust. It is your house. Perhaps your footmen will be watching me, but who will be watching you?"

"You think I will leave the house"—he spread his left arm wide—"looking like this?"

Caroline crossed her arms under her breasts. "You do look quite feeble. Which means you are not in any position to threaten me, Your Grace. You are one step away from toppling over. So you either accept my help, or we can stand here until one of us keels over and we both know it's not going to be me."

"You want to bandage me up?" His lips twisted in a sneer.

"I want to know where you are at every moment. And if that means I have to be the one bandaging you, so be it. Besides, I need some answers from you. And what better way to get the truth out of you than by cleaning your wounds?"

She saw the moment he gave up the fight. For a man like Kensington, who was used to everyone obeying his every single word, for a man who commanded the House of Lords with a single wave of his hand to simply give up control, he must have been in a truly great amount of pain.

He took two steps back and leaned against the side of his bed. "Very well. It seems I'm in your hands."

Caroline smirked, then walked to the adjoining room doors and peeked her head into the room. She asked her lady's maid to bring water, soap, clean strips of linen, alcohol, and some of Rea's salves. And she said to let the duke's valet know that his services wouldn't be needed for the next couple of nights because the duchess would be spending those nights with His Grace.

She didn't expect the valet to comply. She knew Rea wouldn't comply with such a request either, not unless it came from Caroline directly, so she needed to move fast.

"I need to take off your clothes," she said in a matter-of-fact tone as she kneeled before Kensington. "But if you can't lift your arm, I might need to cut the clothing."

"Can't wait to undress me, huh?" His voice sounded hoarse and gravelly, and he didn't resist when she put her hands on him.

"If I wanted to undress you—" she said absently while she ran her hands over him once more, feeling for more injuries.

"Yes, I know. You would've done it while I was unconscious."

"No. If I wanted to undress you," she repeated as she picked up the dagger Rea had left. "I wouldn't have insisted on our current marriage arrangement." With that, she made one swift motion and cut his tunic in two. She carefully lowered it from his shoulder, acutely aware of his warm body beneath her fingers. His muscles bunched at the lightest contact with her fingers and goosebumps appeared on his skin.

This wasn't the first time Caroline had seen naked male flesh, but his was the most beautiful. His shoulders were broad, his arms tied in knots of muscle. His breasts were probably bigger than hers, although they were not soft like hers, but firm, masculine. She pursed her lips so as not to laugh at the thought.

A rusty key was hanging off his neck, only adding more shadows and rugged handsomeness to his chest.

His stomach was flat, showing off the perfect abdomen and an enticing V of muscles that led down into his breeches. Oh, he was beautiful, all right. Not counting the dirt clinging to his body and an ugly wound at his side.

"Perhaps you changed your mind," he said, as though in a sleepy daze.

"I don't usually do that," she said, still studying his body.

Rea brought some of the supplies Caroline had asked for and disappeared once more.

Caroline applied some water to where the tunic stuck to his wound. She carefully peeled the fabric away from his body, opening the view to the angry, bleeding cut. It seemed like it was closing, but she must have disturbed it while peeling away the tunic.

Caroline took the piece of cloth and dipped it in the water before trying to clean the wound.

Kensington hissed but didn't protest beyond that. His eyes were closed, and his face was a grimace of pain. Even so, he managed a light smirk as he spoke. "You insist upon tending to me, but you do realize that my wounds are not the only things that need cleaning. I have blood and dirt all over me. I need a bath. Are you going to insist on bathing me, too?"

"If I do, trust me, you won't enjoy the experience." She got up. "I need Rea's help. Assuming she will agree to help after you frightened her."

"She had a knife at my back," Kensington grumbled and leaned against the bedpost. He was beginning to look pale and his eyelids drooped over his eyes.

Caroline assumed that only the thrill of the chase was what kept him upright for so long. Now, as it all wore down, he was feeling the weakness, and she worried he'd lose consciousness again.

"Let's put you down, more comfortably, on the bed," she said softly. Somehow, seeing him so weak, she felt a pang of regret.

He grumbled something as she threw his left arm over her shoulders and helped him lie conveniently on the bed.

"Mm…you smell good," were his last words before he closed his eyes. Caroline's eyes widened. Had he died? She put her fingers to his pulse and felt it beating against her fingers. Strong. "And your hands are so soft," he murmured again.

Caroline leaned back and studied him with a frown. After a night of running, fighting, carrying him in that abandoned factory, and climbing up the trellis, she definitely did *not* smell good. Neither were her hands soft; they were calloused and rough. He was probably dreaming of one of his mistresses. The thought sent an unpleasant jolt through her.

Rea entered at that moment and looked at her with a raised brow. She had a pitcher of steaming water in her hands.

"Oh, thank you, Rea. You're an angel," Caroline exclaimed and jumped to her feet. "I need your help to clean the wound before it festers."

Rea diligently took out powder and herbs from her pockets. "I'll mix the salve."

Rea's father used to be an apothecary and a healer. He'd worked on Caroline's father's estate, and he'd passed down his knowledge to his daughter before his death.

"Thank you." Caroline went back to the bed and proceeded to clean the wound while Rea prepared her remedy.

"You look worried for him," Rea noted, in a passing manner. Rea always felt comfortable speaking her mind to Caroline.

Caroline had grown up all alone on a huge estate with no friends or family who were her age. As a result, she'd befriended the young scullery maid, then promoted her to be her lady's maid, although she was more like a companion.

Caroline grimaced. "I feel responsible for his current state somehow. I know I am not. And he is probably the villain that I always thought him to be. But he usually looks so strong and formidable. I never imagined I'd see him lying unconscious in bed."

Rea let out a snort. "Not like that, you didn't."

Caroline threw her a narrowed gaze. Rea just shrugged and came closer with her salve. "Are you done cleaning out the wound?"

"Yes, as best as I can."

"Good, now pour some alcohol on it before I dress it."

Caroline nodded and obediently took a bottle of whisky. "To your health, Your Grace," she toasted over her husband's body and poured a generous amount into the wound.

Kensington snarled like a wounded beast and shot off the bed. "Bloody hell!" His hand went to cover his wound, but Caroline took it in hers and held it away.

"You'll get it dirty again. Just lie back down."

"What the devil are you doing?" His face was red, he was panting, his eyes frantic. Caroline ran a finger across the back of his hand, trying to calm him. He looked at their joined hands, puzzled. Caroline took this opportunity to nudge him back into bed.

"Please lie still. Rea will dress your wound. After that, you'll be able to sleep more peacefully."

"I doubt it," he ground between his teeth but didn't protest. He just closed his eyes and soon after drifted off to sleep.

Chapter 4

S oft, warm hands ran over his chest, then up to his shoulder, touching him gently. Dane moaned in pleasure. It had been weeks, if not months since anybody touched him so tenderly. His cock immediately rose to attention, hardening almost painfully. He opened his eyes and looked straight into his wife's green ones. Her eyes were darkened with passion, her lips slightly parted. He tugged on her arm, making her fall against his chest, and immediately rolled them over, so she was beneath him.

"Dane," she breathed as she raised her hand and put it against his face. He scrubbed his cheek against her soft palm like a cat.

He looked down. They were both naked and highly aroused. His cock was rubbing against her wet center. He parted her thighs even more, settled comfortably between them, and took himself in hand. He guided his cock to her center, and she raised her hips to meet him.

They both gasped at the contact.

She was so fucking sweet. He wanted her. He was burning from the want and now he'd finally have her.

Dane rolled onto his right side, still holding her in his arms, and… sharp pain pierced his shoulder.

Dane opened his eyes in the dark, groaning. Sweat covered his body, and he had to grind his teeth to keep from screaming. He tugged on his left arm in an attempt to cradle his aching right shoulder, but it seemed to have caught on something.

He shut his eyes and rolled back onto his back, his breathing still labored. His right hand immediately went to his painfully erect cock. As if it wasn't enough having a shoulder injury, his cock was hard and overly sensitive. He hissed as his hand met the fabric of his breeches that chafed against his sensitive skin.

Why was he still dressed? He squeezed himself with a groan and moved his hand to the waistband of his trousers.

"You're awake."

Dane opened his eyes and jumped in reaction. He braced his right hand against the bed in order to prop himself, only to be hit by a wave of agonizing pain again. He cursed and fell back onto the bed. As if awakening from the erotic dream wasn't embarrassing enough, he had to humiliate himself before his wife.

"I didn't mean to frighten you," the duchess said. He looked at her then, still startled and breathing heavily. She sat by his bedside, her face dimly illuminated by the moonlight spilling from the windows. "It just looked like you might want some privacy for what you had in mind," she said cheekily, "and I'd rather not be an unwilling witness."

The heat flooded his cheeks at her words. She'd seen him stroke himself. What a ridiculous display it must have been. Being startled out of his wits should have subsided his erection. However, seeing the object of his dreams so close to him as he opened his eyes did the opposite. His cock jumped in reaction. He only hoped she didn't notice.

Since when did his wife have such an effect on him? He had never exhibited any interest in her. Perhaps their violent encounter the night before had enticed a physical reaction to her presence. That and the fact that he had not been this close to another woman in months... at least not in the bedroom.

As if reading his thoughts, his wife stood and moved to sit beside him on the bed. Dane swallowed. *What are you doing?*

She was close now, her face only inches away from his. She was wearing a dressing gown, and her hair was collected in a tight bun. She was a genteel lady once more, not a fearless vigilante.

Her scent, orange blossoms, drifted into his nose. Was this still part of his dream? Because if so...

She reached out her hand and touched his forehead, his cheek.

"What are you doing?" This time, he managed the words out loud, although his throat was dry.

"No fever. It looks like you're feeling better," she said and returned to her seat by his bed.

"I am." He jerked his hand, only to realize why he was unable to move properly. His left hand was tied to the bed. "Untie me this instant."

She tsked and shook her head. "I don't quite feel safe in your presence, my dear husband. The last time we were tet-a-tet, you had a knife at my throat."

"And for a good reason," he said darkly.

"Right. So you will be tied up for a good reason, too."

He let out a breath, keeping himself in check. "My valet will untie me."

She smiled slyly. "He won't. I told him that you are not to be disturbed unless called upon."

"Why would he ever listen to you? I am his master."

She shrugged. "I might have implied that I would be spending a few nights in your room."

"And he believed that?" Dane scoffed.

"Well, you can always call him and tell him the contrary." She bit her lip, pretending innocence. It didn't suit her. "Oh, sorry, forgot. You can't."

"You laugh now, Duchess," Dane gritted. "You won't be laughing when I get out of these restraints."

"You understand that threatening me won't get you released, yes? I am not foolish. And you are not getting free until I get satisfactory answers from you."

Dane gave her a dead stare. "You want answers from me? How about your answers? You are the one who needs to give me explanations, not the other way around. You have me tied up." He looked around the room, trying to remember where he was and how he got there. He was following the thugs when the redcoats attacked… They'd attacked just as he stole the scroll that was supposed to have the names of all the members of the Brotherhood of the Crimson Fist.

Right! The scroll. It was tied to his side when he collapsed at the factory. He looked down at himself. He was still wearing his breeches, but other than that, he was completely naked save for a few bandages. He tapped his chest with his palm. The key was still hanging off his neck. Good. At least the key was in place. "Where the devil is my scroll?"

"*Your* scroll?" There was a hint of incredulity in her tone.

"Well, I stole it from a group of criminals, snatched it from their hands, evaded dozens of thugs and redcoats, got stabbed, and then tortured by my wife for it. I think I earned it."

She raised a brow. "Tortured?"

"Well, you called it cleaning my wounds. I call it torture."

She actually rolled her eyes. "I saved you. I could have left you there."

"Right, my goddess and savior. For the love of God, give me the scroll!"

"Fine," she said cheerfully, too cheerfully. Then she picked something up from the chair and dropped a scroll into his hand. "Here you are."

Dane raised his hand as high as he could without causing pain and squinted at the scroll.

"I shall even light a candle for you, my dear husband," she said solicitously and went to do just that.

Dane winced as he adjusted to the light, watching the blots of light disappear before his eyes and turn into writing on a brown piece of paper.

1 lb. Flour

1 lb. Suet

1 lb. Currants

8 oz. Raisins

4 tbsp. Candied Orange Peel

4 tbsp. Candied Citron

2 tsp. Nutmeg

8 tbsp. Brandy

8 Eggs

2 cups Cream

"What the devil is this?" he spat.

"I thought you said it's yours," she answered calmly.

"That is not the scroll I recovered last night."

"Oh, yes. It is."

Dane furrowed his brows. "It can't be," he whispered. "There is nothing there."

Then it dawned on him… It had all been a setup from the beginning. The scroll had never been real. He had been duped. And he'd risked his life for this! He would have realized this earlier, but he was too busy fighting for his life.

"Oh, yes, there is." The duchess nodded eagerly. "It's a quite fine recipe for Christmas pudding."

"Christmas what?"

"Pudding," she said with a straight face. "Our cook is making one as we speak. Well, not literally."

"What the devil are you talking about?" he growled.

She heaved a sigh. "What was supposed to be there?"

He rested against the pillows and watched her with a raised brow. Did she know something about it? "You tell me," he said calmer. "You stole it from me. What did you think would be there?"

"Evidence," she said simply.

Now he just got even more confused. "Evidence of what?"

"Of your involvement with the blackmailers."

Blackmailers? "What? How do you know about—?"

She raised a brow in challenge. "That you're the black-mailer?"

Dane had to shake his head. She was laying a trap for him; he was certain. And he'd almost fallen into it. "What in the world are you talking about?"

"I am talking about how you blackmailed my uncle for you to marry me. How you blackmailed—"

Dane interrupted her with a burst of hoarse laughter. He

couldn't believe it. To be accused of blackmail was one thing, but to be accused by the niece of the person who blackmailed him... Well, this was some kind of farce.

"*I* blackmailed *him*? Is that what he told you?"

"He didn't need to tell me." She tossed her head, baring her elegant white neck.

"He didn't need to tell you," he repeated grimly. "So you have this all figured out, don't you? If I am this villain you paint me to be, then why did you marry me?"

"I told you. You blackmailed my uncle!" She was losing her patience, and Dane rejoiced. The more out of sorts she was, the more truth he would be able to get out of her. He only needed to keep his head cool.

"He was dead when you married me," Dane noted. "So that excuse would not do."

She straightened her spine, although he wasn't certain that was possible. "Because I trusted him that I would be safer as the wife of a monster, rather than being the enemy of one."

"A monster?" What did her uncle tell her about him?

The poor man was delusional for weeks before his death. He forced Kensington to marry his niece, threatening to expose him as a Shadow. He also spoke of him being a monster, or something about monsters, which Dane had just chalked up to his delusions. Kensington would have given up the idea of marrying her once the man had died, except he had said that he wasn't the only one who knew the truth about Kensington and that even after death, he could make Dane's life miserable. Now he wasn't even certain the old man had any proof.

The duchess's nostrils flared. He wondered what was going through her head. She clearly didn't know her beloved uncle as well as she thought she did. Probably not even as well as

Dane knew him. Which only brought more questions to the surface.

Why force an engagement on your favorite niece to a man you claimed to be a monster? Unless he was trying to protect her from even uglier monsters. Dane frowned in thought. He was certain the old man arranged for their engagement so Dane could protect the frail and lonely, innocent lady. Now, looking at his wife, he suspected the marquess had other motives in mind.

"What did he tell you about our union?" he asked.

The duchess stared at him for a moment before answering, "Nothing."

"What do you mean, nothing? Why would you ever agree to marry me?"

"That is none of your concern."

Dane raised a sardonic brow. "Truly? I am tied to a bed by my lunatic wife and it is none of my concern why you chose to shackle yourself to me?"—he threw a glance at his tied-up arm—"or rather me to you. Either way, I beg to differ."

"If I were indeed a lunatic, you would've been dead already. And since you've pointed it out, you are the one tied to a bed, so I will be the one asking questions."

"And will you torture me to get the answers?" He raised a cocky brow.

"If I have to," she said evenly.

"Very well, please, enlighten me. You think I am this big, bad blackmailer. Then in your opinion, what was I doing last night?"

She scoffed. "You were consorting with your accomplices, these lowly criminals."

"If I were blackmailing people, what in the world would I

need criminals for?"

"I don't think you could do it alone," she answered confidently.

"I am pretty certain you just insulted me. Twice."

"Then why were you out there? Shadows are banned from active duty until the rumors die down. Which means you were out there on your own."

"You were out there, too, weren't you?" he pointed out.

"I was following you."

"How do I know that? How do I know you weren't cavorting with criminals?"

"Why in the world would I show myself and help you then?"

He lifted his uninjured shoulder in a shrug. "Perhaps you're not as clever." She gasped and Dane let out a low laugh. "You insulted me, I insulted you. Now we're even." He tugged on his bound hand. "Do you mind untying me? My nose itches."

"I think you'll live through this inconvenience."

Dane lifted one brow. "You know, I am starting to miss the days when we rarely spent any time together."

"That's easily remedied." She stood and nudged the chamberpot closer to his bed with her foot. "I trust you'll be able to reach it?" With a smirk, she turned on her heel and walked to the door. Dane's chest constricted unpleasantly. He wanted to cry out for her to stay.

Why? Only the devil knew.

"Wait," he gritted between his teeth.

She turned toward him. "Yes?"

"Since we are shackled to each other—or at least, I am shackled to this bed—perhaps we should talk."

She slowly walked back. "Do you promise to be pleasant about it this time?"

Dane didn't answer. "He seemed to dote on you, your uncle," he said instead. "Why would he arrange a marriage to a man you barely knew? To a man you didn't want to marry."

His wife swallowed. "As I said, I assumed you blackmailed him."

Dane let out a harsh laughter. "And why would I want to marry you? And so badly that I'd blackmail a peer of the realm for it?"

She squared her jaw. "I am rich."

Dane scoffed. "I am richer."

"Well, then I don't know," she cried. He'd never seen her so out of sorts. "Why did you marry *me*?"

Dane smirked. "Believe it or not, because your uncle blackmailed me."

She scoffed. Dane wished he could see her features more clearly, but she was shrouded in darkness. "Clever. Accuse the dead man."

"Listen, my dear wife. Whether you like it or not, we are in the same boat. Your insane uncle orchestrated this entire thing, and neither of us knows why. Perhaps it's time we found out?" He jerked on his restrained arm and raised his brow.

She slowly walked toward him. Careful, like a cat. "I don't trust you."

Dane smirked. "Can't trust anyone."

Chapter 5

Caroline watched her husband for a long moment, trying to figure out what to do next. They couldn't continue living like this, that was for certain. She couldn't keep him tied up forever, either.

Sooner or later, the valet would come in to check on him, or a chambermaid would notice that something was amiss, and then the rumors would spread and it would do more harm than good.

But she couldn't very well untie him either. He could run off in the middle of the night to his accomplices, or tattle to all who'd listen about his wife, the Shadow. He could get her apprehended by redcoats.

She didn't trust him, obviously. So she needed to come up with some kind of plan to keep herself safe under the roof of her prisoner. For she was his prisoner. There was no other way to say it, even if he was the one tied to the bed.

"If you won't untie me," Kensington gritted out, "then at least bring me some food and drink. Unless, of course, you want me to starve to death."

A drink. What a terrific idea! Caroline smiled sweetly. "Of course, my dear husband."

She walked to the servants' bell and called for Rea.

"My head hurts as if someone hit me with a boulder," Kensington complained. "You didn't hit me with a boulder while I was unconscious, did you?"

Caroline raised a brow. "There is a slight bump on the back of your head, probably from fainting—"

"Please, do not call it fainting."

"But you did faint," she said with a smile. "And there are also innumerable bumps and bruises all over your body. So if someone did hit you with a boulder, they did not restrain themselves only to your head. Which, although I didn't do it, I completely understand the impulse."

Kensington shifted in bed, trying to find a comfortable position regardless of his tied-up state.

Rea showed up at that moment and Caroline hurried toward her. "Please, bring some food for his lordship. And a spot of… *herbal* tea," she added with a wink.

Rea nodded her understanding and scrambled away.

"Now that that's settled, perhaps you would like to answer some questions for me?" she asked as she walked back to the bed.

He let out a tired sigh. "What do you wish to know?"

"If you weren't conferring with your accomplices, then what were you doing last night out on the docks?"

"Looking for the people who abducted the Earl of Payne a few years ago," he answered readily. "Yes, I know, Bradshaw was caught and all the blame was placed on him, but he was not working alone. And I intend to find out who else was involved."

She narrowed her eyes, her mind working on the piece of information she'd just received. "It was you," she finally said. "The one who framed Bradshaw for all the crimes."

The Earl of Payne was abducted, tortured, and then thrown onto an illegal slave ship a few years back. He had managed to escape and return, and the person responsible for the crime was brought to justice a few months ago. But it was all too neat and clean for Caroline's liking even then. And although she wasn't doubting Bradshaw's guilt—the man was despicable—she had always suspected there was more to the story.

He shrugged. "He wasn't innocent. I added a few crimes here or there to make people rest easier. But the whispers were spreading about the Shadows. I had to do something." He shifted again. It was obvious he didn't feel comfortable in the bed, or perhaps the bruises were getting in the way of his comfort.

"But the Shadows are under strict orders to stay inside," she said.

He threw her a suspicious glance. "Yes. And criminals are rejoicing. Or at least, that's what I thought. But I stepped into a trap. It seems that the king put a price on our heads. One thousand pounds. Apparently, we are treated as traitors now."

"That's your own fault," she said. "If you did indeed set up Bradshaw, you're the one who left the Shadows' attire lying next to him. Now people think we are the villains."

"There was no other way. Shadows were already blamed for all sins. It was a logical way out. What would you have done?" He was getting impatient.

She took a deep breath. "What I would have done has no

bearing on this conversation. So you want me to believe that you had nothing to do with the blackmail?"

"I didn't blackmail your uncle." He bristled. "Not to be rude, but I had no interest in marrying. Not you, not anyone else."

Caroline pursed her lips. He could be a good liar. But she needed to know more. To gauge his reaction. "Stay here," she said and walked toward her bedchamber.

"As if I could leave with my hand tied up to the bed," he grumbled under his breath.

Caroline returned just as Rea placed a tray of food in front of Kensington. He took a piece of toast in his right hand and grimaced. "My shoulder still hurts. I can't move my arm," he complained with a grimace. "Either untie my left arm, or you'll have to feed me."

Caroline huffed a breath and sat next to him on the bed. She took the toast from his hand and brought it to his lips. He raised a brow, then slowly bit into the toast. "I really expected you to untie me," he said around a bite. "Tea, please."

Caroline was regretting her life's decisions at this very moment. She could untie him now, could she not? Soon, her husband wouldn't be in a position to go anywhere, anyway. But she found she rather enjoyed his helplessness. So she brought a cup of tea to his lips and tilted it back, forcing him to drink a few gulps of tea, whether he wanted to or not.

"No need to be so aggressive about it," he grumbled.

"Are you done now? Can we go back to our conversation?"

He raised his eyes heavenward. "What do you have in there?" he asked, tilting his head toward her hand.

Caroline handed him the note she brought from her room. The only note she had from the blackmailer addressed to her uncle. She studied his features carefully, looking for any speck of recognition in his eyes. Instead, he just frowned.

"Where did you get this?" he asked, twisting the paper this way and that.

"This came to my uncle. I suppose there were more of these, but I haven't seen any more. This one doesn't shed a light on anything beyond that he was indeed blackmailed."

"It's signed Erebus," Kensington said carelessly. "Perhaps it is him."

"It's not," Caroline said confidently.

"How do you know?" Now it was his turn to watch her carefully as if trying to read her mind.

Caroline picked up the cup again and raised her brow. "More tea?"

"And toast, please," he asked politely, still watching her suspiciously.

She fed him toast and helped him wash it down with her special herbal tea before asking, "You are part of the Shadows, aren't you? Then you know it's not him."

"A man who hides behind two masks can not always be trusted," he said, licking the drops of tea from his lips.

She scoffed. "The same can be said about you."

"And you."

"It can't be him, because the penmanship doesn't match." Caroline snatched the note back.

"How do you know?"

"I checked. Have you not received notes from Erebus? Does this seem like his writing?"

"He could have someone else signing these notes for him." Kensington finished his toast and emptied his cup of tea with the help of Caroline. She removed the tray from his lap as he moved, getting comfortable against the pillows.

51

"It's too risky," Caroline answered after a brief thought. "And these notes are definitely written by the same person. I checked this note against the one that Lavinia received—"

"Lavinia has been blackmailed?" Kensington sat up, genuine concern hitting his features. "Why hasn't she said anything to me?" This last question was addressed more to himself than her.

Caroline blinked. She hadn't expect such a violent reaction to her words. Lavinia had been in love with Kensington for years, but Caroline didn't think that he harbored any feelings toward her. "Because I told her not to."

"Oh, because you think it was me?" He scoffed and tossed his head, disturbing his thick mane of hair. This was the most agitated she'd ever seen him. "Lavinia is my friend. I had made it my business to help her. Perhaps I wasn't always successful in that regard, but I would never mean her any harm." His last words were emphatic, his lips pursed as if he was staving off anger. "Did she believe you?"

"No, she refuses to believe it's you. But she agreed to keep this from you anyway." Caroline hid her gaze. His strong reaction to finding out Lavinia's plight had Caroline doubting her suspicions toward him. "Probably just to keep me happy."

"If you think I truly could have done this…" He gestured to the note, his nostrils flaring, his eyes glinting with anger. "You are mad."

"And if you think that I shall believe you just based upon your word, the madness is yours. Look at the penmanship. I compared it to your letters—"

He raised a brow. "You went through my things." That wasn't a question. He didn't even seem surprised, just annoyed.

"Of course." Caroline raised her chin. "And I looked at your finances. You were dirt poor when you inherited the dukedom at thirteen years old. Your father squandered away the entire inheritance."

"This isn't news to me," he growled.

"Well, how have you managed to amass such a fortune since then?"

Kensington leaned closer to her. Too close. Their faces were mere inches away. His jaw was set, his neck tense, his eyes glinting maniacally. Caroline could not think straight. Her heart thumped loudly against her ribs, and she could not force herself to meet his eyes. "By working hard. Something you know nothing about, Duchess."

He softly put his hand over hers, and she felt the heat rising within her. Then, in one swift motion, he ripped the note from her fingers. He leaned back against the pillow, his brows furrowed as he studied the note. "That's your evidence?" He scoffed. "Erebus, or whoever it is, could have easily forged these."

"Why forge it to make it look like yours?"

"You'll have to ask him." He stared directly at her, unblinking. "Why are you so certain it's not Erebus? Nobody within the Shadows knows who he is."

Caroline squared her shoulders. "I didn't say I did, either."

"No, but you act as if you know. As if you trust him. More than you trust your husband." He placed the note on the bedside table, wincing visibly. His breathing was labored, and it seemed like he was still in pain. Or perhaps his earlier outburst had triggered a headache, Caroline could not guess which. He was too formidable and looked too virile to suspect he was hurting. He was obviously very good at hiding things.

"I don't have any reason to trust you, husband. I don't even know you."

"Yes, but you know *him*. Is he your lover?" He didn't seem angry, just curious. Or perhaps he was tired. Drifting off to sleep. Perhaps the tea had started working.

"What if he is?" She swallowed, her entire body tensing.

He shrugged. "He could be using you."

"He's not."

"Untie me, Duchess," he pleaded weakly. "So I can get a comfortable night of sleep. I am not going anywhere."

"No, you're not," Caroline agreed, watching his drooping eyelids. He was already under the effects of her tea. She leaned in and untied his hand.

Kensington turned away and tried to make himself comfortable against the pillows. Caroline supposed the conversation was over. At least, for now.

She stood and quietly walked toward the adjoining room doors.

"You know, Duchess," he stopped her with his slurry words.

She turned toward him. He was watching her beneath his heavy eyelids. "You are not as good at keeping secrets as you think. For you to be so certain of him, he has to be someone you trust implicitly. Or…" He paused, while his eyes closed. He was quiet for a while, and Caroline thought that he'd fallen asleep when he finally spoke. "It's you."

Chapter 6

C aroline put on her soft, silk nightgown after a nice steamy bath. She had left Kensington alone—well, not truly alone, Rea was watching after him—hoping he would fall into a deep sleep.

The herbal tea Rea prepared had a bit of skullcap in it. A sleep-inducing herb that Caroline used during her deep insomnia after her uncle's passing. From her own experience, she knew that the herb made a person drowsy in minutes, but it would take a bit longer for them to fall into a deeper sleep. And Caroline definitely needed the duke to be more than just drowsy for what she had in mind.

Not to say that his well-being was not among her priorities. After all, he had been in a great deal of pain, and sleeping soundly was the only way for him to heal without suffering. Or at least that's how Caroline tried to appease her conscience for drugging her husband.

Caroline collected her hair into a neat bun, covered her body with the dressing gown, and quietly tiptoed back into her husband's room. Rea sat there, in the dark corner, sewing. How she did that in complete darkness, Caroline couldn't fathom. There was a light from a dying hearth and a single candle by the duke's bed, but those sources of light didn't reach Rea's corner.

"How long will he be asleep?" Caroline asked.

"I don't know," came Rea's hushed voice. "A few hours, perhaps."

"Good." *Just enough for what I have in mind.* "Stand guard at the door and do not let anyone inside."

Rea nodded and left the room.

Right after marriage, she and Kensington had agreed upon one important thing. Their bedchambers were out of reach for the other. Neither was to cross the other's bedchamber threshold.

Since she had already broken that agreement, she didn't want to let that opportunity pass in vain. God only knew when she would have access to his bedroom again without the interference of his servant and while the duke was in a peaceful slumber.

Since their marriage, she had scoured his every study in all of their estates and looked through all the documents she found there. But she'd found nothing incriminating in those documents.

It was logical to conclude that if he wanted to hide anything from her, surely, he'd keep it here. The room always guarded by his valet or by himself. The room she'd agreed never to enter.

Caroline was intrigued by the idea of a truce between her and her husband. There was a possibility—however slight—that he was innocent. That he wanted the same things that she did. And in that case, she could use a powerful duke as an ally.

But Caroline wasn't naïve. She wasn't foolish either. She needed to make certain that Kensington posed no threat to her. And what better way to do that than by rummaging through his things?

So she walked toward her husband, softly treading on the thick Turkish carpet. He was sleeping peacefully, she assumed, based on the even rise and fall of his chest and his soft snoring. She only hoped he wouldn't awaken any time soon.

Nodding to herself, Caroline took the candle from the bedside table and proceeded to go through his things. She inspected all the surfaces first, then rummaged through his drawers before moving to his dressing room and looking through the shelves among his clothes.

There was nothing of note in either of those places. Caroline huffed a breath, disturbing the locks of hair that managed to escape her bun. Then she turned and surveyed his chamber once more. Kensington was still sleeping, seemingly undisturbed by her quest to find anything that would prove that he was the blackmailer.

Her gaze slid along the room, carefully assessing the dark corners and illuminated surfaces.

She had hidden his scroll under her floorboards, so maybe the duke had found a hiding place of his own. After inspecting the floors and the walls and turning up nothing, Caroline moved closer to the bed.

Right above it hung a portrait of the duke's horse, Midnight. *Who hangs a portrait over one's bed?* It could fall and crack the skull easily. Hmm… the idea seemed utterly enticing.

But more to the point, she realized it would be the perfect

place to hide something very important. She looked at her husband's peaceful features.

"Please, don't awaken," she whispered as she hiked up her skirts and climbed onto the bed, careful not to touch him. The bed dipped and made a creaking sound, but the duke didn't move a muscle.

The painting was hanging right in the middle of the wall, which meant Caroline needed to stand in the middle of the bed to be able to take the painting down. And it wasn't a tiny bit of art either. The frame was massive, carved out of wood. If it did fall, it would certainly split the duke's skull. Caroline scrunched up her nose. *Let's call it Plan B.*

As her luck would have it, her husband turned to lie on his back right in the middle of the bed.

"Of course," Caroline grumbled under her breath. "Dane, if you awaken now… Well, let's just say you have no one to blame but yourself," she said as she stepped on either side of his head.

She took a deep breath and lifted the painting off the nails it had been hanging on. She peered at the wall to realize that she was right. There was a safe embedded in it. Caroline stepped down and carefully lowered the painting to the floor.

Now to figure out how to open the safe.

Caroline narrowed her eyes, thinking. Then her gaze fell to the duke's bare chest and the tiny key hanging off his neck.

That must be it.

Caroline kneeled before him, ran her fingers gently against his chest and neck, picked up the key, and dragged it over his head.

Kensington groaned and swatted at the place Caroline's fingers had just been.

Chapter 6

She grimaced, her hands still in the air, holding the dratted key and trying not to breathe. The duke let out one more sigh and resumed his quiet snoring. Caroline softly removed the chain with the key off his neck before finally letting out her breath.

One issue resolved. Now to climb the bed again...

Caroline hiked up her skirts and mounted the bed again. She had no problem opening the safe and peeking inside as she balanced on the soft mattress, the duke's head between her legs.

His soft snoring was tickling her ankle as if reassuring her that he was still in a deep sleep. Caroline plunged her hands inside the safe and brought out pieces of jewelry.

Family heirlooms.

All the jewelry that by any right belonged to her, yet her husband had not bothered to give them to her. Not that she blamed him, although her throat burned a little from the discovery.

She placed them back and took out an oblong box. She opened the lid and beheld the most beautiful emerald choker and matching earrings.

Duchess's jewels.

The jewels every duchess before Caroline had worn for their formal portraits that now hung in the family gallery.

Caroline placed the box back, her heart heavy. She'd never wanted a marriage or a family. Somehow, the arrangement she found herself in had never bothered her... before tonight.

She had married the duke because she thought he was a traitor of the Shadows. She'd married him because she thought he was a dangerous blackmailer. She'd thought that she could find out all his secrets while being his wife.

And despite all that, she strived to be a perfect duchess.

But it seemed like her husband had never thought of her as his duchess. And even if she had a reason to mistrust and loathe him, he loathed her simply for her.

She let out a breath and shook her head. The sadness she felt would pass. It was a momentary lapse of judgment, she was certain.

Caroline dipped her hands inside the safe one more time to find a small leather ledger. Another ledger? Why did he keep it here and not among the ledgers in his study? Caroline felt that she was onto something. She got down from the bed and came closer to the bedside candle as she leafed through it.

Unfortunately, there were no incriminating details, no names of possible accomplices. Actually, there were no names there at all. Only the list of expenses.

Caroline turned page after page. Many, many expenses. She couldn't possibly go through them all in one night, and she was already quite exhausted. But she couldn't very well take the ledger with her. Kensington would immediately suspect her, rightly so, and then there would be hell to pay.

The only solution would be to find something of substance and quickly. She leafed through to the last page with scribblings on it and squinted, trying to make out the words.

> *Make an addendum to the will: Four thousand pounds upon my demise to P.*

Did he want to change his will and bequeath four thousand pounds to this person? Who was this P? Caroline was certain it was a partner in crime, or possibly several partners. But no matter how hard she looked, there were no names in this journal. Only one address was written on one of the first pages. Caroline quickly jotted down the address, folded the piece of paper, and placed it into her pocket.

She climbed onto the bed one last time and replaced the items in the safe. She successfully hung the picture on the wall and smiled to herself. "Voila!"

Just at that moment, Kensington turned in bed, disturbing her balance, and she fell right onto his chest.

Caroline stifled a screech as she landed against her husband's warm body. Kensington groaned as she was certain she had crashed into his dislocated shoulder. She only hoped she hadn't injured it all over again.

But that was not what she should have been worrying about, because at that moment, Kensington opened his eyes.

Caroline froze, her hands on his chest, her hair falling down her face, tickling his chin. Her skirt hiked up right to her thighs, and she should have been embarrassed and horrified. But she was just frozen in panic.

Instead of raging and screaming, and perhaps even letting out a surprised yelp, her husband looked her right in the face, then tightened his arms around her body and buried his face in the crook of her neck.

What is going on?

He turned onto the side, taking her with him, and kissed her neck. He kissed her!

Caroline was so shocked that she couldn't even gather her wits enough to react.

What in the hell is going on?

She placed her palms against his burning chest and pushed. Hard.

The duke growled and bit her shoulder in protest.

"What are you doing?" Caroline asked, her voice curiously breathless.

"Let me enjoy the dream, just this once," her husband begged. He weaved his fingers through her hair, then pulled her head back and whispered, "Once."

Then his mouth was on hers. Hungry, insistent. His tongue probed at the seam of her lips, and his hands glided against her body, plastering her flush against him.

Caroline's mind became completely foggy. She had no understanding of what was happening at all. It was all like a dream. And perhaps, for him, it was a dream.

For her... a nightmare?

Kensington caressed her buttocks and jerked her closer to him. Her pelvis rubbed against his hard manhood. Her lips parted open on a sigh or a gasp... some kind of exclamation. Then her husband's tongue was inside her, sweeping along the edges of her mouth.

Then it all stopped.

The duke's body relaxed and became as heavy as lead, crushing her onto the bed. And then his snoring resumed.

Chapter 7

D ane woke up with a bitter taste in his mouth and an unpleasant feeling in his body, as though a building had been dropped on him the night prior. He stretched, his muscles aching and protesting against the movement. Well, at least he wasn't tied up this time.

He rolled off the bed, completely forgetting about his aching knee, and almost slammed face down onto the floor. He caught himself with his hands, his right shoulder giving another dull ache.

He slowly straightened, his pulse pounding in his head, and stretched his back again. Then he slowly moved his shoulder to make certain it was still mobile. He twisted his neck until it cracked, then his back, his fingers. Yes, his body was truly falling apart.

He brought his fingers to his temples. Why was his head pounding so much?

He called for his valet, trying to move as slowly as he could. Then he looked around the room with narrowed eyes.

Something was different.

"And how was your night?" Victor, the valet, asked as he walked in, a huge grin on his face.

"Very well, thank you," Dane croaked. "But my entire body aches."

"Oh!" Victor blinked, opened his mouth to say something, then quickly closed it shut, his cheeks reddening.

"Are you going to stand there, or are you going to help me shave and dress?" Dane raised a brow.

"Of course, of course." The flustered valet hurried to pick out clothing for Dane and prepare the shaving implements.

"Have you been here since last night?" Dane asked. "Something is different."

His valet turned toward him, somewhat confused. "No. The duchess said not to disturb you on account of her spending the night in your rooms."

Of course! His wife had been in his room. And suddenly the memory of the night before came screaming back to him. The boring musicale, the chase at the docks, the encounter at the docks, and the torture that his wife had disguised as cleaning his wounds.

He was in pain and felt so groggy that he didn't even know how many days had passed. Two? Three?

The duchess had said that she'd informed his valet she'd be spending a few nights with him. The poor chap probably believed that the stay was of a romantic nature. Let him think that. It would be rather embarrassing if he found out that not only he'd been duped, but that his master had spent those nights tied to the bed. And not in any pleasant way.

His valet approached Dane with soap and lathered his chin and cheeks. Dane eyed the room carefully while the valet was busy grooming him. Something felt truly different about the room. No doubt his wife had taken the opportunity to go through his things. Although their agreement clearly stated that neither of them was allowed in the other's chambers.

Well, if she had no issue breaking their agreement, neither would he.

"Please, let the housekeeper know that I shall be breakfasting in my room today."

His valet gave him a startled glance before responding with a meek, "Of course."

This was the first time since his marriage that Dane had requested this. He had always breakfasted with his duchess until now.

Well, there would be a lot of changes people in this house would have to get used to. All the people in this household, including his duchess.

The valet scraped the last of the soap from Dane's chin, then handed him the towel to wipe himself off.

"And then have the coachman prepare the carriage. I shall be leaving right after breakfast."

The valet bowed and left the room. Dane turned toward the bed and noted the crookedly hanging painting. His gaze dropped to the bed. It was badly rumpled. Ah yes, he'd had some heated dreams of her last night. He smirked.

His duchess wanted their agreement broken, did she? Then Dane would make certain it was broken in every single way.

* * *

Caroline sprung out of bed as she always did in the morning and called for her maid. She had a lot of work to do. With the

Christmas feast approaching, the list of things that needed to be taken care of grew by the minute. Add to that the predicament she was in with her husband and she didn't have enough hours in the day to accomplish all the items on the list.

Now that her husband knew that she was a Shadow, and he knew that she thought him a blackmailer, she needed to be careful, and she needed her wits sharpened.

How was her husband this morning? Was he awake? Did he feel better?

She was anxious about facing him. She was anxious about a lot of things.

Last night might not have solved any mysteries, but it had certainly changed the way her future would unfold.

She took her morning ablutions just as Rea walked into the room. "Good morning, Rea," she said with a smile. "You're just in time to help me dress. Is the duke up already? I don't want him waiting for me in the breakfast room."

They had agreed at the beginning of their marriage that to avoid the servants' gossip, they would breakfast together every morning, as well as attend all the social functions together, even if they separated shortly after.

Rea paused and looked at her strangely. "Um… The duke has already breakfasted."

All Caroline could do was blink in surprise. "He has?"

"I assumed he informed you of his actions."

Caroline pursed her lips. Is that how he wanted to proceed? Well, she could ignore the rules, too.

Caroline walked up to the adjoining room door and opened it without knocking. She expected her husband to be lying in bed, still drowsy. The injuries he had sustained that night at the dock did not heal easily. They'd need a few days to mend. But what she saw as she stared into his chamber was a made-up bed and an empty room.

"He left after breakfast," Rea said from behind her.

Caroline slammed the door shut and sharply turned to face Rea. "Oh, that's how he wants our truce to go," she murmured.

Rea shrugged. "I think you both have a very skewed idea of what a truce is."

Caroline rolled her eyes and sat at the vanity. "Please untangle my hair. I have places to be, dukes to strangle."

* * *

After instructing the footmen to watch their duchess's every step, Dane quickly got dressed and slipped away.

He took his walking stick to mask his limp and held his right arm close to his body, although he refused to wear a sling. He didn't want people to notice his injuries.

He reached the familiar townhouse, knocked, and waited in agitation for the door to open.

"Your Grace." The butler bowed and let him inside. The fact that he was so easily let inside without the butler checking with his masters meant a lot to Dane. It meant he was welcome in this house despite everything that had transpired before.

The butler led Dane toward a drawing room before bowing out.

Kensington looked around the room. He hadn't been in this house a lot. Maybe once or twice before marrying Lady Caroline, definitely not after. The walls were covered with beautiful paper, but there was evidence of missing paintings in some places. The paper was lighter, and there were bare nails on the wall.

"Dane."

Dane turned around at the soft call of his name. "Lady Roth." He sketched a bow.

Lavinia, Dane's long-time friend, smiled and stretched out her arms as she walked toward him. "I am so happy to see you."

Lavinia and Dane had lived on neighboring estates growing up. As luck would have it, she had met Caroline as a debutante and quickly became good friends with the future duchess. And then a few months ago, she'd married Sebastian Devis, the new Marquess of Roth, Caroline's uncle's heir.

Dane took her hands in his and squeezed. "I am glad that you're happy to see me. I wasn't certain if you were still angry with me."

Lavinia did indeed look happy. She had a healthy pink in her cheeks, and her eyes were sparkling.

"Angry?" She shook her head. "Why would I be angry?"

"Well, the last time we interacted, I punched your now-husband in the face. And before that, we had quite an unpleasant altercation."

She bit her lip and grimaced. "Please, sit."

Once they both were seated by the hearth and Lavinia had carefully smoothed her skirts, she finally looked up. "I am not angry with you. Quite the opposite. I believe you saved me a great deal of pain."

"How is that?" Dane tilted his head.

Her smile turned wistful. "You know I feel so foolish about my outburst that night…"

The night you told me you loved me. Dane smiled in turn.

He loved Lavinia, too. Like a sister. But that night, a

few weeks ago, during the Roth house party, when Lavinia screamed at him in anguish that she'd been in love with him her entire life, something within him shifted.

Of course, he'd known. How could he not? The way she colored every time they spoke, the way she stole glances at him at any opportune moment. He'd known it, but he ignored her because his feelings weren't the same.

But that night, when she'd told him the truth, he'd wished he could have looked at her differently. He'd wished he had married *her*, not his current wife. Because that way he'd prevent the things that followed: the blackmails; his cold marriage.

Now, as he looked at Lavinia, he had to concede that he had made the right choice, after all. Because perhaps with Lavinia *his* life would have been better, happier even. But not hers.

"I don't regret it," she continued. "It's as if with that outburst, with those words, I let go of all the pain and bitterness and opened myself up for happiness."

"And are you? Happy, that is."

"Extremely." Her smile, the shine in her eyes, didn't lie. She was telling the truth.

Dane swallowed and forced out a smile. "I am glad."

A housekeeper came and set the table with tea and biscuits and brioches, giving Dane time to collect his thoughts. "But we are still friends, yes?" he asked the moment they were alone again.

"Of course. I shall always be your friend." Her face was open; she was sincere.

"So if you were in trouble, you'd tell me?"

Lavinia lowered her eyes and chewed her lower lip.

Dane watched her in silence for a moment before saying, "I

know you have a husband now, who, hopefully, takes care of you to the best of his ability."

"He does."

"But as a friend, I would appreciate it if you still let me help you…" He paused. "Unless you don't trust me anymore."

Her head shot up. "I do trust you."

Dane gave a tiny shake of his head. "Then you're not being blackmailed?"

Lavinia clamped her lips shut, her brows furrowed. She looked down, her fingers crimping the folds of her gown. "How do you know about that?"

"The duchess," he bit out and stood. He walked toward the window and looked out.

"Caroline told you?" Lavinia asked from behind, surprise evident in her voice.

Dane turned back, then leaned his good shoulder against the windowpane. "Well, let's just say that she did not have much of a choice. But it's not her who I should have heard it from. You should have told me."

"I wanted to!" Lavinia cried. "I truly did… Well, not at first, but that was different. Once I got married, I was determined to ask for your help. Sebastian and I even came to your house."

Dane let out a chuckle. "And got intercepted by my wife."

"She asked me not to tell you. She is my friend, too, Dane."

Dane nodded and stalked back toward Lavinia. "She asked you to keep silent because she thought—thinks that I am the one blackmailing you. Do you believe so, too?"

"Of course not!" She leaned toward him, her features sincere.

"You say that, but your actions speak louder." Dane was unable to hide the bitterness in his tone. It chafed that people he cared for so much kept things from him. Thought the worst of him.

"I know it isn't you, Dane," Lavinia said emphatically. "Please, sit."

Once Dane resumed his seat and Lavinia refreshed his cup of tea, she continued. "You have to understand. Caroline needs someone to blame for her uncle's death. It's part of her grief. I couldn't betray her. She wouldn't listen to my reassurances, so I'd rather she figured out that you're innocent on her own."

"And in the meantime, the real blackmailer can wreak havoc on your life?"

"It's not your concern. I am a married lady now. I have a husband whose job it is to protect me."

"And he is probably the one they intended to blackmail all along! How much leverage do the people have blackmailing a lady? And a destitute one at that. None! But they can use you to make your husband do whatever they want. Especially a lord with honor. And especially now, since your union is a love match!"

Lavinia's cheeks reddened, and her eyes glistened with tears. "When the blackmail letters started arriving, I wasn't even married. I hadn't even met Sebastian yet! He had just returned from France to assume his rightful place as the new marquess."

Dane wanted to retort but quickly changed his mind. Instead, he reached into his pocket and handed Lavinia a handkerchief. "Apologies," he said, forcing himself to calm down. "I didn't mean to upset or insult you... And I didn't mean the callous words—"

Lavinia dabbed at her cheeks and then handed the handkerchief back to him. When she spoke next, her voice was soft. "You are right. Why would anyone want to blackmail an impoverished young lady with no prospects?" She let out a chuckle, then reached for a piece of pastry. Instead of biting it, she rotated it between her fingers, deep in thought. "Of course, my guardian at the time would not let me remain with no prospects. Did I tell you he wanted to marry me off to Lord Pembroke?" She chuckled, then finally popped a piece of pastry in her mouth and washed it down with a sip of tea.

Dane straightened. "Did anybody else know about that?"

Lavinia nodded. "Everybody knew about that. He told everyone short of printing it in the morning paper."

I didn't know about it. Dane picked up a cup and took a sip, trying to gather his thoughts.

The Earl of Pembroke used to be a part of the Shadows. His name was no longer on the roster, but it used to be. He had retreated to his estates after the tragic deaths of his wife and child and hadn't been back to London since then. Until now.

He was also a distant relative and heir presumptive to the Duke of Wolverstone. A powerful title for a young and virile man. And Dane could easily see people wanting to blackmail him.

"Why does it matter? Surely you don't think someone anticipated me marrying Pembroke and blackmailed me in advance. Why not just blackmail him?"

Dane nodded. "You're right. It's probably unrelated." Unless this was exactly the connection he had been looking for. "And I had no right coming here demanding answers from you. I am not a part of your life anymore. Your husband is."

Lavinia smiled softly. "You will always be a part of my life. At least, if you still want to be."

Chapter 7

After a quick breakfast, Caroline got dressed and summoned a carriage. She knew that the coachmen and the footmen following her would tell Kensington everywhere she went and everything she'd done since she woke up this morning, so instead of investigating the address she found in her husband's safe on her own, she decided to turn to her friends for help. Especially when one of her friends was married to a fellow Shadow.

Caroline's carriage stopped in front of Viscount St. John's townhouse. She disembarked and before she even knocked on the door, it opened, St. John's butler welcoming her with a flourish.

And before she even stepped into the hall, Olivia, Lady St. John, Caroline's friend, rushed to greet her. "Caroline! How good of you to visit!"

Helen, Mrs. St. John, Olivia's cousin-in-law, appeared behind her and curtsied demurely. "Your Grace."

"We were just going out for a walk, but now that you're here." Olivia's nose twitched as she considered their options. "Would you like to sit?"

"Actually, a walk would be lovely," Caroline said with a smile.

Olivia's lips spread in a smile. "Marvelous! Let's go then."

The trio set out at a sedate pace toward the park.

"How is marriage treating you, Olivia?" Caroline asked.

"I quite enjoy it," Olivia exclaimed. "There was a slight adjusting period. I had to arrange things to my liking, but Helen helped me immensely."

"I doubt I was of much help," Helen said meekly.

"Of course you were. I don't know what I'd do without you. I love Jarvis. But whatever problem I came to him with, he would just… kiss me and think that it solved everything."

Caroline let out a chuckle. It wasn't something ladies discussed, even among themselves. But Olivia wasn't bothered with social etiquette. She just spoke her mind. Caroline found it quite refreshing. Especially since she herself was all about etiquette.

"Sometimes kissing does solve things," Helen said softly.

Helen had lost her husband, whom she loved very much, a few months ago. And since then she lived with Olivia and her husband Jarvis St. John. Caroline couldn't imagine it was easy for Helen to witness the happy union of her husband's cousin. Or perhaps it was exactly what she needed. Caroline didn't pretend to know.

When she was grieving for her uncle, she'd required solitude. But people dealt with grief differently.

"And how are you?" Olivia asked. "Any progress unmasking your husband?"

Caroline smiled. "In a way, yes."

Caroline had told Olivia and her other friends about her fears that her husband was the man behind the threatening letters—the man responsible for her uncle's spiral into madness and his eventual untimely demise.

"You did, truly?"

"I found him bleeding in an abandoned building and confronted him," Caroline said with a chuckle. "It's a long story. He denies it all, of course. But I found something that may either incriminate him further or clear his name. And I need your help in uncovering that piece of information."

"My help?" Olivia's eyes widened in surprise.

"Yes, there is truly no one else I can turn to with this."

"That's terrific!" Olivia exclaimed enthusiastically. Then her cheeks colored. "I meant it's terrific that I can help, not that you're in a dire state with no one else to turn to."

Caroline laughed. "I understand, dear. And I am also very happy that you might be able to help me with this. Although, perhaps it's your husband's help that I truly require."

"Jarvis will be just as excited to help you. I assure you."

Caroline nodded and rummaged through her pockets. She fished out the piece of paper with an address and handed it to Olivia. "Please, be discreet with this."

Olivia peeked at the writing on the paper before carefully folding it and slipping it inside her glove. "I have no pockets," she clarified. "And I will lose it otherwise. But what is this address supposed to tell us?"

Caroline shrugged. "I do not know yet. But he kept it hidden in his secret safe. It must be something important, right?"

Helen cleared her throat before speaking. "It could be something important. But it could equally be something mundane. Please, do not have your hopes up."

"You are just saying that because you don't believe Kensington is guilty." None of her friends believed his guilt.

Helen shook her head. "I am saying this because I hope with all my heart that he is not guilty. He is a powerful duke, Caroline, and he is your husband. He can either become your biggest protector or the worst of the villains. And I truly hope it will be the former."

Chapter 8

Kensington was absent the entire day. He had not come home for dinner, and he was still away even though it was past bedtime. Of course, he was a duke, and he had a lot of things to keep him busy.

And yet something nagged at the back of Caroline's mind, warning her that his absence was not incidental. That he had not been just frolicking about or taking care of his lordly business—he had been cleaning up the evidence of his involvement with the blackmailers.

However, lying in bed alone and watching the fire dance in the hearth, that was not what she was dwelling upon. She should have been. She should have been doing everything in her power to catch her husband or to find more implications for his guilt.

Yet, as she lay in her lonely bed, the only thing she could think about was last night's encounter. And not the moment she found him unconscious in a factory. But that startling moment when she fell against her husband's chest and he held her tightly in his arms.

It wasn't about his erotic touches and his hungry kisses. Very well, perhaps it was a little about that. But mostly, it just made her realize that she hadn't felt the warmth of a human body for quite a while.

When was the last time she'd been held close to another human's body? When was the last time she'd experienced a loving, familial embrace?

Years.

Her uncle, as much as he loved her, was not a tactile person. At most, he would pat her on her head, sometimes he would squeeze her fingers. Wolverstone, the family friend, had hugged her exactly once. When her uncle died. Not a warm, full-body embrace either, but a pat on the shoulders. And due to circumstances, an embrace she would happily erase from her memory.

Her friends would sometimes attempt to wrap their arms around her and, in that case, she would be the one to keep her distance. She wrapped her arms around others when they needed consoling. A half-hug, a shoulder to cry on.

But the last time she'd experienced a real, full-body embrace, full of love and warmth, was when her mother was still alive.

Caroline shivered and burrowed further into her warm bed. She missed that. And she felt incredibly sad that the first time she'd experienced it in years was from her cold husband, who was convinced he was dreaming... And probably wasn't even dreaming of her.

There was a knock on the adjoining room door.

Caroline sat up straight, her mind racing. This was the first time since she'd moved in with her husband that anyone had knocked on that door.

Another knock.

Caroline climbed out of bed and threw a dressing gown over her nightgown. She tied it around her waist and slowly tiptoed toward the door.

One more knock. Steady, patient, not even that loud.

She opened the door.

Kensington stood before her in a shameful state of undress. His coat and waistcoat were off, the cravat nowhere in sight, his neck and throat were completely open to her gaze and even a few dark hairs peeked out from the open V of his shirt, the sleeves of which were rolled up to his elbows, showcasing his muscled forearms and his popping veins.

And that wasn't all!

His boots and stockings were off too, leaving him barefoot.

Caroline raised her chin to look him in the face—as that was the only proper body part she could allow herself to look at—and even then, his hair was down, framing his face in haphazard locks. She had never seen her husband thus if one did not count their encounter last night. Which, of course, didn't count! It was under the shadows of the night, and he was dirty, injured, and bleeding from various places. Now, he was completely clean and, apart from his breeches, wearing nothing but his undergarments!

"Yes?" she asked, trying to keep her wits about her.

"You weren't sleeping, I hope," he said, studying her from head to toe.

"Not yet." She paused. "You were out rather late."

He raised a cocky brow before leaning his shoulder against the doorframe and crossing his arms over his chest. "You were never interested in my whereabouts before."

I am always interested in your whereabouts. I was just more circumspect about it. "And you never knocked on this door before. I suppose this is a week of firsts for us."

"You drugged me," he accused.

Caroline opened her mouth to protest, but she found she had no words.

"We agreed to call a truce"—he pushed off the doorframe and stepped toward her, forcing her to retreat into her room—"and then you turned around and drugged me."

"I did it for you," she lied. "You were groaning in pain. You couldn't sleep." Caroline stopped retreating after a couple of steps and refused to budge.

"Please, step aside," he said and raised a brow.

"I don't remember inviting you in." Caroline defiantly raised her chin. "Especially since we have an agreement."

Kensington chuckled. "Ah, yes. The agreement. The one you violated last night?"

"You were injured. Under the extenuating circumstances, I think it's allowed."

Kensington placed his hands over her arms, squeezed, picked her up, and actually moved her out of his way, bodily! Caroline's mouth opened, but no sound emerged from the shock.

"Quid pro quo," he said slowly as he moved around the room.

"How dare you?" Caroline finally found her tongue.

"Are any of these paintings or books from your previous home?"

Caroline bristled in indignation. But she knew that, unlike her husband, she could not possibly lift him and move him back into his room. "Yes," she bit out. "Why?"

He moved closer to her uncle's favorite painting—one of

the few he had instructed her to take with her in his note to her before he died—and reached out his hand toward it.

"I would thank you not to touch it," Caroline said.

Kensington turned toward her. "Oh, so it is completely fine for you to ransack my bedchamber, but I cannot touch one measly painting?"

Caroline's eyes widened, her cheeks burning. He knew? He knew that she'd looked through his things! Had he not been asleep? And what about the moment when he'd grabbed her in his arms and kissed her? Was he awake then, too? The burn from her cheeks spread to her entire body, and she felt like she was on fire.

"Ah!" Kensington smiled slyly. "So you do possess shame, after all, Duchess. Did you think I wouldn't notice the misplaced items, the crooked painting?" He raised a brow.

Caroline closed her eyes in relief. He hadn't been awake, he'd just noticed that the items were out of place.

"You would have done the same thing," she said in a mere whisper.

He shook his head. "Oh, no, my dear wife. I *shall* do the same thing."

Caroline straightened her spine. "Please do. And then get out."

Kensington narrowed his eyes and stepped closer. Too close for her comfort. "I would watch the way you speak to me, Duchess."

"Or what?" Caroline raised her chin. She had to if she wanted to look him in the eyes. He was incredibly tall. "You'll kill me?"

His face contorted in disgust. "You misjudge me, Duchess."

"I doubt it very much."

He turned away and walked back toward the painting. "You know, I went to your old home today."

Both of Caroline's brows climbed of their own volition. The home she lived in with her Uncle Roth. The home that now belonged to her cousin Sebastian, the new Marquess of Roth. *Lavinia's home.* "Oh?"

"Yes, you see"—he took the painting off its nail and studied it carefully, ran his palm against the back of it—"I thought that I might learn something interesting about your uncle. Which perhaps would help us recognize why he forced us into this farce of a marriage."

"And did you?"

He shrugged, then hung the painting back and proceeded to the next one. "I noticed the missing paintings."

Caroline threw up her hands. "He instructed me to take these with me. They belong to me. Why is that odd?"

He threw her a glance before continuing to look through the paintings. "Perhaps it isn't. These are very expensive, valuable paintings, are they not? When did your uncle acquire them?"

"Before he inherited the title," Caroline said sharply. "What exactly are you trying to find?"

"Here's your problem, Duchess," he said as he continued going through the paintings one by one. "If you look for something in particular, you risk missing something you didn't expect to find."

"Well, whatever you expect or don't expect to find, there is nothing there." And she knew that for certain. Because looking through her uncle's paintings and books was the first thing Caroline did upon his demise.

He shrugged, replaced the painting, and moved to her bookshelf.`

"Are you going to look through all the books?"

"You don't mind, do you?" he asked without turning toward her.

"I don't care one way or another. Just don't ruin anything. They are very important to me. It's the last thing I have of my uncle." She said the last sentence quietly, almost inaudibly. But he paused and turned to look at her.

"I can feel your animosity, my dear wife."

"Oh, do you?" Caroline rolled her eyes.

"Yes, and while I understand it, understand this. Your uncle is the key to our problem. He married us. He was blackmailed. So whatever you're looking to find, it would be among his things." He ran his finger along the spines of the books, then turned around, leaning his back against the bookshelf.

"Are you satisfied, husband?" she asked coldly once he was done.

He looked around, his gaze thoughtful. "Not exactly the word I would use, no."

Caroline let out a sigh of exasperation. "If you want to know more about my uncle's life, you shouldn't be looking through my things. You should be looking through his."

He raised a brow. "Such as?"

"The ledgers?" Caroline folded her arms across her chest. "Cousin Sebastian has them all. Perhaps you can charm him into giving you access to them." She offered him a fake smile. *If you have any charm, that is.*

"And you wouldn't be throwing me off the scent, would you, wife?" He narrowed his gaze on her.

Caroline raised her chin. "I see no benefit in doing that. But since I came up with the idea, I would appreciate it if I were involved in the process of studying my uncle's ledgers."

"You mean to tell me that you went through my books, but you didn't go through your uncle's?"

Caroline gritted her teeth. "It is your idea to look into my uncle. I, for one, am convinced it's a waste of time. However, I wouldn't want you misconstruing whatever you find there as meaningful."

He scoffed. "Fine. You want to spend evenings cuddled up with me by the hearth, looking through your uncle's books, I am happy to oblige."

Caroline huffed a breath. "Whatever will get you removed from my chambers is good for me."

He immediately took two giant steps toward her. "You entered my chamber; I repaid the favor. You ransacked my room; I looked through your things. But do not forget, my duchess, that you tied me up, too." He stepped even closer as he spoke. "Rest assured, I shall make certain to get even with you for that."

He winked, turned on his heel, and walked away. Only when he was already at the door did he pause and turn his head toward her. "You are free to do whatever you please from now on, my dear. Consider our agreement voided. But remember, quid pro quo."

Chapter 9

Dane dreamed of Caroline again.

It was not surprising. Ever since he'd found out she was part of the Shadows, he'd been unable to take his mind off of her. She was a secret he wanted to unwrap, a mystery he wanted to unravel. His mind was consumed with her by day, and the fact that those thoughts turned erotic by night was natural or so he rationalized. His body told him he needed a release, and his mind presented the only woman he thought about all day.

Who was she, the woman he'd made his wife? A spy? The infamous Erebus? He doubted it. But that did not make her any less intriguing, or her life any less dangerous.

She was embarking on a journey no lady should have embarked on. The blackmailers would not differentiate between a duchess and a harlot if they thought their livelihood was in danger. So he needed to find out the truth before she did. For his own peace of mind and for her safety.

For she *was* his duchess. And Dane protected what was his.

They had spent several days looking through the ledgers of her uncle and so far had found nothing of consequence. Dane was getting desperate, and it only meant one thing. They needed to change their approach to this matter.

He rolled out of the bed and prepared for the morning ahead. He was oddly looking forward to breakfast. Yes, he needed to speak to his duchess about their search, but that wasn't the only reason for his excitement.

Ever since Dane was thirteen years old, he had always broken his fast alone in silence. Even before that, his family was always quiet during the mornings. His father would read a paper, and his mother rarely, if ever, joined them.

When he'd married, his wife acted much like his mother, and he, he now realized, acted a lot like his father. He was brief, polite, and distant. She was a perfect duchess, but cold and absent.

They always breakfasted together due to their agreement, but their meals were filled with silence. They always attended social events together, but never spent a moment more in each other's company than necessary.

To outsiders, their marriage looked perfect.

On the inside, it was as cold as a winter chill.

But that was what they had agreed upon, and that had worked perfectly well. Until a few days ago. Now their life was turned upside down. And although he bemoaned his wife for thinking the worst of him, he quite enjoyed the banter-filled meals, her scathing looks, her wit, and intelligence as they spent evenings in his study, going through the ledgers. It almost felt as though it was a real marriage.

Almost.

Dane performed his morning ablutions, got dressed, and

walked toward the breakfast room.

His wife was already sitting at the table. She looked at him briefly as he entered the room and then resumed her meal.

With a quick bow toward her, Dane assumed his seat at the head of the long sixteen-foot table.

"I trust you slept well?" he asked.

"Quite well, thank you," she answered briefly. Perhaps he was wrong about the morning banter. It seemed impossible to tug the words out of his wife's mouth this morning.

"Do you have any plans for today?"

She looked at him strangely across the length of their breakfast table. "Since we are hosting a Christmas feast in a few days—which I am certain you have forgotten about—I shall keep busy."

Dane pursed his lips. She was right. He hadn't remembered the Christmas feast. In fact, he didn't even know that it was Yuletide, although all the greenery in the house and the merriment on the streets should have reminded him of that. The fact was, he had never celebrated it.

When he was younger, he was always left out of any celebration, locked in the house—in his room, while his parents were elsewhere. When he became the master of the house, he didn't see the necessity of such a celebration. Although his stepmother often prepared a feast for the villagers in the country seat, Dane was just always... absent.

His wife, on the other hand, seemed to celebrate everything. In the mere five months of their marriage, she'd organized a masquerade ball, helped Lord Roth host a house party, and now she was preparing a Christmas feast.

"I did not forget," he lied. "I have just been preoccupied with other thoughts. About the blackmailer."

"Yes, me too." His duchess visibly perked up.

"You have? Well, by all means, I am eager to hear your thoughts."

"Well, I was thinking about something. My uncle's ledgers all seem rather meticulously documented. Nothing is out of place. I don't think we'll find anything there."

Kensington cocked his head to the side. "Do you propose we give up the search?"

She waited to finish chewing before she answered. "Not quite. I was thinking… since we have all the ledgers for as long as my uncle was the marquess and we are not seeing anything in them, perhaps it's not about what's in there, it's about what isn't."

Kensington popped a piece of food into his mouth and chewed thoughtfully. "You mean before he became the marquess?"

"Exactly. You said… or at least, you presumed that he might have been blackmailed for a long time. What if it was going on his entire life?" She paused, her face turning grave, her voice lowering. "That would drive anyone mad. But that would mean that whatever mistake of his past that the blackmailer used, we won't find it in the ledgers we have."

Dane wanted to soothe his wife. He knew that her uncle meant a lot to her. And thinking about his suffering probably hurt a lot. But he wasn't good at consoling people, so he opted to lighten the mood. "Does that mean you no longer suspect it's me who is responsible for the blackmail?" He flashed her a smile. "I was a mere lad back then."

The duchess huffed an annoyed breath. "You are not beyond suspicion still. But we can't do the same thing over and over, looking through these ledgers that have nothing and expecting to find some kind of outcome."

"If you're right," Dane said around a bite, "that could mean that whatever we are looking for might not even exist. All notes and documents could have been burned years ago. It's not like we can dig up the ashes."

"No," she agreed. "We can't. But we can ask someone who was there."

Dane raised a brow. "Do tell."

"When my uncle inherited the marquessate, the Duke of Wolverstone, our family friend, was the one who helped him ease into the title. He's been a family friend forever. He might know if my uncle had any issues, or perhaps he was helping him even before. He might even have notes that could help us. He is very meticulous."

"You are rather clever, my duchess." Kensington smiled. "How come I never knew that?"

His wife's cheeks glowed red in the morning light. "Because you always underestimated me," she said evenly.

"I shall do so no longer. I promise," he said, being utterly serious. "I can talk to Wolverstone tomorrow at—"

"No." She shook her head. "Let me. It's a family affair. Besides, there's a ball tomorrow, which we are both attending, by the way."

"Is there?" He smiled.

"Yes, and your valet shall remind you of that tonight, as he always does," she stated as she set her teacup down.

His smile widened. "That he does."

* * *

Dane lifted his head the moment he heard the footsteps on

the grand staircase. He knew when he looked up he was going to see his wife, yet he was not prepared for the vision before him. She quite literally took his breath away.

She wore a beautiful emerald green gown that contrasted wildly with her dark mahogany red hair. Simple white gloves and a fan complemented her ensemble. The duchess's emeralds would fit perfectly on her bare neck.

She didn't wear any jewelry, in fact. As though she'd left her skin bare on purpose for people to feast their gazes upon.

Her slippers hit the floor, and she flipped the fan open. "Shall we?"

Dane cleared his throat. "We shall."

She tentatively placed her hand on his sleeve, just like she always did, barely touching. Dane covered her hand with his and pressed it to his forearm.

She looked up at him briefly, confusion shining in her eyes. Dane averted his gaze. It was better if she never knew what lurked behind his eyes. She looked away, too, and they proceeded toward the carriage in silence.

In silence.

That's how they spent their entire journey to Wolverstone's townhouse. That's how they made their way into the house. And that's how they joined the guests in the ballroom.

They approached the host and after the brief greetings, Wolverstone took the duchess's hands in his and squeezed. "How good it is to see you. I have not seen much of you since your wedding. I trust you're looking out for her?" This last was addressed to Dane.

"The best way I know how," he said with a polite smile.

"Roth trusted you with the most important thing in his life. I sure hope you are doing your best to keep your wife happy."

Is that why the late marquess had blackmailed him into marrying his niece? Dane doubted it. So he just inclined his head.

"And how are you faring?" the duchess asked with a polite smile.

"Good, good. My cousin Gustava helped me put together this ball, but I would appreciate it if you took part as a second hostess, if you please. I am afraid Gustava and I are both too old to keep the youth entertained. And perhaps you could introduce my heir apparent to a good lady or two?"

The duchess pursed her lips to hold her smile. "Of course, Your Grace. Now let us move. We are holding up the line."

"See, you are already acting like a hostess!" He winked and welcomed another set of guests as Dane maneuvered his wife away and into the throng of people.

The moment they moved away from the host, Caroline tugged her hand away. Dane leaned his head closer to hers so she could hear him. "Is something the matter?"

His wife looked at him as though he was mad.

Dane suddenly understood her confusion. Since the start of their marriage, every time they came to a social function after they greeted the host, they separated, not to be reunited until after the function was over. His wife obviously expected the same pattern to continue. But Dane had no interest in resuming their life the way they'd been living before.

"If you don't mind, I shall go about my business," she said.

He couldn't very well detain her now, Dane decided. But he'd find a way to change the way she looked at him before the night was over. For now, he let go of her hand and inclined his head. "Of course."

Caroline gave him a confused smile and disappeared among

Chapter 9

the crowd.

Chapter 10

Caroline let out a deep breath. It felt as though she hadn't breathed freely since she'd descended the grand staircase at her house.

She wore a beautiful emerald green gown with golden lace on the bodice and an overskirt. Her hair was up in an intricate chignon, yet she wore no jewelry. Only white gloves and a white fan completed the ensemble.

She'd done it on purpose. She wanted to accentuate the absence of the duchess's emeralds on her neck and ears. She wanted her skin to be bare, to show to the world, or at the very least, to her husband, that he'd neglected his duty as a husband to pass on the family heirlooms.

She shouldn't have cared about it at all. She didn't want to be part of this family. But they had agreed to be civil. They had agreed to show to the world a false facade that spoke of their amicable marriage. And that meant passing on all that by law belonged to her.

Perhaps, she did care. And that made her even more bitter.

Chapter 10

Because as much as she distrusted her husband, she still had the desire to belong somewhere, to belong to someone. To have a family.

She and her husband did not share much. And wearing the duchess's emeralds would signal to the world that she did indeed belong. To *him*.

But the moment she'd descended the stairs back in their townhouse, she'd regretted the display of her skin. Because now her husband was watching her so closely she was certain his gaze would burn through her clothing.

Things had shifted between them in the past few days. They seemed to have a lot to talk about, and yet, tense silence still dominated most of their interactions.

It wasn't just in her head. Her husband was just as confused as she was. But as always, when she felt confused or out of sorts, she did what she did best. She worked.

So she went to greet the guests, and act as a hostess during her family friend's ball, all the while from the corner of her eye watching her husband interact with others.

He seemed relaxed—although one could never tell with the duke—he was always rigid and controlled. But he didn't look around the room in agitation, he didn't look for an escape. In fact, the only thing he constantly looked for was her.

Was he afraid she'd slip away? Or was he watching her merely to unsettle her?

Because if so, it worked. Caroline tried to act as nonchalant as she could, but it seemed like every time she turned, she crashed into her husband's burning gaze.

Caroline spotted her friends, Lavinia and Victoria, the Princess of Mecklenburg-Schwerin—Cousin Sebastian's niece, and a sister to Russia's regent—standing in the corner of the ballroom.

Lavinia was fanning herself vigorously, her cheeks rosy, her eyes glinting with joy. Ever since she married Sebastian, a look of happiness rarely escaped her features. Victoria was standing beside her, a lovely smile on her face, as a row of suitors lined up for a glimpse of her, and a hope for a dance.

Caroline smiled and was about to join them when she noticed that Wolverstone had moved away from the crowd and was heading toward the exit of the ballroom.

Her friends could wait. This could be a perfect opportunity for her to speak to him about her uncle.

She slowly glided toward the exit and then looked around the corridor, searching for any sign of where the duke might have gone but could not see anything. So she walked leisurely toward the grand staircase, peeking inside every door. Then the sounds of murmurs caught her attention by the staircase.

"This is not why I came back," said the man's hoarse voice.

"Why did you come back?" She recognized the second man's voice as that of the Duke of Wolverstone, so she moved closer.

"Because a lady was in trouble. Or so I've heard. That was the only reason I even agreed to marry."

"You have to marry to ensure—"

"The continuation of the line. Yes, I've heard that before. But I do not owe you anything, old man. I do not have an obligation to your title or any other legacy you think I should be part of." The sharp, rude voice was followed by retreating footsteps.

Caroline stepped out onto the staircase landing and cautiously made her way down. Wolverstone stood on the steps, just below the landing. He looked troubled.

"Your Grace," Caroline called softly, and he turned.

His face immediately lightened. "Yes, my dear?"

"Is anything amiss?"

He shook his head. "No, everything is perfect. You are doing an amazing job, not that I should be surprised. You always have."

"Thank you."

"Let's return to the ballroom." He waved a hand for her to proceed.

"Wait... Pardon me." Caroline smiled, feeling slightly awkward. "I wanted to talk with you about something."

"Yes?" The duke caught the balustrade and leaned against it.

"I wonder if we could do it in private?"

He frowned. "Is something the matter?"

Caroline let out a nervous laugh. Wolverstone was an old friend of her family. But whenever she had tried to talk to him about her uncle's death in the past, he had always dismissed her concerns. And whenever she brought up the blackmail, he had always warned her to stay away. She didn't want him to dismiss her now. So she felt awkward and uncertain of how to proceed. "No, no. It's just... it's about my uncle. I was wondering if perhaps you could help me with some ledgers of his."

His frown deepened. "To what end?"

"Well..." Caroline looked around again, then stepped closer. "I don't want to speak out in the open. It's about the threatening notes. I was hoping that his activities might help me decipher who is behind them."

The duke waved her worries away. "I thought I told you to leave it alone. Your uncle died because he was obsessed with this."

"And that's exactly why I can't leave it alone," Caroline insisted. Tears burned at the back of her eyes as they did every time she thought of her uncle. She blinked them back. "He was so distraught that he took his own life! I can't let the people who taunted him get away with it. And this isn't the only reason for my search, either. My friend is in trouble as well."

"I have no answers for you," he said and, as if the conversation was over, dismissed her and climbed the stairs toward the ballroom.

Caroline picked up her skirts and followed after him. "Does this mean you don't know anything? Because I am fairly certain my uncle did. And that's why he married me to Kensington."

Wolverstone paused as he reached the landing and turned toward her. "Kensington is a wealthy, powerful duke. He is also as honest as they come. Who else to guard his beloved niece than a man like that? Please, Caroline. Do not look any further. I can't lose you. Not you too."

The duke grimaced, hunched over, and placed his hand over his heart, breathing in deeply.

Caroline leaned toward him. "What's wrong?"

He chuckled. "Nothing, nothing dear. I am just getting old. And old bodies do hurt sometimes."

"I hope I wasn't the reason—"

He straightened and patted her hand. "No, dear. You could never be the reason for anything bad. Now go back to your husband and enjoy your night."

Caroline wanted to protest, but at that moment, a young gentleman, Mr. Townsend, appeared out of nowhere. "Your Grace." He bowed. "Would you do me an honor of this dance?"

Wolverstone winked at her and walked away, leaving Caroline no choice but to accept the invitation.

Slightly annoyed, she forced a smile to her lips and placed her hand on Mr. Townsend's sleeve. They walked into the ballroom together and immediately she could feel the burn of her husband's stare on her skin. She tried to ignore it while Mr. Townsend escorted her onto the dancefloor.

As the music started and everyone moved into the dance, Caroline studied Mr. Townsend's thoughtful features.

"I must apologize," he said finally, "for my lack of polite manners. I feel quite awkward, but I have a reason for seeking you out."

"You do?" Caroline smiled politely as she moved around him on the dancefloor.

"And this is something I shouldn't feel embarrassed about, and yet, I cannot help it. I wasn't raised to walk among the lords, although I am a gentleman." He cleared his throat.

"I am certain you have no need to be embarrassed. What did you want to ask me?"

"I would love it if you could perform introductions to a young lady I have my eye on."

"Oh!" Caroline beamed at him. "I would be honored. Who is the young lady that caught your eye?"

Mr. Townsend stumbled slightly before straightening. "Apologies. I do hope I did not tread on your toes."

"Not at all," Caroline said softly. "But you were about to tell me the name of your intended?"

"Ah, yes." His cheeks pinkened, and his eyes flickered somewhere behind Caroline. "I understand that perhaps I am not exactly the match she deserves, but I am very much hoping to at least get acquainted with your beautiful cousin,

Princess Victoria."

This time, it was Caroline's turn to stumble. Mr. Townsend caught her against him and discreetly helped her straighten as they twirled in rhythm with the dance.

Caroline, an accomplished dancer as she was, had never stumbled before. But he wanted to court Victoria!

She understood his awkwardness. Victoria was a Princess, and Mr. Townsend was an earl's untitled cousin. However, what Mr. Townsend didn't know—what nobody except for the closest circle knew—was that Victoria was already married. And to a duke's bastard, no less.

Caroline could not tell him that, could she?

"I would love to make the introductions," Caroline said carefully. "But I have heard that the princess is planning to go back to Russia soon."

His brows crinkled in thought. "Well, perhaps she will change her mind. For a husband."

Caroline stretched on a smile. "Perhaps."

The rest of the dance they spent in silence. Her—figuring out how to introduce him to Victoria and at the same time dissuade him from courting her. He... she could not even begin to fathom what occupied his thoughts, but he seemed lost in them completely, his expression quiet.

As soon as the music ceased, Caroline searched the ballroom for Victoria. She found her standing by Lavinia's side, chatting animatedly.

She was wearing a beautiful deep blue gown, her dark locks framed her face perfectly, and a smile shone on her beautiful face.

Blast.

Mr. Townsend was bound to fall in love with her. Because

although she was still a bit naïve—very well, a lot naïve—her character was flawless and more beautiful than even her delicate face.

With an inward sigh, Caroline took Mr. Townsend's arm, and they both proceeded toward the princess.

* * *

Dane watched his wife float from one group of peers and peeresses to another. She kept herself straight and composed at all times. She spoke to people always with a polite smile on her face. Dane should have seen her perform this function, a hostess, a few times by now. They'd held a masquerade together. She'd helped her cousin, the new Lord Roth, hold a house party just a few months ago. And yet Dane had never really noticed her until now.

He had never been interested in her whereabouts, or even in her abilities as a hostess. He knew she was accomplished because she managed to run his household without a single question, without a single complaint. Yet he'd never seen her do it.

For some reason, he was now mesmerized by the vision of her. And he was absolutely curious to see her wielding her power as a mistress of his lands rather than wielding a dagger. He imagined she would be just as impressive, if not more so.

In the entire time he'd been watching her, she never made a gesture out of place. She'd never picked on her fingertips as many were wont to do, never fidgeted with her gown, and never swept a lock of hair away from her face. Now that he noticed, she never had a hair out of place either. She was absolutely perfect, and it aggravated him.

Her overall appearance left Dane lurching from one extreme to another. On one hand, he had the urge to cover her up, wrap a blanket around her, hide—no, protect—her from other's gazes, throw her into their carriage, and drive her away.

On the other, he wanted to rattle her. He wanted to walk right up to her, take out all the pins from out of her coiffure and tousle her hair, rip her bodice, and cover her milky skin with his mouth, claiming her as his.

For some unfathomable reason, he had a violent, almost animalistic need for his duchess. Where had it come from? And would it easily subside?

She wasn't exactly his. She thought him a monster. And yet, and yet, and yet, he had the urge to prove her right.

Right now.

In the middle of the ballroom.

Just then, she drifted toward the exit and a few moments later disappeared behind the ballroom's closed doors.

Dane wanted to follow her, but he curbed the urge for now. She probably followed Wolverstone. She needed to speak to him privately, and Dane would allow her that. Besides, he was halfway across the ballroom.

He edged his way toward the ballroom doors nonetheless. But before he made a few steps, he was approached by lords and ladies from every corner blocking his way. He was forced to make polite chit-chat, while his duchess was out of his sight.

Dane was getting irritated, making his way through the throng of people. But before he even reached the edge of the ballroom, his duchess had already returned. And she wasn't alone.

Chapter 10

Mr. Townsend, the Earl of Payne's cousin and all-around nice gentleman, had her on his arm. He was saying something, leaning close to her ear, and she was smiling.

Dane took an involuntary step forward, his fingers curling into fists.

Nobody should be allowed to touch his duchess.

Just at that moment, she threw Dane a discreet glance before stepping onto the dancefloor with her partner.

Dane watched them dance, smile at each other earnestly, catch each other as they stumbled... Stumbled! His duchess never stumbled. What had Mr. Townsend said to her to rattle her so?

Was he her lover? Were they just outside having a tryst? Dane bristled on the inside, while his gaze followed his wife in the arms of another man. As the dance finished, she weaved her arm through the gentleman's elbow and led him away.

Dane followed them.

They walked around the ballroom before approaching Lavinia and Princess Victoria.

Dane couldn't watch any longer. The agreement they'd established when they'd married was void. There was no reason why he couldn't approach his wife and scare away any man who dared to come close to her. So he strode toward her, not paying any heed to the people who started to stop him on his track.

A moment before he reached his wife, Lavinia was swept away by her husband and Mr. Townsend took the princess onto the dancefloor.

The duchess watched the couple leave, her lips pursed, her unblinking eyes the only indication of her agitation.

Dane walked up to her from behind. "Are you nervous that

he might actually like her?"

"Yes, I am. Very much," his wife answered without turning to look at him. "Victoria is very likable."

Dane stepped to stand beside her. "Hm… So you're afraid to lose one of your lovers?"

She turned toward him, her brows furrowed. "How dare you."

"You are offended." He smiled wolfishly. "Good. I just wanted to see if my suspicions were correct. I am glad to say that they weren't."

She turned away again, her chin lifted in defiance. "Why would you care?"

I wish I knew the answer to this question myself. He shrugged. "You are my wife."

"Not in the strictest sense."

He craned his neck to look at her. Her nostrils were flared, her eyes glinting with candlelight. "Do you always have to be so… prickly?"

She narrowed her eyes. "Why would I be nice to you?"

"I am your husband."

"Not of my own desire."

He grimaced. "I would argue that was exactly your desire."

"You know nothing about my desires," she said, meeting his eyes.

No. But I wish to. "The day we married," he said carefully. "You said something that I was never able to forget."

"What is that?" She spoke through her teeth as if even talking to him was taking a great deal of self-control or effort.

"You said that you married me because you didn't want anyone else to."

She raised a brow. "You remembered that." Now her full

attention was on him. Finally.

"That's not something a gentleman forgets."

She shifted slightly, almost imperceptibly, but visibly for him because he was watching her so closely. He'd rattled her. "I didn't want anyone to suffer being married to a monster," she finally said.

He sniffed. "So you martyred yourself?"

"I can take care of myself."

Dane had the urge to roll his eyes. "Obviously."

"Do you always have to be so… annoying?"

He let out a loud laugh and in turn beheld her surprised expression. "Is something amiss?"

A slow smile crept up her face. "No. It's just… I don't think I've heard you laugh since the day we married."

Dane's features sobered. Nobody had ever said anything like this to him. Nobody was in a position to notice. He had to clear his throat before he could speak again. "Did you get to talk to Wolverstone?"

"Yes." Her tone was filled with annoyance. But it was not directed at him.

"What did he say?"

"In a nutshell? To enjoy my night."

Dane frowned. "So he knows nothing?"

"Either that or he won't tell me."

Dane rubbed his chin in thought. So another night, wasted. But perhaps it could still be salvaged. "Duchess…" he said slowly. "We are both in a situation that we would rather have avoided. Married to people we didn't choose. Stuck at a ball we would have rather avoided."

"We had to be here," she protested.

"And we had to marry each other, although we didn't want

to," he interrupted swiftly. She pursed her lips in disapproval, her gaze piercing. "I have a proposition for you. We can't do anything about our animosity just now. But we can try and salvage the evening."

She raised her brows. "How?"

"How about we pretend as if... we like each other?"

She didn't miss a beat. "I wouldn't know where to start."

He stretched out his arm. "We can start with a dance."

Chapter 11

Caroline placed her hand on her husband's arm, and he swept her away in a dance.

She didn't know whether he read the emotions on her face—people rarely could decipher her thoughts—or whether he too was tired of their distance, of the cold, silent townhouse, and the absence of the feeling of home.

Caroline didn't know if he even considered any of their dwellings a home. But for some unfathomable reason, on the day she felt most lonely in the world, on the day she felt like she didn't belong to anyone, he offered her a reprieve.

He offered his hand, and she took it. Not without apprehension. A tiny voice in the back of her mind said that he wanted to lull her into a false sense of security. She needed to stay alert. And yet...

It felt nice not worrying about her husband scurrying off into the night, not worrying about blackmail and other nefarious plots. For one short moment, they were husband and wife dancing during a ball.

Not that that was customary. People attended balls to get away from their spouses and to socialize with other people. In that way, their alliance was a perfect replica of the marriages of high society. Not today.

"Why didn't you wear any jewels?" he asked suddenly as they moved through the dance.

Caroline looked at him, startled. Ah, so he noticed. "I don't own any emeralds," she said evenly. "And I didn't think anything else would accentuate this gown."

He opened his mouth, then closed it like a fish out of water before finally speaking. "You have all my resources at your disposal. You can afford to buy some."

Caroline's chest felt heavy. She didn't expect him to offer the duchess's emeralds on the spot. This ceasefire was, after all, a farce. A one-night deal. A short escape from their miserable existence. But the reminder of that still hurt.

"Is green your favorite color then?"

Caroline narrowed her eyes at him, that tiny voice in the back of her mind screaming that this felt very wrong. "You want to know my favorite color?"

"We agreed to try and be"—he cleared his throat—"pleasant to each other tonight. And—"

"Yes, I remember that."

"—since we didn't have a proper courtship, why not try to imitate it now?"

Caroline turned in the dance, which gave her a moment to school her features because otherwise, she imagined she looked quite shocked. "You want to court me?"

He shrugged. "Just for tonight."

Caroline chewed her lip as she watched her husband carefully. What was he doing? Was this some kind of plan of his to lower her guard? *It's just a color, Caroline! Do not overthink it.* "Very well," she conceded slowly. "My favorite color is red."

"Ah, that color would look good on you, too. Perhaps you should consider acquiring some rubies." Caroline let out a laugh at the sheer foolishness of their conversation. Kensington faltered for a moment, his gaze trained on her. "Have I ever told you that you have a beautiful laugh, Your Grace?"

Caroline paused mid-dance, too. Then she smiled widely. "No. But if your idea of courting is to shower me with compliments, I quite like it."

A wicked grin blessed his lips. "Then I shall do exactly that."

Caroline stepped toward him and their hands touched just as the dance dictated. Only something electric passed through Caroline's hand. Her husband had felt it too. She could see it in his eyes that glinted with something unfathomable.

The music stopped and everyone around them bowed, while Caroline and Kensington still stood, their hands touching, their gazes locked. Caroline averted her gaze and attempted to step away, but Kensington tightened his fingers around hers. "Not yet," he said in a low voice that made gooseflesh cover her skin. "We'll dance another."

Caroline's eyes widened. "That's not proper."

"Tonight is not about proper," the duke answered with a wink. "Tonight is about me courting you."

A burst of laughter left her lips. This night promised to be interesting.

* * *

Their two dances back to back sent town gossip into a frenzy.

The Duke and Duchess of Kensington, the perfect society couple, have gone out of their minds. Dane could just see the gossip columns rambling in the morning.

His wife had a few cups of wine, so she was very relaxed, her cheeks rosy.

Had she always been this way and he just never noticed? Or had she reserved this side of herself for people she actually liked?

If so, was he one of those people now?

For the rest of the night they exchanged meaningless gossip, they laughed about anything and everything, and they spent the entire evening just enjoying each other's company. As it turned out, his wife's company was quite pleasant. They failed to talk about anything substantial. But that wasn't the point of the night, was it?

So then, what was the point?

Dane knew what *he* was trying to escape that night. The loneliness, the trifling conversations, another boring evening which he'd experienced every night for as long as he'd been a duke. Usually, he took off to seek danger under the guise of the Shadows. Tonight, he tried a distraction of a different kind.

At least Dane thought that was what it was about. Until his wife snuggled close to him in the carriage and placed her head on his shoulder.

At that moment, he forgot everything he thought he knew about life.

She heaved a sigh and closed her eyes as the rattle of the horse hooves and carriage wheels lulled her into sleep.

She had probably had too much wine, now that he thought

about it. Because, in her sensible mind, surely she would never have willingly sat so close to him. She never would have trusted him enough to press her cheek against his shoulder.

He turned toward her. Her breaths were deep, her mouth slightly open, and her lashes fluttered with her every exhale. Was she asleep so soon?

An errant lock of hair traveled its way out of her perfect coiffure to tickle her nose.

There. She wasn't as rigid and perfect as she was at the beginning of the ball. One mission of his accomplished.

He smiled to himself. Then he leaned closer and swept the errant lock away from her face. He watched her as she slept peacefully, trusting him to take care of her, trusting him not to hurt her, and something within him constricted in pain.

The carriage swayed, and the door was thrown open, awakening his duchess. He mourned the loss of her warm touch as she raised her head and blinked a few times, trying to understand what in the world was going on.

"We've arrived," Dane said softly. "Home."

She blinked up at him at his last word and stared at him for one long moment. And then she nodded. "Lead the way, Your Grace."

Dane exited the carriage, helped her onto the street, and then led her into their townhouse.

The butler had a self-satisfied smirk on his face, which he couldn't hide when he greeted them. Dane didn't know what the butler could have seen to have him act that way. He couldn't have seen the duchess leaning against him in the carriage. But then, Caroline's hand was no longer hovering over Dane's forearm, her fingers were gripping his coat. And she was not walking a foot away from him, but leaning into his side.

They made their way up the stairs in silence. But this was no longer the cold silence that had occupied their marriage from the day of their wedding. This was a charged silence—not with animosity, but with something else. Something new.

They stopped before the duchess's chambers, and Caroline turned to look at him. "Thank you for a lovely night," she said.

There was a slight slur to her speech. Was it from sleep or wine? At that moment, it didn't matter. Because there was a change in the lilt of her voice and the cadence of her tone. Not from being intoxicated. But different somehow. Warmer.

Silence again.

Dane had a hard time putting his words together. More so because he knew if he said goodnight, he'd have to leave. But there was nothing more to say. Was there?

"I wish to do it again," he blurted out.

Her gaze turned vulnerable. As though she'd hoped he'd say those words. As though she was afraid he wouldn't.

She placed a hand on his chest. Warm. Hot. Burning through his waistcoat and shirtsleeves. He stepped closer.

"Why?" she asked.

"Because perhaps we misjudged each other."

She stepped closer still. Now they were mere inches away. "What if we haven't?"

Dane lowered his head and stopped only when his lips grazed hers. "What if we have?"

There was a long pause where their breaths mingled, his heart drumming in his ears. "I want to kiss you," he said.

She didn't say anything. Her gaze was concentrated on his mouth, her fingers curled into his waistcoat. He could feel her breath on his face, and that was the only thing that stopped him.

Her breath smelled of alcohol. She wasn't in complete awareness of herself. And if he kissed her—when he kissed her—he wanted her to be of a completely clear mind.

He stepped away. She swayed, and he had to catch her by the arms to steady her.

"But you said—" she started, looking confused.

"I know." He smiled. "Tomorrow. If you still feel the same."

He slowly let her go and took two more steps back. She stood there, watching him for a long moment before finally nodding and turning away. Only when the door behind her closed did he have the courage to speak again. "Goodnight."

* * *

Caroline woke up with a terrible headache... but in a good mood.

Where did that come from? How can one be in a good mood when one's skull felt as though it was cracked open? She closed her eyes and pretended to be asleep for a few more moments while trying to remember what led to her current disastrous state.

And the memories of the night before penetrated her mind.

"Oh, God!" She shot up, then winced at the sharp ache in her head.

Had she really almost let Dane kiss her?

Let him? She'd practically begged him to do it!

This was bad. Bad, bad, bad, bad, bad.

Wasn't it?

Caroline fell back onto the bed and covered her face with her blanket. She didn't want to face the day. More than that, she didn't want to face her husband. What was she going to say to him?

Would he gloat that she'd so easily fallen for his charm?

Of course, she could always lie and tell him that she did not remember anything because of her deeply inebriated state the night before.

But oh, she remembered. The heat of his chest beneath her fingers, his warm breath on her cheek. His full, sinful lips oh-so-close to hers.

She groaned aloud.

Then she pushed her covers aside, her mind working on the solution to the problem.

What am I going to do?

Well, she couldn't very well stay in bed all day, could she? It would help her avoid the duke, but it wouldn't help her with anything else, and she had way too much on her plate with the upcoming Christmas feast.

Maybe if she pretended that she was busy all day… She needn't pretend. The list of tasks for her to do was so long, she could bury herself in them and not see the duke until the twelfth night.

Yes, that was the best solution. Keep herself busy and not think of her husband… Or else, just keep herself busy.

She slowly scrambled from the bed and rang for her maid. Then she sat back on the bed, her head in her hands, her elbows propped against her knees.

"Good morning!" Rea sang as she entered the room and Caroline shushed her. "Had too much wine, have you?"

Caroline nodded, then immediately regretted the action. "Yes. Too, too much."

"Well, I have the perfect remedy for that. It shall be waiting for you at breakfast."

Caroline winced. "Is… Did the duke awaken?"

"Oh, yes. A few hours ago."

"Hours?" Caroline looked around and then winced again. She shouldn't move her head for a while now. Not until the headache subsided. "What time is it?"

"Past noon, I believe."

Caroline groaned.

"Are you certain this is just the effects of the alcohol?" Rea placed the back of her palm against Caroline's forehead.

"I am fine." Caroline swatted her hand away. "Just a bit… out of sorts."

"Come." Rea took her by the hand and led her to her vanity table. "Sit." Rea proceeded to take the pins out of her hair. It felt nice.

"Perhaps I should have my breakfast here," Caroline said. "But nothing greasy. A couple of pieces of toast should be fine."

Rea reared back and looked at her, shocked. "That's it?"

Caroline chuckled. She was known for her great appetite, but this morning she just didn't feel like it.

"Well, you need to rest up. You have a busy day today."

"I do?"

Rea gave her a sardonic look. "More Yuletide greenery arrived. You need to decide where to put it all. And then you scheduled a visit to the draper. I believe you wanted to order childbed linens for Lady Payne. And today is Thursday, which means that ladies are coming here for the nuncheon."

Caroline stifled the groan. "Oh, no, I completely forgot about the nuncheon."

"Yes, I thought so."

Why did she have to drink so much wine last night? There were too many things to take care of. And she also needed to speak to her husband.

Did she?

Yes. She did. She needed to tell him that last night was a mistake and they shouldn't do anything of the sort until they figured out this whole blackmailing business.

Right?

Caroline knew that the melancholy she'd felt the night before was the reason for her irrational thoughts and action. She longed to be in the bosom of a loving family. Being alone during the holiday season was never easy. And that was interfering with her objectivity.

Caroline stopped Rea's ministrations. She needed to clear her mind. "Bring me the breakfast and the remedy. And then a bath. And if the duke asks about me... I am very, very busy."

Chapter 12

D
ane waited for his duchess to show up at breakfast in vain.

At first, he thought that perhaps she wasn't feeling well after drinking the night before. But after a few hours passed and she was still nowhere to be seen, he realized that she was avoiding him.

He had a lot to do today, places to go, but he didn't want to leave the house without seeing Caroline, without talking to her, and without kissing her.

He might not have fully trusted her yet. And he might not have fully reconciled with the idea of her being his true wife. But he had enjoyed their time together the night before. And the memory of it promised a brighter future.

Trust wasn't born in a day. It was earned. And they both had a lot of earning to do.

But at the very least, they could stop being hostile to each other. At the very least, they could start working on their strange, yet curious, relationship. And 'curious' was something he could live with.

"Is the duchess up yet?" Dane asked the butler as he left the study in search of his wife.

"Yes, Your Grace. She is in the kitchen."

"Great, great." Kensington nodded and hurried toward the kitchen.

Caroline was standing in the middle, wearing an apron over her day gown. His duchess in an apron was not something he expected to see. She was standing over already prepared dishes, waving her hands and explaining something in response to the cook. Kitchen maids were running around her, bringing the dishes, taking them away. It looked like a mill in the middle of the working day.

Dane leaned his shoulder against the doorjamb and just observed his wife doing what she probably did daily: performed her duties as a duchess.

"Yes," Caroline said in answer to the cook's concerns. "Please, prepare blancmange in advance and store it in the dairy room. And then we shall have a goose, turkey, and venison prepared on the day. We won't have many guests, as I said, but the more food we have, the more you get in your Christmas box the next morning. It's our first Christmas celebration with me as a duchess, so I want the table to be laden with food."

"Absolutely." The cook bowed her head.

"And how is our figgy pudding?"

"I brandied it just an hour ago, my lady."

"Brilliant!" Caroline exclaimed. "I think we are all ready for our first Christmas together!"

Dane's smile grew at his wife's enthusiasm and burst out in applause at her grandiose finish. The entire kitchen went quiet for a moment as heads turned toward him. Caroline's eyes were wide, and she turned as red as a beetroot.

"Oh, I wasn't supposed to clap?" Dane asked.

Caroline stepped closer to him and hissed in a low voice, "What are you doing here?"

He shrugged. "I wanted to see my duchess work. Is that wrong?"

She discreetly waved him to the side. "Is something amiss? Why are you looking for me in the kitchen?"

He watched her with an intense stare. "No, nothing's amiss. Perhaps I just missed you."

"Your Grace—"

"Dane. Please, call me Dane." From the corner of his eye, he noticed the servants gathering around them.

She pursed her lips in disapproval. "I am very busy."

"I can see that," he said, then turned his head toward the servants.

Caroline also turned toward them, confused. "Why are you not working?"

The chef cleared her throat. "It's... Nothing. It's just..." She raised her eyes toward the ceiling. "You're standing under a mistletoe."

Dane carefully raised his eyes, as if afraid that some monster was above his head. No. Just a mistletoe leaf. "So?"

"Well, sir..." The chef crumpled the apron in her hands. "It's a... Well, people say that if two people are caught beneath a mistletoe, they need to kiss."

Dane glanced toward his wife. Her eyes widened in horror. "There will be no kissing," she said emphatically. She seemed quite offended at the idea. And if normally that would bother him just a little, now she was showing her distaste in front of their servants, and his pride got slightly injured.

Dane tilted his head to the side as he watched his wife with a raised brow.

"I wouldn't dream to contradict milady, but"—the cook looked utterly uncomfortable—"it is said to be bad luck if the lady refuses the kiss."

"You don't want bad luck, do you, wife?" Dane said with a grin.

She narrowed her eyes at him. "Do not encourage them!"

"Why not? You don't want to be the reason for bad luck in this house, do you?"

"Fine." Caroline straightened her spine. Then she elegantly offered him her hand.

Light groans and whispers of disapproval sounded from the crowd, but as Caroline turned toward them, they all seemed to find an utter interest in the floorboards.

Dane smiled, took her hand, and tugged on it until Caroline crashed against his chest. Then he took her by her chin and planted a quick but hard kiss on her lips. Before letting go, he whispered in her ear, "I promised you a kiss yesterday. I don't go back on my promises."

Caroline retreated two steps, not taking her eyes off him. Dane couldn't quite tell if she was shocked, horrified, or simply speechless. Then she ordered the servants to get back to work, turned on her heel, and fled.

* * *

There was a knock on Caroline's door a few minutes after she stormed into her room. Probably her husband.

How could he humiliate her so before the kitchen staff?

Lords and ladies did not kiss in front of their servants. Actually, they did not kiss in front of anyone. Some lords and ladies did not kiss at all!

Another knock. More insistent this time.

"Caroline, may I speak with you?" Her husband's voice came from behind the door.

Caroline, she mouthed. "Yes, come in."

She leaned her hips against her bed and crossed her arms over her chest, waiting for her husband to enter.

He came in and looked around, tugging on his cravat. "Apologies if I made you uncomfortable."

"You acted like a gentleman," she said and registered surprise on his face before she continued, "yesterday."

"Ah, you mean when I did not kiss you?"

"Yes, exactly. I should have known that wouldn't last."

"I couldn't disappoint the servants." He slowly started moving around the room. "So… can I assume you didn't enjoy the kiss?"

Caroline blinked, her mind going completely blank. What was it about this man that he always managed to render her speechless? He turned toward her with a grin, then raised both brows.

"I think it is better if we keep our association purely… businesslike," she said and licked her lips.

His eyes lowered to her mouth, his lids heavy. "Businesslike, you say?"

Caroline stiffened. "Until the matter with the blackmail is resolved, I don't think we should… talk about kisses."

A slow smile appeared on his face. "You didn't answer my question."

"Oh, for God's sake!" She turned away to hide her blushing

119

cheeks. At least, she was certain she was blushing because her entire body burned hot.

"Fine," he said as he continued prowling about her chamber. "Then let's talk business."

"Yes?"

"Christmas dinner," he said.

She turned toward him and watched his slow approach toward her. "Did you pick out your Christmas attire?"

"I did." She nodded for emphasis.

"Is it that green gown you wore for the Wolverstone's ball?" He was uncomfortably close now. She had to crane her neck to look him in the eyes. But his posture was non-threatening. He had his hands behind his back, his features thoughtful.

"No, I have another one that I think is more appropriate for the occasion."

"Hm… pity."

"Why is that?"

"Because I have something for you. And it would fit perfectly with that gown." He pulled his hand from behind his back to reveal a rectangular box.

"A gift?" she asked, breathless. "But it's not St. Stephen's day yet…"

"It's not really a gift," he said with a slight grimace. "It belongs to you. I just didn't think to give it to you earlier."

Caroline took the box in her hands and opened it. She already knew what she'd find there. And yet she felt emotions welling up inside her as she saw the duchess's jewels.

Caroline cleared her throat. "Thank you."

"Let me put it on—" he started, but she interrupted him, shaking her head.

"No. Not yet. I don't… I don't feel like I can wear it now

with my current attire."

He gave her a roguish smile as he took out the emerald choker from the box. "You're my duchess. You can wear it all the time." He walked behind her. "Whether you're wearing an apron over your gown." He laid the necklace against her neck. "Whether you're wearing a nightgown." He attached the clasp. "Or whether you're not wearing anything else at all."

Gooseflesh covered her body at his last words as his breath worried the wisps of her hair at the back of her neck.

They stood silent for a few long moments before she sharply turned toward him. He didn't step back, so they were toe to toe now, their faces only inches away. "How does it look?" she whispered.

His gaze traveled down to her neck, and he swallowed. "Like it belongs to you." He met her gaze. "Like you belong to me."

Caroline caught her breath.

He lowered his head.

Caroline's pulse drummed loudly in her head. "I said—"

He kissed her.

Caroline's eyes fluttered closed, her hands grabbing at his broad, steady shoulders because if she didn't clutch onto him as hard as she could, she would've fallen. His hand went to gently cup her cheek while his lips worked their magic over hers.

It wasn't Caroline's first kiss. Not even the first kiss from him. And yet it was the first one that made her knees weak, and her entire body burn with need. Need to be close to him. Need to experience more.

Caroline stood on her toes and kissed him back.

Dane groaned, his arm weaving around her waist and pulling her closer. His mouth opened over hers as his tongue probed at her lips. His thumb caressed her cheek, his fingers tickling her jawline, her neck.

She surrendered with a sigh, opening to him, drawing his tongue further inside, tasting his salty essence.

What am I doing? Her mind finally screamed at her.

Caroline pulled away, still gripping his shoulders tightly. Dane's eyes were still closed, his breath heavy. He leaned in and pressed his forehead against hers.

"Thank you," he breathed.

Thank you?

Then he smiled and pressed a kiss against her forehead. "Good day, Caroline." With that, he turned away and walked out of her room.

* * *

Caroline still wore the duchess's jewels as she made her way downstairs for the nuncheon. She didn't know why she was loath to take them off, and she was afraid to question her decision.

Instead, she decided to forget all about her troubles and join her friends in the drawing room.

Just like every Thursday, Caroline's drawing room was filled with female chatter. The ladies were animatedly exchanging greetings and compliments as they laughed and bantered before finally sitting down in a circle around the table, laden with nuncheon treats.

"Oof!" Annalise settled down in her chair, her every movement punctuated by her grunts. "My midwife says I have at least a month to go, but I feel if this babe grows more, I won't be able to walk. I'll simply be toppling over all the time."

Caroline patted her hand. "But are you still fine to go to the draper today? I can do it myself. I am not sure you'll like what I pick out—"

Annalise's eyes watered, and her voice was high as she spoke. "I'll love everything you pick out. I trust you more with this than I trust myself!"

Caroline squeezed her fingers. "Then do not worry about it. I don't want to drag you around town if you're uncomfortable."

"Oh, I don't feel comfortable at all," Annalise complained. "And to make matters worse, my mother arrived yesterday."

"Your mother?" Lavinia grimaced.

"Yes, and she insists we move to the Blakehurst manor on the outskirts of the city. She says that the town smoke and the smell from the Thames are not good for the babe. And since I am not supposed to leave my house the last month of my pregnancy, she insists we leave tomorrow."

"You can't leave tomorrow!" Caroline exclaimed. "The Christmas feast is in three days. And I am specifically not inviting anyone other than us and your husbands so that you don't even have to dress up. Nobody is going to care what you look like or if you decide to take a nap halfway through."

Annalise wrinkled her nose. "My mother would want to come too. And I truly don't want to ruin your Christmas feast."

Caroline pursed her lips. "I won't insist, because it can't be easy for you. But just know that I would love for you to be there."

Annalise nodded. "We shall probably move to Blakehurst tomorrow. I truly can't argue with Mama. But it's only an hour away. I shall beg Blake to take mercy on me and bring me here for Christmas."

Everyone chuckled.

"But enough about me." Annalise suddenly turned to the other women in the circle. "Anyone else have news?"

"Only grievances," Victoria grumbled.

"Grievances?" Caroline raised her brow.

"Victoria is still adamant about leaving for Russia," Lavinia said with a grimace.

Oh, yes. Victoria's home country. Ever since her marriage to a bastard, Victoria wanted to escape England and go back to her motherland, citing that there was nothing more here in England for her, since the only reason her uncle brought her here was to marry her off. Advantageously. And since that plan had failed, she didn't want to remain in England any longer.

"I am just going home to my sister!" she exclaimed.

"Yes, and Sebastian and I want to accompany you," Lavinia said softly.

Caroline stifled a smile. Sebastian, the Marquess of Roth, was Caroline's distant cousin. He had inherited the title from Caroline's dear late uncle. Cousin Sebastian was a lovely man and Caroline was glad that Lavinia seemed happily married to him. Especially since she still felt guilty, even if justified, for stealing Kensington away from her.

"I can do it alone."

"Sebastian doesn't think so and I agree," Lavinia said. "You should not go anywhere alone. Besides, we are going to leave anyway. Just as soon as I find Matilda. And there is also the matter of Sebastian's aunt, who is too frail to go anywhere. I don't want to leave her alone."

Matilda was Lavinia's stepmother. Before Lavinia married advantageously, her guardian had time to wreak havoc on her life and expel Matilda from her home. Now Lavinia was adamant about bringing her stepmother home.

"You want to go to Paris," Victoria whined. "I know that. It's Uncle's favorite place. But I am going to Russia."

"We can go with you to Russia for a few weeks and then go back to Paris, can we not? Or do you not want us with you at all?"

Victoria cleared her throat. "Uncle just doesn't trust my sister. I know that. But she is running the entire country all by herself. She can take care of me, not that I need taking care of. I am married now."

Caroline pursed her lips. "I don't think you should use that as an example of your independence, dear. I don't mean to be unkind, but you went around everyone's back and married a bastard and a criminal."

Victoria straightened. "I didn't know that at the time."

"And that's exactly the reason why you shouldn't be going anywhere alone," Lavinia chimed in, then threw Caroline a cautious glance. "Besides... With the blackmail letters I received, I am not planning on staying in England for long."

"We shall figure this out, I promise," Caroline said and patted Lavinia on her hand.

"Any news on that front?" Annalise asked.

"Or on some other front, maybe?" Lavinia asked, with a strange glint in her eyes.

"What front?" Olivia frowned.

"Oh, I forgot. Neither of you was at the ball last night," Lavinia said. "Caroline had quite the night, didn't you, darling? With her *husband*."

125

Caroline's cheeks burned intensely, which was probably noticeable to all. Curse her fair skin.

"You did? What happened?" Annalise's mouth fell open.

"Nothing," she said with a timid smile. Then she repeated it more emphatically as she turned to Lavinia, "Nothing."

"Right, nothing." Lavinia nodded. "Except you danced two full dances and laughed for most of the night."

There was a murmur of surprise and awe, and Caroline hurried to intervene. "We called a truce for one night. That is all. I suppose we were both tired of the tense atmosphere in the house and decided to... ignore it for a few hours. And I might have over-imbibed the wine."

"Mhm..." Lavinia watched her with narrowed eyes, although she was pursing her lips from smiling.

Everyone else was openly grinning, except for Olivia, who just seemed shocked.

"That doesn't change anything," Caroline insisted.

"The lady doth protest too much, methinks," Annalise said with a satisfied grin.

"Can we talk about something else, please?" Caroline threw up her hands.

"Does this mean that Kensington is no longer under suspicion?" Victoria asked.

"He is. And I shall continue my inquiry into him just for this reason."

"I am certain that there could be no other reason for your inquiries," Annalise said with a cheeky smile, and everyone laughed.

"Well, since we are on the topic of Kensington," Olivia said. "Jarvis gave me this and told me to give it to you."

She extended her hand with a note in it. Caroline took it

and proceeded to open it. "What is this?"

"The information you asked for," Olivia said. "I don't—I didn't open it. He just said to give this to you. And to be with you when you open it."

Caroline paused at the act of unwrapping the paper, startled by St. John's words. Was it bad news then?

"What does it say?" Helen spoke for the first time since their nuncheon started.

Caroline opened the note and read.

> *The house under the address you sent me is occupied by one Miss Nicolette Burk. She is a known actress and a courtesan. No criminal ties.*

Caroline's throat constricted, and her vision darkened.

"What is it?" Annalise asked. "Is something wrong?"

Caroline swallowed and shook her head. "No," she said and tried for a smile. "I suppose it's good news."

"Good news?" Lavinia echoed.

"You don't look like you received good news," Victoria confirmed.

Caroline let out a deep breath and read the contents out loud.

"A courtesan?" Victoria repeated, looking confused.

Caroline nodded. "Probably his mistress." *Definitely his mistress.*

The silence lengthened, everyone frozen in an awkward tableau.

"I am sorry, Caroline," Olivia finally said. Even someone who didn't understand the necessity of social etiquette and who wasn't good at recognizing the nuance of human emotion

127

somehow understood that it was unpleasant to learn of your husband's infidelity.

Of course, Olivia was in love with her husband, whereas Caroline had barred hers from her bed.

"Mistresses are quite common," Helen added. She knew that firsthand.

Caroline put on a smile. "It's all irrelevant. And it's not like we— Kensington and I are not—" Caroline grimaced. She wasn't going to divulge their private arrangements with everyone, was she? But she found she had nothing else to say.

"Would you like some water?" Victoria offered.

Caroline shook her head. "No, it's not necessary." She stood. "As I said, that's good news then."

"Good?" Annalise asked stiffly. Everyone looked confused.

"Well, it means that Kensington probably isn't involved with the criminal element, just as you all suspected. It also means that you do not have to worry about me any longer."

"Yes, absolutely," light murmurs followed from every woman.

"I heard from Jarvis that many gentlemen keep their mistresses in separate townhouses," Olivia said. "He said that most don't even bother to hide it."

Caroline nodded, knowing Olivia wasn't trying to be unkind. She was merely stating facts as she saw them. And Caroline had asked Dane to be discreet. Well, she should have been thankful for that.

"Yes." Caroline tried for a smile, but her heart felt heavy.

She didn't know why. She truly hadn't expected him to be faithful to her, had she? They'd barely spoken a word to each other in over five months of their marriage, let alone spent any time together. There should have been no surprise that his loyalties lay elsewhere. But after the ball, the mistletoe kiss, and the way he had given her the duchess's jewels, she had a hard time wrapping her head around the truth.

Suddenly it all made sense, though. Perhaps that was it. Perhaps Kensington's secrecy, all those missed dinners, and the nights he had spent away from Kensington townhouse had nothing to do with blackmail or even the Shadows. He was simply spending his time in another woman's arms.

"You know that Payne had a mistress before," Annalise said and let out a deep sigh.

"Before he got some sense knocked into him?" Lavinia offered.

Annalise laughed. "No, before we married. But he fully intended to keep his mistress even after our marriage. He had a very… um… traditional father. He raised him with some awful views on life. Luckily Payne grew to realize that. He was never unfaithful, but our marriage was still rocky in the beginning. Even if he loved me. If I weren't a naïve debutante, perhaps I would have stood up to him earlier. Right away. And then perhaps our marriage would have begun better than it did."

"You can't blame yourself for his actions," Caroline protested.

"I don't. I am just saying that we were both young and quite stupid, I'm afraid. So we made a lot of mistakes. You are neither young nor stupid. So perhaps you can avoid my fate."

Caroline frowned. "Kensington and I have a mutually beneficial arrangement. We don't—That's not a part of our agreement."

"But it hurts you," Helen said softly, her brows crinkled in thought. "I think Annalise is right."

Caroline shook her head. This was madness. Anyone would react to the news of their husband's mistress the way she did. She didn't want him. She'd just lost perspective for one moment. Theirs wasn't a real marriage.

"This is foolish talk. All of your marriages are love matches."

"Perhaps," Helen agreed. "But it doesn't mean it hurts you less. You should tell him if it hurts you." She paused, and then added quieter, "I know. I wish I did."

Caroline snapped her head toward Helen. Her eyes were filled with pain. She had always been sickly, as long as Caroline knew her. And her husband was always having affairs, as long as they'd been married. Or at least, that's what everyone said.

Suddenly, it wasn't about Caroline anymore. It wasn't about her pain and about her revenge. It was about regret. Every woman in this room regretted something. Caroline was always the one to give advice and to help her friends when they were going through difficult times. Perhaps this time, it was her turn to listen.

Chapter 13

It was late evening, and Dane was looking forward to going home. He'd had a busy day, and to his utter surprise, he looked forward to coming home to his duchess.

Dane didn't even try to fool himself into pretending that he wasn't thinking about their kisses. He quite enjoyed them. His duchess was rather sweet and pliant in his arms. She was a constant revelation, that woman, and he was looking forward to finding out more.

What surprised him was the fact that he felt this desire for her that went beyond physical. Something drew him to her. Something more than the need to find physical relief.

She didn't feel the same, though. He was certain of it. Perhaps she felt the physical draw, but her reluctance to meet his eyes, her attempts to avoid him, told him that she still didn't trust him. Not that he trusted her completely either. She was hiding things, he was certain. But not anything as dire as being a secret criminal.

And he knew exactly how to make *her* trust him.

All he needed to do was to find the real blackmailer by himself. Once he did that, he could demand more of her. He could demand answers and perhaps hope for a more friendly relationship with his wife.

He didn't know exactly why he wanted that. But after discovering the true face behind the duchess's mask, after experiencing her witty retorts and seeing the scorching fire behind those green eyes, finding out more about his wife excited him. And he hadn't been excited in a long time. Perhaps, never.

So instead of directing his carriage homeward, he rapped on the roof and barked, "To Ford Gunning's."

A few minutes later, the carriage stopped in front of a dark, imposing building. Dane jumped out of the carriage and walked toward the door with a sign that read *Lion's Head Coffeehouse*.

Dane walked inside and was welcomed by immediate stares his way. Then a few moments later, Ford Gunning, the infamous thief-taker, appeared from the back door.

"Your Grace," he said with a slight bow. "An honor."

Dane gave a sharp nod. "Can we talk in private?"

"Of course." Gunning led him into a small, dark office at the back of the coffeehouse and waved to a chair. "Coffee?"

"No, thank you."

"What can I help you with?" Gunning asked as he settled across from him.

"I am looking for someone. A blackmailer."

Gunning raised a brow. "You'll have to be more specific than that."

Dane shrugged. "Deals out threatening notes. Targets either

powerful lords or helpless ladies. Does it sound like anyone you know?"

"If you're implying Hades, then it is definitely not him."

"Definitely?" It was Dane's turn to raise his brow.

Gunning let out a chuckle. "Let's drop the pretenses, shall we? You and I both know that Hades is one of the most notorious blackmailers in London. The difference is every single person he blackmails knows it is him. They never question who is behind the threats. And all that threatening is always done in person. Now, I am not fond of him, you know this, but he does not cower behind notes. And he most certainly does not blackmail innocent ladies."

"Right." Dane nodded sharply. "He just kidnaps them."

Gunning curled his fists. Hades had recently kidnapped the thief-taker's sister. Subsequently, they fell in love and married. However, there was no love lost between the in-laws.

Mr. Gunning's sister was not the only victim of the kidnappings, though. Helen St. John had also been a visitor of Hades' mansion. It had nothing to do with Mrs. St John though, but everything to do with her scoundrel of a former husband.

"As I said. I do not condone his actions, nor am I his avid defender. But there is one thing Hades is not, and that is a coward."

Dane scratched his jaw. "The bastard I am talking about is impersonating a Shadow."

Gunning studied him curiously. "That doesn't help a bit. Everybody hates the Shadows at the moment."

This was true. A few years ago, the rumors started about the Shadows and equated them to criminals for no reason. And then after Bradshaw—an actual criminal—had been caught with the Shadows' uniform by his side, the rumors exploded, leading to the current situation where even the King was after them.

"But can you ask him? I am convinced that Hades is not involved, but he knows almost everyone in the criminal world. Perhaps he's heard rumors we're deprived of."

"I don't know what kind of impression you have about the relationship I have with Hades. We don't exactly like each other."

Dane smirked. "You're family. Perhaps you will be spending the Christmas feast together?"

Gunning let out a burst of hoarse laughter. "You want me to show up at a family dinner and ask my brother-in-law to help poor defenseless toffs? I'll be thrown out on my arse and never let in again. And I might not like him even a bit. But I won't risk not seeing my sister again for you, Your Grace."

Dane stood and paced a couple of steps in the cramped chamber.

"There is something I heard," Gunning said thoughtfully.

Dane immediately turned on him. "Yes?"

"A rumor around St. James about a man who grants favors. Claims to take revenge on aristocrats who wronged them. Calls himself… I don't recall, but not a Shadow. I'd remember that."

"Erebus?" Dane raised a brow.

Gunning shrugged. "Could be. I don't really recall."

Hm… Could be something of value. But a rumor? Not much to go on.

"Perhaps you know something about this?" Dane took out a list with names of paintings that were hanging on his wife's wall.

Gunning squinted at the names, then shrugged. "I am not that familiar with art."

"These are unknown works of very popular painters. But they belonged to a man who had no means of acquiring them about fifteen years ago."

Gunning twisted the paper in his hands. "Fifteen years ago is slightly before my time as a thief-taker. But I know someone who deals with art theft, underground auctions, and forgeries."

Forgeries? Interesting. "Who?"

"The Brotherhood of the Crimson Fist."

The Brotherhood? The same people who had abducted and tortured Lord Payne. The same people who dealt with slave ships were behind art forgeries? This sounded more than confusing. And even more unbelievable.

"The Brotherhood of the Crimson Fist is one of the oldest secret societies. An elite order bent on world domination and furthering secret agendas I know not of. It seems far-fetched at best they would be behind art forgeries," Dane said out loud.

Gunning cocked his head. "You seem to know a lot about them."

One side of Dane's mouth kicked up in a smile. "I studied secret societies at school. Beginning in the thirteenth century, many elite societies started popping up like the Orange Order and the Masons; some benevolent, others bent on world domination; some religious, others not really."

What Dane neglected to mention was that the Shadows were one of these societies. But unlike the others, their agenda was ridding the world of secret societies, as strange as that might have sounded.

The Shadows were created to stand up for the people. A group of vigilantes sworn to protect the people of the land and to ensure no secret agendas against the people were conducted within the House of Lords.

But did Caroline's uncle have anything to do with either of these groups?

"I don't know much. Just that there's a secret auction house dealing with stolen and forged art which only admits the members of the Brotherhood. I came across them by accident and learned as much as I could without getting killed. Apologies I can't help more," Gunning said as he relaxed in his chair. "Although I am not the one you should be asking about this."

Dane raised a brow. "Oh?"

"You come here asking me to approach my family with your questions, saying it's yuletide." He shrugged. "And yet, you have a family member who would probably know a lot more than me. Someone who ran with The Brotherhood some fifteen years ago."

Dane stiffened.

Gunning smiled slyly. "Someone like your brother."

* * *

"Is the duchess home?" Dane asked the butler as he took off his coat and handed it to him.

"Yes, Your Grace. She is in your study."

Dane faltered for a moment before a smile stretched his lips. *My study?* She wasn't even hiding her snooping ways anymore. Well, if she went through every document he had in his possession, perhaps she would finally believe that he had nothing to do with the nasty crimes that she accused him of. And today he especially needed her to believe him. Because she would not like what he had to say.

After the Wolverstone ball and the mistletoe kiss, he'd hoped that things between them had started to shift for the better. And there was hope on the horizon that their marriage could become real.

Why he wanted that, he couldn't say. But the desire to have that was undeniable.

He moved swiftly toward the study and paused at the door. He was looking forward to seeing his wife, and yet he stalled because the conversation would not be an easy one. Taking a deep breath, he turned the handle and entered the dimly lit room.

Caroline was curled up in his grand chair by the hearth, reading. He paused at the door, just watching her, soaking her in. Her eyes ran down the page for a few brief moments before she finally raised her head.

She looked at him, seemingly stumped, as if she wasn't the one who was encroaching on his territory. As if he was the one out of place.

"Good evening, Duchess." Dane inclined his head. "Anything interesting on those pages?"

"Not particularly." She closed the book but kept her finger in place. "You're home rather late."

He raised a brow. "Were you waiting for me?"

"No." *Oh.* His spirits dropped a little. "But since we have this truce, I decided to find a cozy place for myself to spend some reading time other than my bedchamber. Monotony gets boring after a while. So I thought why not exploit one of the many chambers of this spacious townhouse? And well, I settled on this chair."

Dane undid his cuffs as he walked toward his desk, then slowly started rolling up his sleeves. "I am glad you're making yourself comfortable after five months of marriage," Dane said with only slight sarcasm in his voice. "Are you feeling more at home then?"

"Is there something in particular that you wanted?" his wife asked suddenly.

For a moment, Dane was startled into speechlessness. He thought their marriage had become amicable, yet his duchess's tone was anything but friendly.

"If I am holding you back from working, just say the word and I shall be out of here in a pinch." She made a motion to leave.

Dane leaned his hips against the desk. "Actually, I would very much like it if you stayed. We have some things to discuss."

"Oh?"

"Don't you think?" He watched her, trying to gauge her mood. She seemed rather angry with him, or even worse. Indifferent.

"No, not particularly," she said with that cold, unfeeling tone that she had used for most of their marriage.

"When we parted today, I dare say you felt differently." He hoped she would blush at his words, or look away, give him a timid smile. No such luck.

She stared with that glacial gaze of hers. "Then, I am afraid you misread my sentiments."

"Did I?"

The kiss under the mistletoe might not have been welcomed by her, but the kiss after he gave her the duchess's emeralds was passionate on her side. He couldn't have mistaken that. He thought things between them started to shift.

Not that he expected her to run into his arms and demand he kiss her—although he secretly dreamed of that—but he did expect a more tender greeting. At the very least, he'd earned a smile. Or so he thought.

"Right. Well, then." Dane directed her a glacial stare of his own. "Let's at least talk about business."

"Absolutely," she agreed readily.

Dane crossed his arms over his chest, every muscle in his body tensing. Perhaps this way it would be easier to tell her what he needed to say. He needn't be afraid of ruining their relationship. It seemed there was nothing there to ruin.

"I was thinking deeply about the core of our issues."

"Were you?" Caroline lowered her feet to the floor and adjusted her skirts as she spoke.

"Yes, and that would be your uncle."

"Or so you say." Her words were mild, almost indecipherable. She straightened and met his gaze.

"Well, *you* said you thought that perhaps he was blackmailed prior to inheriting his title."

"Yes?"

"And I thought to myself, if we can figure out what he had been blackmailed with, we might somehow get to the bottom of this."

"How?" Her tone was incredulous. "We know what Lavinia was blackmailed with, and how does that help?"

"I don't know yet," Dane conceded. "It might be connected somehow. Or it might not be. But I think I have an idea about your uncle's plight. I went to a thief-taker tonight—"

"A thief-taker?" Caroline's nostrils flared. "You went behind my back to investigate my uncle with a thief-taker?"

"I didn't think you'd mind. And I wanted to have some answers before I came to you."

"And do you have any answers?"

Dane took a deep breath, getting agitated. "Maybe."

"Maybe?" Her tone was sharp.

"Listen, please. While looking through Roth's ledgers, I found one interesting thing. Your father apparently had cut your uncle off. There was not a single penny allocated to him, according to those ledgers. He didn't receive an allowance. Your father didn't pay any of his bills."

"What does it mean?"

"It means that he had some other way of earning funds."

She stood sharply. "Criminal ways."

"I didn't say that." Dane straightened before the desk.

"But you meant it, and I don't think I like your implications. The blackmailers are criminals, not my uncle."

"I came into the title without a penny, and you assumed I was a criminal. Yet I don't take as much offense in your accusations as you do to mine. So I will thank you not to jump to conclusions about anything. Not about me, not about your uncle," Dane said coldly.

"My uncle is—was a good person," she insisted.

"Lavinia is too." Dane threw up his hands. "And yet they found something to taunt her with."

Caroline took a deep breath. "And what exactly do you think my uncle was involved in?"

Dane stepped toward her, slowly. "Well, the paintings in your room got me thinking. You said he had them even before he became a marquess. And they are by very popular artists. They couldn't have been cheap."

"You think he was an artist?" Caroline looked utterly confused.

"I think he dealt with stolen or forged art." He stepped even closer.

Her nostrils flared, but she remained silent.

"The thief-taker thinks he might be a part of the Brother-hood of the Crimson Fist."

Caroline stepped back. "The same people you think are responsible for Payne's abduction? If so, you're insane to even consider it!"

"We should consider every angle, I thought we agreed on that." He stepped even closer but she raised a staying hand. Imploring him to stop advancing.

"And I think you're just trying to throw suspicion off of yourself. You're painting my uncle to be a criminal so that I stop looking for the people responsible for his death."

"That was never my intention!" Dane ran a hand through his hair, bristling from the inside. He turned away from her and paced to the other side of the room. "You have been hostile toward me since the moment I came through that door, and yet all I wanted to do was please you."

She let out a bitter chuckle. "Please me? You went behind my back! You steered the investigation toward my uncle's dealings. You've been doing that from the start." She waved her hand angrily. "You disappear at all hours of the day and night, while I know you have me followed everywhere I go!"

"Caroline—"

"Your Grace!"

Dane stared at his wife's angry gaze for a moment before letting out a sigh of defeat. "Your Grace," he bit out. "I am not going to account to you for every step I take before I take it.

141

You are most busy during the day and the thief-taker's office is no place for a lady. I thought I was saving you the trouble. My mistake."

"And I thought we were partners in this. It seems the mistake was mine. And be warned that I will absolve my uncle of your suspicions. And from now on, I won't be fooled by your offers of a truce."

* * *

Caroline couldn't sleep.

This had been a night of unpleasant revelations, and she just could not lie peacefully in bed when everything inside her screamed with agony. What was she supposed to do now?

Caroline sat up and blew a stray lock of hair away from her face. She was hot, and the air inside her chamber didn't let her breathe. She needed to get out of the house.

So she pulled on her stockings, threw a dressing gown over her nightgown, and wrapped herself in a cloak. Before leaving her room, she walked up to the paintings on her wall, studying the expressive brushwork.

Could her uncle have truly been a criminal?

She had been too angry with her husband to seriously entertain that possibility before. She'd just learned of his infidelity and every word out of his mouth just reminded her of his lies and treachery.

But it wasn't true treachery, was it? Their marriage was not real. It was a farce. Yet he'd made her care for him before hurting her so badly.

She walked out of her chamber and along the hall in silence, studying the dark walls. The suffocating feeling didn't abate.

On the contrary, it just intensified.

This wasn't her home. This didn't even feel like her house. She'd spent five months trying to be a perfect duchess while proving that her husband was a monster, and as a result, she didn't feel a kinship to this place.

She'd thought she'd started healing the more time she spent with her husband, but all of that was lies. He'd never cared about her. He'd kept a mistress all this time. He was still keeping a mistress.

And that wasn't even the only thing he did behind her back. He hid things from her.

Caroline used the servants' stairs to reach the exit and went outside. The chilly wind blew in her face, and she huddled deeper into her cloak. Perhaps the cold would force her thoughts to a different avenue. Maybe the wind would blow them out of her mind. Or a brisk walk would deplete her energy, thus halting her ability to think.

She walked toward the stables, just because it was the only place besides the garden that was available to her. She couldn't very well leave the premises and go gallivanting about town in her current attire.

Caroline entered the stables and walked along the stalls with sleeping horses in them. Was she an idiot to ignore Kensington's words? Or was she an idiot for believing him? The paintings hanging in her room corroborated his words, but that wasn't proof enough, was it?

Conflicting thoughts rioted in her head. Her husband could have just been lying. He could have been steering the investigation to where he wanted, so she wouldn't suspect him anymore.

And that explanation might have worked fine for her a few

weeks ago, but not after everything that had happened. She had doubts, but then her jealousy would rear its ugly head and scream at her that he was a terrible liar.

But if he were, indeed, not lying, what did it mean for her? What did it mean for the memory of her uncle?

Perhaps her job was to discover the truth no matter what it was. No matter how painful. Either her husband was a liar or her uncle was. And the way things stood just now, Caroline doubted either answer would bring her peace.

She just needed to follow the breadcrumbs of evidence to find out what had really happened. And she would do it without the help of her husband.

The husband whom she'd started to trust during the short span of their truce. The husband she believed when he put emeralds around her neck and told her she was his true duchess now.

The husband who had been seeing his mistress on the side this entire time.

She leaned her back against one of the stalls, feeling defeated. She didn't know why that bothered her so, why she cared if her husband was unfaithful, but she did. A large lump stuck in her throat that she couldn't get rid of.

At that moment, something moved behind her and a moment later, Midnight's head appeared from within the stall. She nudged Caroline on the cheek with her nose and then leaned her head against Caroline's shoulder.

"Hello, Midnight," Caroline murmured and patted her cheek while leaning into Midnight's embrace.

The mare puffed in answer.

A single tear traced its way down Caroline's cheek. The beautiful mare's kindness was the last straw that broke the resilience of Caroline's overwrought nerves. So she turned into Midnight's neck and wept.

She wept away the grief she still held for her beloved uncle. She wept away all those months when she'd had to pretend to be a perfect hostess when she didn't know how to avenge her uncle's death, while simultaneously residing under the roof of a man she thought to be a monster.

She wept away the pain of causing grief to Lavinia when Caroline married the man her friend had loved. And she wept away all the dreams she had started to build in her head when the hope arose that perhaps her husband wasn't as bad as she thought.

She wept and wept, all her strength escaping her, leaving her leaning against the powerful beast that showed her the silent kindness she had needed all this time.

Caroline stood like that, just breathing, her mind slowly working on the dilemma at hand. Then she wiped away her tears, looked at Midnight, and said, "Thank you, dear, for letting me be weak for a moment." She rubbed the horse's mane and smiled. "We both feel trapped here, don't we?"

Midnight puffed a breath as if in agreement, and Caroline rubbed the horse's neck. "We can help each other, then." She bit her lip, thinking. Midnight was an active horse, she would love the exercise. And after all these days sitting on her arse, Caroline could use a punishing ride.

Her mind made up, Caroline patted Midnight on her cheek. "Now stay here. I'll be right back."

Caroline turned on her heel and hurried toward the house. She silently made it to her room, donned her Shadows attire, and returned to the stables within a few minutes.

With lifted spirits, she saddled Midnight and raced off into the night.

Chapter 14

C aroline hadn't felt this kind of freedom since the day her uncle died.

Every action she'd made since then had a purpose. She was either watching her husband, or she was hosting a function, perhaps she was shopping for her friends. But she never let herself be idle. She never let herself process the grief.

She had almost forgotten how freeing it was to just gallop around town a few hours before sunrise, when everyone was asleep and no one was in a position to stop her.

She wore her Shadows uniform because of the ease of donning it but also because it hid the fact that she was a lady, since most people tended to stand away from a dark figure.

Midnight also seemed to enjoy their outing. Caroline just urged her horse on, not caring where they were going.

The brisk ride with the wind in her face did make it easier for Caroline to think. It did clear her mind. But it didn't stop her heart from hurting.

Her husband had a mistress, her uncle was quite possibly a criminal, and she had always just been a pawn in those two men's lives.

She pulled on the reins, halting Midnight and taking a break.

"Good girl." She patted the mare on the side.

Caroline took a deep breath and let it out, white puffs of air leaving her lungs. The frost was climbing up the walls of the buildings around them.

She looked around only to realize where she was—the abandoned factory where she'd found her husband a few weeks ago. Back where it all started.

"You know, Midnight," she said conversationally. "This is where I found your master bleeding on the floor a few weeks ago." She paused. "Perhaps I should have let him bleed out."

Midnight whinnied, shaking her mane.

"No? You don't think so?" Caroline let out a chuckle. "Of course, you don't. You probably love him. Just like every other lady I know." She patted her horse on the side. "Very well, Midnight, I think it's time for us to go back."

At that moment, a huge wall of a man appeared before her. "A Shadow," he said in a hoarse voice. "Hey, I was just saying that it'd be mighty fine coming across a thousand quid. Wasn't I, Garry?"

Caroline pulled on the reins to turn Midnight, only to notice three more thugs appearing from different sides, surrounding her.

"Yes, you were," another man—presumably Garry—said and spat on the ground with a loud smack.

Midnight was getting panicked in the constrained space and among strangers. She huffed and puffed, moving around in a circle and whinnying uncontrollably.

Caroline tried to calm her horse, at the same time calculating the route of escape.

One of the men let out a battle cry and charged at Midnight with his dagger. Midnight whinnied and reared before taking off in the opposite direction, almost trampling the other men in her way.

Caroline held on for dear life, keeping her body close to Midnight as the horse raced with all her might. The voices of the bandits grew distant, and they would have probably escaped just then, except that the alley narrowed and turned sharply before them. Caroline turned Midnight, forcing her to skid into the crooked alley.

But the speed of the animal was too great to turn in time, causing Midnight to fall and successfully dislodging Caroline off her back.

I was looking for a punishing ride, Caroline thought grimly as her entire body ached. *Well, looks like I got it.*

* * *

Dane lay in bed, staring at the canopy above his head.

Had he been a fool for thinking that things had changed between him and his wife? Had he ignored her hostility toward him because he wanted their relationship to transform?

Or was there something else he hadn't noticed all this time?

Caroline was right, of course. He shouldn't have done things behind her back. He shouldn't have investigated her uncle without telling her, without taking her with him.

He was just used to doing things on his own. He never had to account to anyone. But if he wanted his marriage to shift and change, then he had to change, too.

No use lying in bed and contemplating things he could have done. It was time to do what he knew was right. He needed to apologize to his wife. And then perhaps he should stop steering the marriage and the investigation and let her decide how she wanted to proceed next.

His mind made up, he walked up to the adjoining room door and knocked.

No answer.

Dane wasn't surprised. She probably didn't want to speak to him.

He knocked again.

Still no answer.

"Caroline—Duchess. I'd like to speak to you. Please?"

It was dead quiet inside the room. Was she asleep?

He tried the door handle, but it was locked.

Dane let out an irritated breath. He left his room and knocked from the corridor. Still no luck.

He turned the handle and pushed open the door. "Caroline. Are you asleep?"

Dane walked inside the room and realized why Caroline was ignoring him.

She wasn't there.

He frowned. Where could she have gone in the middle of the night?

Right then, the beat of horse hooves sounded from outside the townhouse. Dane rushed to the window only to catch a glimpse of Midnight disappearing over the bend.

Devil take it!

Where was she going?

Dane froze. No. She wouldn't try to investigate the

Brotherhood on her own.

Normally, yes, she was a lot smarter than that. But she was extremely upset.

No. Even if she did decide to seek out the Brotherhood, she couldn't possibly know where to start. She probably just went to rid herself of frustrations by galloping around town while everyone was asleep.

Yes. This was probably what she'd done. Except Dane couldn't risk the possibility that she had gone to seek out the dangerous Brotherhood. Because whether she found them or not, that way lay trouble. Shadows had a price on their heads. Criminals roamed the town at night. So whether Caroline was looking for trouble or not, she was bound to find it.

So he hurried back into his room, and got dressed before rushing out to follow his wife on foot.

Following Midnight's hoofprints on the freshly laid snow wasn't a difficult task. They led the way up to the factory where Caroline had found him bleeding all those weeks ago.

Dane smiled, remembering the night that changed their lives.

But his smile promptly turned into a shocked grimace when the hoofprints disappeared, smudged by the signs of struggle.

Dane rushed from one alley into the next, but there were no more signs of his wife or his mare.

The moment he despaired to ever find them, he heard loud hoofbeats. And then out of nowhere, Midnight appeared galloping right at him.

Dane's eyes widened, his heart squeezing at the sight. Midnight, alone, running wildly.

As Midnight raced past him, Dane whistled low and managed to grab at the reins. Midnight slowed her pace, letting

Dane hop onto her saddle. He pulled on the reins, forcing Midnight to a stop. He rubbed her neck and whispered soothing nothings in her ear.

"Why are you alone, Midnight?" he asked. "Where's your mistress?"

Midnight whinnied and shook her mane in agitation.

"Show me," Dane whispered again. "Show me where you left her."

He urged the mare to a start and Midnight cantered back to where she'd appeared from. Dane only hoped she would bring him to an unharmed Caroline.

Let her be angry. Let her be mad at him. Let her not want to have anything to do with him. He deserved it.

But only if she was alive and unharmed.

* * *

The cold had touched Caroline to the bone.

Every Shadow knew that the best way to evade thugs was to find higher ground. But her wrist ached, forcing her to just walk in circles, evading her attackers, hiding in the narrow alleys.

Her entire body hurt from the fall, which meant that Caroline couldn't run. So her only other options were to hide or fight.

And hiding hadn't seemed to work out well for her thus far. It seemed like she'd been evading her followers for hours. She was tired, hungry, and freezing.

She was also cursing herself for her thoughtless actions. The one time she acted irrationally, and this would be the time she died? It seemed rather unfair.

She remembered the warm bed that awaited her in her room and stifled a groan. If only she were back at the house.

Very well, Caroline. You can act like a helpless damsel, or you can act like the duchess that you are.

This wasn't the first time she'd been stuck in a perilous situation. And hopefully, it wouldn't be the last.

She rubbed her hands together for warmth, her wrist giving a dull ache. She knew that the thugs had split up to cover more ground and to keep her trapped. She could use it to her advantage.

Caroline tiptoed from one alley to the next, watching for any approaching bandits. She peeked her head around the corner and noticed one such man coming toward her.

Caroline crouched down, waiting for the thug to pass her.

Her pulse drummed loudly in her ears, and she tried to hold her breath, so she wouldn't alert her enemy of her whereabouts.

Just when he stepped around the corner, she plunged the dagger into his foot. When he bent over in pain, she hit him in the trachea, causing him to fall down, gagging. Caroline lowered his jacket from his shoulders and used it to tie him down before skittering away.

One down. Four to go.

Just as she anticipated, two more men followed the sounds of their gagging friend and while one of them stopped to help, another one continued his way to look for the evasive Shadow.

Caroline hid again, and this time, she tripped the thug and hit him over the head with her elbow.

"Oi! He's there!" The voice came from somewhere behind Caroline. And there was no point in hiding anymore.

Caroline collected all the strength she had left and sprinted away. Perhaps, she could just outrun them.

She barely managed to finish her thought when a huge man stepped out of the corner. Using her own method against her, the man had just waited for her in an alley and grabbed her just before she passed him by.

He caught her easily by the shoulders and slammed her against the wall.

"I got 'im!" he yelled and then sneered, showing his rotting teeth. "Now, let's see who's behind the mask."

Caroline tried to get out of the gigantic man's hold, but being trapped the way she was, she couldn't move her limbs. The man took her mask off, dislodging the hood of her cloak in the process, and revealing her hair, which was already falling out of her coiffure.

"Huh?" The thug's confused features would be a treat in any other circumstance, but now it just made Caroline grimace.

He pulled down the handkerchief and then took her by the chin. "You're a woman."

"And you're a disgusting boar," she spat.

He raised a brow. "A mouth on you." And then he sneered. "Would love to taste it."

"Get your hands off me!"

"Or what?" he asked almost gently, his face getting closer and closer to hers. "Hm, I am going to enjoy you before collecting my thousand quid."

"You are going to regret touching me," she whispered furiously.

"Am I?" He sneered. "Let's test it then."

He leaned toward her, and Caroline fought with all her might to dislodge him, to no avail. And that's when she heard the sound of hoofbeats. And in the next moment, Midnight appeared from the mist.

Chapter 15

Seeing the huge, dirty man touching his wife made Dane's blood burn through his veins. Without thinking, he jumped off Midnight before she even came to a stop.

Midnight reared and whinnied, scaring the man enough to distract him. And that's when Dane plunged his sword through the bastard's middle. "Are you regretting it yet?" he asked as he looked into the devil's eyes.

The thug fell to the ground, looking absolutely flabbergasted. Two men appeared from the side and rushed toward Dane. He easily evaded their attacks, countering their every move with a ferocity he hadn't felt in a long time.

He slit one man's throat, the blood spurting onto Dane's hands and sword then turned sharply to concentrate on the sole opponent he had left. But the man trembled before him, dropped his weapon, and fled as fast as his feet could carry him.

Dane's breath came in huge gulps. He wasn't winded or

tired. He was fucking mad. And not at the thugs, but at his dear, disobedient wife.

He turned to her sharply. She still stood, her back to the cold wall, her eyes round in shock or fear, her breathing ragged.

Dane walked toward her and patted her limbs. "Are you hurt?" he barked.

"I am fine," she breathed softly.

"Are you certain?"

"Don't bark at me!" she cried and pulled away from his touch.

"Don't you ever go into this part of town alone, do you hear me?" His voice was harsh, the puffs of air hitting her face with his every word.

"No! I don't hear you," she said angrily. "You don't get to dictate what I can and cannot do!"

"Can't I?" He waved toward the dead thugs at her feet. "They could have killed you! And since they realized you're a woman—" He looked away in frustration. He didn't even want to think what would have happened if he'd arrived a minute later.

They stood like that, their breathing and Midnight's quiet puffs the only sounds in the alley.

"Where did they hurt you?" Dane finally asked, slightly calmer. "Show me."

"Why do you care?"

"Why?" He stomped toward her angrily, so he was only a few inches away. "You are my duchess. You are *mine*. Nobody is allowed to touch you. Nobody but me."

He grabbed her by her chin, his bloody fingers marking her silky-white skin with the thug's blood, and kissed her savagely.

157

She went limp for a short moment, her lips yielding to his, her mouth opening enough to let in his insistent tongue. But the next moment, she stiffened and started pushing at him, beating at his chest.

Dane only held her firmer, his hands stroking her body, his lips urging her to calm down. Instead, she pulled away violently and then slapped him in the face.

Dane's face turned sideways with the resounding smack. He huffed out a breath. "I suppose I deserve that."

"Yes," she agreed, "you do." Then she took his face between her palms and lowered it to hers.

Dane didn't have time to react before her lips touched his and then, he forgot all his anger. Because her soft, plump lips were moving over his, her sweet tongue probing at his mouth and demanding entrance.

He pulled her closer to him before slamming her hard against the wall, trapping her between the building and him. She brought him closer, kissing him wildly, biting his lips, then soothing them with her tongue. Dane caught her tongue and drew it into his mouth, tasting her, delighting in her warmth.

He pulled his mouth away to trail kisses down her cheek, to her jaw, and then her neck. He bit her skin, rejoicing in the tiny sound she made. Then his arms traveled down her body, grabbing her buttocks. She raised her leg and hooked it behind his knee.

"Let me," he whispered as he kissed her mouth again.

He grabbed her thighs and raised her, pinning her against the wall with his weight. She immediately wrapped her legs around his hips.

"Dane," she breathed his name like sugar on her lips.

"You're mine," he whispered against her skin again. "And I'll prove it to you, right here."

Then he possessed her mouth in a soul-scorching kiss. His thigh was moving against her center, forcing tiny mewling sounds to erupt from the back of her throat.

"Yes, darling," he murmured as she started moving her hips in rhythm with his, her hands curling into his shoulders. "Tell me you're mine."

"I'm yours," she said without missing a beat. And she was.

As he kissed his way down to the pulse in the side of her neck, his thigh still rubbing against her, the sounds she made grew louder, her rhythmic motions more desperate.

"Again," he growled, increasing his speed, sucking on her sweet skin.

"Ah!" she cried out, her fingers scratching at his back.

"Say it."

"I'm yours," she breathed. Then her head fell back, giving him more access to her neck.

Dane suckled on her sweet skin, his hands stroking the peaks of her breasts through her clothing, his thigh still working at her center.

Their pants and moans grew louder as he quickened his rhythm and the next moment, she cried out in ecstasy.

Dane felt a rush of pleasure flood his body. He paused, still pinning her with his body, letting her calm her breaths.

When she looked up at him, her eyes were dazed, her mouth swollen from his kisses, and her cheeks rosy. She looked sated and felt languid in his arms. Dane nudged her nose with his before giving her one more slow kiss on the mouth.

She cupped his cheek enthusiastically, returning his kisses.

Dane pulled away and shook his head. "Enough," he said.

More to himself than to her. Just so that he would have the willpower to let go of her.

He slowly lowered her to her feet and stepped away, letting her bear weight on her own. His cock still pulsed with need and chafed against his breeches. But he knew he couldn't take her. Not in the middle of the alley on a cold winter night with the dead bodies of the thugs right beside them.

Already, he'd taken more from her than he'd given. He tilted her chin up and kissed her again.

The sound of hoofbeats sounded somewhere nearby. Dane cursed under his breath. Probably redcoats. Probably looking for them.

"Let's go home now," he whispered hoarsely. "And then I'll get back at you properly."

* * *

What in the devil was that?

Caroline sat with her husband's sturdy body behind her, his arms holding her steady and keeping her balanced atop Midnight. Her mind was jumbled, and she had a hard time untangling her thoughts and feelings.

Getting attacked by thugs was something she'd expected. Something she had gotten used to by now. And she had always been able to count on herself to get out of a situation like this.

But tonight was different. She was already tired, her wrist hurt, her entire body was bruised, and then that huge thug had whispered repulsive things, his rotten breath clouding her mind.

And then her husband had appeared out of nowhere like an avenging demon, killing the thug right before her eyes.

160

If that wasn't excitement enough for one night, he had to kiss her right in that alley and make her... and have her...

What in the devil was that?

She wanted to scream the question out loud, but she doubted her husband would hear her. She doubted he would understand her confusion because she didn't understand it herself. Her mind was just so muddled.

He stopped by the side of the house and helped her down. Then he slapped Midnight on her rear, and she cantered away.

All of it felt very familiar.

"Can you climb?" he asked, the first thing he'd said since they mounted the horse.

"No. My wrist... it's... I think I sprained it."

He frowned and took her hand gently, circling her aching, swollen wrist. "Bastards," he growled. "I'm going to kill them!"

"Y-you already did," she stammered.

"All of them," he growled again. Then his tone turned gentle as he met her gaze. "Come, we'll use the back stairs."

Caroline bit her lip. "There's another way."

She took him by the hand and led him toward a trapdoor a few feet away. She raised a brow, and he opened it. Caroline slowly made her way down and waited for him to join her. He looked around the dark, cold room in silence. He didn't seem to understand where they were.

"It's a dairy room," Caroline said, holding on to a chuckle. She waved a hand toward one side of the room. "That door leads to the kitchen. And this one"—she opened a narrow passageway—"leads to the staircase closest to my chambers."

She stepped onto the cramped stairwell, and her husband followed behind her.

"That's how you sneak in and out of the house undetected,"

he mused.

"One of the ways. The other one requires me to climb through a library window, and I don't feel like doing that," she said softly.

He let out a chuckle.

They walked the rest of the way in silence.

Only when they entered her chamber and Dane quietly closed the door behind them did he finally speak. He turned on her sharply, rough emotion playing out on his features. "What were you thinking?"

"Pardon me?" Caroline looked up from trying to untie her cloak. Her hands were shaking, and her swollen wrist wasn't helping either.

Dane stalked toward her and pulled her hands away. "I'll do it." He started untying her cloak carefully, gently, although his breathing was ragged. "What were you doing out there all alone?"

"I needed to clear my head." Her voice was shaky.

"Well," he scoffed, "that worked quite well, didn't it?"

He took off her cloak and placed it on the back of a chair, then came to stand in front of her again.

"You can't just expect me to easily believe that the uncle I loved all my life, the uncle who was like a father to me, was a criminal," Caroline said evenly. Or at least, she tried, but her voice gave a tiny crack at the end.

"I don't give a damn about that!" Dane threw up his hands. He raked a hand through his hair. "I care that you're home and safe. I care that you don't storm away to the most dangerous place in London in the middle of the night without telling me."

"You might not care, but I do," Caroline said emphatically.

"You led us down this path, trying to convince me that my uncle was a criminal, but he was not! He can't be."

Dane let out a breath of frustration. "What if he was? Is that going to change the fact that he loved you? Cared for you? *No!* I have not insisted upon this path to make you give up the search for the blackmailer. That is all I want, too. I want to get to the truth, no matter what. And I can't do that and keep you safe if you keep running off like that."

Caroline lowered her head, feeling like a chastised school-girl. "I was just angry."

Dane tipped her chin up with his fingers, forcing her to look at him. "Why? Why were you so angry with me? Why risk your own life to prove me wrong if you don't even believe me?"

Caroline chewed her lip. She couldn't explain her actions. Her mind was too muddled for that. She was angry with him for going behind her back. She was angry at him for keeping a mistress. And yet, none of that justified her recklessness.

Luckily, she didn't have to explain anything. Instead of waiting for her to answer, Dane started patting her limbs to check for more injuries.

"Ow!" Caroline exclaimed, swaying from his not-so-gentle ministrations.

Dane pulled the sleeve of her tunic up and his eyes widened. "You're all bruised!"

Caroline snatched her hand away. "I fell from a horse."

Dane closed his eyes as if praying for patience. "You'll be the death of me," he whispered. "I can't talk to you right now without getting angry every second."

Caroline pulled down her sleeves and rubbed her arms, feeling vulnerable.

"I suppose I should ask your healer maid to take care of your injuries and give you a warm bath," he said with a sigh.

"I suppose." They both stood motionless, as if not willing to step away from each other.

Then he lowered his head and pressed his lips against hers.

* * *

Dane left Caroline in the care of her lady's maid and returned to his chamber.

He was angry, frustrated, and irritated all at the same time. In his current state, he was not the best company.

Her maid was going to undress Caroline. She was going to help her bathe, while Dane was barred from her bedroom once again. With a groan, Dane went to his dressing room and washed with a pitcher of water.

He had been covered in the thugs' blood. And he had dared to touch his duchess in that condition. No wonder she was shaking.

Dane put on his banyan over his naked form and trotted to the bed.

He was an idiot for kissing Caroline that way in the alley. He was an idiot for bringing her to completion there. And he was an even bigger idiot for not finishing what he'd started once they got home.

He should have been the one to undress her, to care for her, to bathe her. Then he would have laid her down on the bed and worshiped her body...

His cock sprang to attention, and his entire body tensed. Dane tipped the banyan off his shoulders and propped himself on the bed, his eyes concentrated upon the door through which his wife was sitting in a tub, naked.

Bathing.

He ran his hand along his cock, imagining her soft hands on him. He would spread her legs and sit her down across his lap as he lowered her onto his engorged length, her wet center enveloping his hardness as he filled her completely.

The idea of her on his cock almost undid him. The image of her wet, hot core, welcoming his hardness drove him wild.

Dane moved his hips, as he now envisioned entering her, moving in a slow sensual rhythm until she was moaning in his arms. He'd look into her eyes, those expressive emerald eyes of hers. So deep and so sparkling. He would taste her sweet lips, sipping on them like on the juiciest of sweetmeats. He'd squeeze her buttocks with his fingers, running his hands up to touch her breasts, taste them, roll those hard nipples with his tongue while she rode him, clenching at him, gliding up and down his length.

The climax hit him hard and unexpectedly. His breathing labored, the memory of Caroline still on his tongue, as if he truly was kissing her mere moments ago.

"Oh, Caroline," he groaned and spilled his seed into his hand.

He paused, breathing heavily.

God, that felt so good… and it was just the vision of her, the dream. What would it be like to feel the real thing?

His cock moved again, from the mere thought of having her in his arms.

No, he wouldn't be able to get rid of his need so easily.

No, this was no temporary sickness. This was something direr. Something he hadn't felt before.

Chapter 16

D ane did not see his wife for the next two days.
He barred the windows of her bedchamber and
ordered his valet to watch her whenever Dane was
not at home.

Their violent encounter the night before had truly scared
the devil out of Dane and awakened a beast within him. So
for the past two days, he had made it his mission to find the
remaining thugs and make them pay for daring to attack his
duchess.

He also made it his mission to spread the word that the
Shadows did not tolerate attacks on one of their own. That
vengeance would find whoever was brazen enough to try.

Once he was done with that, he decided to finish the
nonsense with the blackmailer. It was time to catch the
bastard and make him pay.

And he knew the one person who would be in a position to
help him.

So Dane woke up early in the morning, sneaked out of bed,

saddled Midnight, and braved the winter storm.

The weather that day was unforgiving. Harsh wind beat against Dane's face, and frozen droplets of water—not quite rain, not quite snow—scratched his already irritated skin. It's as though the universe whispered, *Do not go there. There are no good answers for you. Only misery and trouble await you at the end of the road.*

But Dane persisted. He reached what looked like a medieval castle on the outskirts of town in under two hours. He jumped out of his mount and waited for a groom, or some servant, to appear and take Midnight.

Nobody did.

Dane frowned, huddled closer into his coat, and walked toward the stables. Nobody was there, either. Not a stable boy, no stable master. What was going on?

Dane tied down his horse into one of the stalls and quickly strode toward the house.

He raised the knocker and let it fall a few times, burrowing closer and closer into his coat against the cold.

No answer.

Had he made all this journey for naught? Was nobody home?

He raised the knocker again and tapped his foot in agitation. "Devil take you… Where the hell did you go?"

He raised the knocker one last time and already turned away when the door finally opened.

"You are not leaving, are you?" a familiar voice said behind him. "I was so looking forward to the company."

* * *

Christmas morning started like any other, except that footmen lugged in the Yule log, the entire house smelled like evergreen branches, and the smoke from cooking spread around the entire townhouse.

Everyone was in a good mood, all the preparations were on time, and everything was just... perfect.

Caroline was incredibly excited about her own Christmas celebration. Of course, she missed her uncle—she always did and she always would—and memories of her parents flooded her mind. But she couldn't spend the day yearning for something she could no longer have. Instead, she concentrated on starting a new chapter in her life's book with her own holiday traditions.

Or at least she tried to.

She wore a beautiful red gown with purple underskirts, matching lace on her sleeves, and little bows on her bodice. Her hair was collected in an intricate coiffure, and the duchess's emerald set completed the ensemble.

Now she was ready.

She sat in the parlor, anxiously awaiting her guests. It was already time for dinner and yet nobody had arrived. Which was completely fine because her husband was nowhere to be found either.

She had not seen him since the night of their encounter with the thugs. At first, she was happy for the reprieve, because she could not quite face him either. But now she'd started to worry that his avoidance would turn permanent.

After all, today was Christmas and he was not even in the house.

How could a man who claimed to worry about her this much just leave her alone for three days, including a holiday feast that they were supposed to host together?

She wasn't worried, because he appeared from time to time and closed himself off in his study, or a butler would say that he'd been at home, so he wasn't in trouble. But he didn't join her for breakfast anymore, and he wasn't at home most of the nights either.

Caroline refused to imagine where he spent all those nights, although a persistent image made its way into her head, whispering to her ever so lightly that he spent that time with his mistress, and had even gone to her on the most important day of the year.

Caroline tried to curb her panic and jealousy, but it wasn't easy.

After the kisses they'd shared the other night, she had hoped he would come clean about his mistress, promise to never visit her again, and ask Caroline to make their marriage real.

It turned out, she was still a little girl deep inside, dreaming of fairy tales.

She should have known better. Her husband was not the prince of the romantic fables. He was a monster.

And it would have been fine, for she was not a fragile damsel. If she had to choose between a prince and a monster, she would have chosen the latter. Except this monster—her monster—did not choose her back.

Caroline grunted, then stood and started pacing the parlor.

Where in the world was everybody else?

If her husband's abandonment wasn't exactly surprising, everybody else's failure to appear made her question herself.

Was she wrong? Was today not Christmas? Then why would the servants not tell her? Or perhaps, this was some elaborate joke.

She pictured every eventuality in her mind, starting with the one where everyone forgot about the dinner and finishing with the one where they were mugged along the way or died.

She tried to push the anxious thoughts aside and concentrated on fixing every little thing in sight to return some semblance of power into her own hands.

It didn't work.

Caroline looked at the clock for the third time in as many minutes and that didn't help her either. Because it was already past dinner time. And yet nobody was about.

She paced the parlor in agitation, not quite knowing what else to do.

When the time was half past the assigned dinner time, Caroline had despaired to ever see her guests. She was certain that some awful misfortune had taken place that simply made all of them disappear.

She plopped into a seat, rested her elbows on her knees, and lowered her face into her palms.

This was a disaster.

And then she heard the door open downstairs and low, but friendly chatter. Finally!

Caroline sprung to her feet and ventured downstairs to meet her guests. She smiled as she saw the friendly—albeit reddened—faces of the Roth family.

"I am so sorry we are late," Lavinia said as she shed her coat and squeezed Caroline's hands with her cold fingers. "But we received last-minute correspondence that couldn't wait."

"You are not late," Caroline said with a smile. "Well, you are. But you are actually the first ones to arrive."

"We are?" Victoria appeared by her side. "Merry Christmas, cousin. But where is everyone?"

Caroline licked her lips. "I have no idea."

"Caroline," Lady Elinor, Victoria's great aunt, finally approached her with a warm smile. "Such a pleasure to see you again, *Kindchen*."

Caroline curtsied, Roth bowed low, and they all proceeded upstairs.

"With the weather like this I won't be surprised if Annalise decides to stay in," Lavinia said.

"I would not blame her." Caroline forced on a smile. No, she wouldn't blame her, but she would be upset.

They reached the parlor, and Lavinia looked around the room, squinting. "Where's Dane?"

Caroline swallowed, then cleared her throat and tried to assume as gentle a tone as she could. "I don't know."

* * *

Dane turned slowly and beheld his bastard brother's smug face. He stood only an inch or two shorter than Dane, his golden mane of hair tousled, a grin on his face, a tumbler of whisky carelessly hanging between his fingers. He wore a banyan over his breeches and, Dane assumed, nothing else as his chest peeked out of the open V of his banyan.

"Welcome, brother," William said with a smirk and stepped aside.

Dane swallowed and entered his brother's dwelling, already regretting that he had come.

"To what do I owe this unexpected surprise?" William rubbed his chin in thought. "I suppose if it was expected, it wouldn't have been a surprise now, would it?"

"This is not a social call," Dane said.

"Oh, no?" William feigned surprise. "But it's Christmas!"

Dane closed his eyes against the unpleasant reminder. *Christmas!* He had completely forgotten. His wife was hosting dinner tonight. Well, if he hurried, he might still make it on time.

William laughed then and waved for Dane to follow him. "Don't worry, brother, I didn't hold out hope that you would deem it necessary to bring a gift."

William led Dane into a—Dane didn't quite know what to call the room. A library? A study? An erotic parlor? All of the above?

The room was vast, with a single large fireplace in the middle of the back wall. A cross between a mattress and a carpet lay on the floor by the hearth, filled with pillows. It looked like something out of the stories of Turkish Sultans, a place where they claimed to keep their harems. A few crystal decanters stood on the brass footman by the side of the carpet. A few books were strewn about on the floor. More books took their place on the shelves that filled the entire wall opposite the fireplace.

Cozy.

William tumbled onto his carpet and waved his glass of whisky toward Dane. "Please, sit."

Dane grimaced. "No, thank you."

William let out a laugh. "Afraid to hurt your knees, old man? That's fine. You can stand." He propped himself against the pillows before refilling his glass. "I'm listening."

Dane leaned against the side of the hearth. "I need a favor."

William chuckled. "How interesting. Interesting, indeed. And what can I help you with?"

"Does the name David Fitzgerald Langley mean anything

to you?"

William raised a brow. "That's your beloved duchess's uncle, isn't it?"

Dane cocked his head. "So you did know him."

"I did. A few of us did. I was just dipping my toe into my criminal ways, but he was a professional by then."

"What are you talking about?" Dane growled. He felt protective of his wife's late uncle somehow. Although the confirmation that he was indeed a criminal was not surprising.

"Tsk, tsk, tsk." William sat up. "Do not growl at me, brother. That tone won't get you much in this house. It might get you whisky. Are you sure you don't want a glass?"

"William!" Dane snapped.

"Barking won't help your cause, either." William shook the tumbler in his hand before taking a gulp.

"Fine," Dane said softer. "I need to know what you know about my wife's uncle."

William grimaced. "I gathered as much. But I don't quite get what's in it for me?"

Dane prayed for patience. "I don't suppose you like my interruption of your..."—he looked around—"solitary Christmas. So I will leave you alone as soon as you tell me all I need to know."

William frowned. "Hm. I am pretty certain I'll get that, whether I tell you anything or not."

"Fine," Dane said between his teeth. "What do you want?"

William pursed his lips in thought. "I heard your wife is hosting a Christmas dinner today."

Dane stiffened. "She might be." *To which I shall be late if you continue tattering on.*

"And I heard that my wife is invited."

Dane gritted his teeth. "Don't even think about it."

"Ah, yes. I think I shall. What I want from you is an invitation to this Christmas dinner."

Dane shook his head. "You don't want to come to my place for Christmas, believe me."

"Why is that?"

"A lot of people whom you angered greatly are going to be there."

William placed a hand against his heart. "Your concern for me is greatly appreciated, brother—"

"Stop calling me that," Dane bit out.

William just smirked. "What do you think they are going to do to me?"

"I am not so much worried about what they are going to do to you. Rather, I don't want you upsetting my wife on Christmas."

William's smile turned sly, and Dane immediately stiffened. He shouldn't have mentioned Caroline. William could see into people's souls. And he always found a way to exploit that.

"Then I shall tell you nothing." William lay back against his pillows and took a big gulp of whisky.

That Dane could not risk. William was his last hope. If he didn't help him, Dane risked his wife running off again and doing things on her own. He needed to finish what they'd started, and he needed to finish it alone.

Dane looked around the room once more in agitation. "Why is no one here? I had to stow my horse in your stables by myself. There was no groom, no stable master, not even a stable boy."

William raised a brow. "I gave them all a day off. Come

now, it's Christmas." And then he let out a burst of hoarse laughter. "Ah, but your servants do not get to go home to their families for the holidays, do they?"

Dane stiffened. "Their families live under my roof."

"But of course!" William took another sip. "And do they get to celebrate? Or do they work, perhaps even harder than on any other day?"

"Oh, get off your high horse, William. And don't pretend as though you're better than me."

William tsked. "But I am better than you, *brother*. And I know things you want to know. So, what shall it be? Will you invite me for a family dinner or do you prefer to seek other sources?" He cocked his head to the side, watching Dane as though he was a curiosity he hadn't seen before. "But you have no other sources, do you? Because you would not darken my step otherwise."

"Don't be absurd."

William grinned. "I told you my condition. Either we are both leaving for your cozy townhouse to enjoy the family Christmas dinner, or you can pucker up and kiss my glorious arse."

Chapter 17

The St. Johns arrived a few minutes after the Roths, and together they were seated in the parlor, waiting for the host of the dinner party to arrive.

"Helen had a fainting spell," Olivia explained.

"It wasn't a fainting spell so much as just dizziness," Helen chimed in with a pained expression. "And a headache. I am so sorry. I did not mean to hold up the dinner."

"You have nothing to worry about," Caroline said. "Especially considering that the duke is nowhere to be found."

"Surely he wouldn't just disappear," Lavinia said, looking worried.

"Well, you've seen the roads," Olivia said. "Our poor driver struggled to get us here and we live a few streets down."

"That's true," St. John offered. "The roads are icy, which can't be good either for the horses or the carriages. And it happens so rarely that it's enough to spook the horses. Depending on where Kensington went, he might be simply stuck on the road."

"Yes," Caroline agreed tightly. She had the urge to ask St. John how far his mistress's place was since he knew. But she managed to keep silent. "I am guessing Annalise wisely decided to stay at home. So now that you're here, we can actually start eating," Caroline said." The duke will have to join us when he can."

St. John raised his brow, looking confused. "Are you certain? You don't want to wait for your husband?"

"Lady Elinor is already sleeping by the hearth. And I am starving," Caroline said, determined to keep the irritation out of her voice.

"Well, do you want some good news first?" Victoria interrupted, turning very excited.

"Yes, please," Helen agreed readily.

Caroline's stomach was growling, but since Victoria interrupted her with her cheerful tone, she decided some good news could liven up the atmosphere. "Of course, dear."

"Well, I am so incredibly happy to say that we are finally going to Russia!" Victoria beamed.

"You are?" Olivia asked. "That's wonderful news!"

"After Yuletide, of course. We wouldn't want to celebrate on the road," Victoria continued.

"Does that mean that you found Matilda?" Caroline turned toward Lavinia.

"Yes," Lavinia answered with a smile. "Apparently Matilda ran off to look for her childhood sweetheart—a quest I full-heartedly approve of. I just wish she would have told me so I wouldn't be this worried and could have assisted her. But of course, Mr. Atwood—my then guardian—threw her out on the streets while I was at the house party, so she had no means of passing the message to me."

"And did she find her sweetheart?" Helen asked, looking awed.

"She did indeed. I received a letter from her just as we were about to leave for dinner. She apologized profusely for the way she ran off, but I am just happy to hear that everything is well. I had to pen her a response right away. I couldn't wait."

"That's wonderful!" Caroline said, absolutely thrilled for her friend. She'd been worried about her stepmother all this time and now, just in time for Christmas, she'd received the best gift.

"So as soon as I find a companion for Lady Elinor"—Lavinia dropped a quick glance toward the older woman who was peacefully sleeping by the hearth—"we are going to leave for Russia. She doesn't want to travel, especially not in winter. And she said she is content to stay here."

"Yes," Victoria beamed. "And I am just so happy to be going home soon and be far away from the vile, lying bastard that is my husband." She shuddered.

"Couldn't be possibly talking about me, could you?" the familiar voice said from the doorway.

Every person in the room froze for a moment before turning in slow unison.

William, Kensington's bastard brother, and Victoria's unfortunate husband stood in the doorway, a smirk on his face.

* * *

Dane regretted bringing William into his house the moment he had agreed to it. But there was nothing he could do. He needed William's insights. William had already proved to know a few useful things about Caroline's uncle while in the carriage and insisted on telling the rest only after his demands were met.

However, Dane knew that Caroline would not be happy. She was already looking at him with murderous intent in her eyes. And knowing his wife now, he didn't even doubt that she was capable of doing it.

This was why Dane had asked William to stay in the corridor while he talked to her first. But *no*. The moment the bastard heard his *beloved's* voice, he pushed Dane aside and strode into the room.

Now they both stood like a couple of idiots with all eyes turned toward them.

"Greetings," William continued with a grin, enjoying everybody's discomfort immensely. "What was it you said about leaving, *wife?*"

Roth stepped in front of his niece, his fingers curling into fists.

William tsked. "No need for that. I am just here for the festivities. What a nice small circle of friends. Family, truly."

"William," Dane warned.

"Oh, don't worry, brother. I promised to behave, didn't I? I would just like to speak to my wife."

"You'll have to kill me first," Roth growled.

"That won't be a problem," William quipped.

"*Podonok!*" Victoria cried and everyone turned to her, their eyes wide. "*Merzavets! Lzhets!*" she continued, taking a step with every word. And then there was a flurry of Russian words that Kensington had no hope of ever deciphering.

His wife quietly walked to Victoria and touched her on her arm. "Dear, I think that's enough."

"No, it's not! He ruined my life!"

"Did I?" William raised a brow.

"William?" Lady Elinor, who seemed to have been dozing before the princess' outburst, stood and narrowed her eyes on him. "You defiled my dear great niece. You are going to pay for it. You better leave now before I shoo you away with my walking stick."

"I am afraid that's not going to happen," William said confidently. "See, I was invited."

And that's when all the heads turned toward Dane.

"You *invited* him?" his wife bit out.

"Let's not discuss it here. William, Duchess, let's adjourn to my study. We have a few things to talk about."

"Oh, no!" William rested his shoulder against the hearth and crossed his arms over his chest. "I am quite comfortable here."

"My study... Now!" Dane growled.

William laughed. "No need to turn into a beast, brother. All you need to do is ask nicely."

Dane walked up to him and stood very close so the others wouldn't hear. "I promised to bring you here, *brother*. But I didn't say I wouldn't kick you out on your arse if I wanted to. So move."

William raised his arms in self-defense, then winked at the princess before heading out of the parlor. Dane waited for Caroline to follow the bastard and then left the room.

The moment he stepped out into the corridor, Caroline turned toward him. "What are you doing?" Her eyes were filled with rage and... disappointment.

What was he doing, indeed?

He wanted to gather his wife in his arms and tell her that everything would be fine. He had missed her, he realized suddenly. Her warmth at his side brought him peace. And he would happily endure her beratement if only William was not staring at them curiously.

Instead, he took her hand and placed it in the crook of his arm. "Come. I'll explain everything. But I promise you, I wouldn't have brought William to our house if it wasn't absolutely necessary."

"But did you have to do it during the Christmas feast?" She couldn't hide the disappointment in her voice and Dane's heart squeezed. *Yes, I mucked up. I am so sorry!* "Couldn't it have waited a day or two?"

"It could. And I apologize for ruining the festivities. But after your last… um… adventure, I couldn't waste time. And I suppose I lost track of time."

She looked at him, utterly confused. "Did you forget it was Christmas?"

Dane smiled stiffly but didn't answer and they walked in silence the rest of the way.

The moment they stepped into the study, Caroline disengaged from him and stepped a few feet away, as if she didn't want anything to do with him. "Now explain, please."

"I apologize for doing it this way," Dane said.

"Behind my back," Caroline said icily. "Again."

"I wouldn't be the only person doing things behind the other's back," he reminded her.

She opened her mouth to argue, but Dane quickly interrupted her. He didn't want to draw unnecessary attention to their quarrel. Especially not in William's presence. "Besides, I needed to be certain that William would help, and that he actually had helpful information."

Her eyes lit up in anger, but she pursed her lips before taking a deep breath. "And does he?"

"Yes, he does," Dane answered hoarsely.

"But *he* also has conditions," William chimed in.

"What are your conditions?" Caroline finally turned her attention to the bastard.

"I just want to speak to my wife."

Caroline let out a low chuckle. "I am sorry to disappoint, but it's not going to happen."

"Listen, darling—" William stepped menacingly toward Caroline.

Dane immediately blocked his path. "Watch your tone."

"Do not speak. In fact, do not even look at my wife. If I catch a wayward glance her way, I'll have you drawn and quartered!"

"My, my. Have caught feelings, have you?" William narrowed his eyes.

Dane pressed his lips into a thin line. William knew how to rattle people, how to make them show their weaknesses, and then he exploited those weaknesses against them. "She is my duchess. And I won't have my property threatened." Dane didn't dare meet Caroline's gaze as he said so.

"Property?" William raised his brow, then craned his neck to look at Caroline, an unpleasant smirk on his lips. "I know something about properties. You do not speak of your wife as one. You do not speak of her as a possession."

Dane's nostrils flared. "What did I tell you about looking at her?"

William's eyes glinted as he bowed. "As you wish. But I shall only tell you everything I know if you let me talk to Victoria. I am not asking for much. Just five minutes. Five minutes and I'll be out of your way. Otherwise"—he shrugged—"I will stay for dinner, perhaps even longer."

"Who says she even wants to hear anything you have to say?" Caroline scoffed.

"Because she's my wife," he answered simply.

Caroline let out a soft laugh. "Your wife. And therefore, she should listen to your lies, suffer through your speeches, and tolerate your despicable behavior. Is that it?"

Dane grimaced. Somehow he doubted she was speaking about William.

"I told you my conditions," William said nonchalantly. "Five minutes or five hours. That's up to you."

Caroline watched William for one long moment. She was fierce, his duchess. Perhaps even more fierce than he was. "You'll get your five minutes. But you won't get it alone with Victoria. If you want to say something to her, you'll say it in front of everyone."

"I don't think that's a good idea," William waved his hand. "I might be the duke's brother, but I am not a lord. I do not have experience talking in front of crowds. I am more of a one-on-one person if you will."

Caroline pursed her lips, her eyes narrow. "Either you speak to Victoria in front of everyone or you don't get to speak to her at all. You can stay here as long as you like, but it doesn't mean that she has to. *That* is up to you."

* * *

Caroline tried very much to pretend that her husband's actions didn't hurt her. She directed her anger toward his bastard brother, she concentrated her thoughts on Victoria and her plight, but it just didn't work.

183

How dare he disappear for three days without a word, only to show up late to their own Christmas dinner! And with his bastard brother in tow, no less. She supposed she should be grateful he had come at all, as he seemed to have forgotten what day it was. Nevertheless, Caroline could not muster an ounce of gratitude.

Perhaps William had pertinent information about her uncle, perhaps he didn't. But the least Dane could do was warn her about his plans.

Throughout their entire marriage, they had not talked to each other much, and they barely saw each other all day, but at least, when it came to important decisions, decisions that affected them both, they always made them together. They might not have known how each other's day went, or if the other was ill, but if something affected Kensington, she always brought it up to him.

Now, with their cold arrangement seemingly ended, he'd stopped considering her opinions at all.

And it hurt.

But there was nothing she could do about it now. So once again, she took her husband's arm and walked back to the parlor, his brother, William, following them a few steps behind.

As they entered the parlor, Caroline immediately disengaged from her husband and walked toward Victoria. "Dear," she said. "He insisted on speaking to you."

"I don't want to hear him speak," Victoria said, raising her chin.

Caroline took a breath to argue, to cajole, and then she glanced at her husband, the person she was mad at for doing exactly the same thing she was about to do to Victoria, and she stopped. "I understand," she finally said, after thinking for a moment. "And if that is your final decision, then I shall tell him to leave."

Victoria crinkled her brows. "You will? But why did you agree to it in the first place?"

"Because he promised to tell me something about my uncle that I might not find out otherwise. But it's not your burden to bear. If you don't want to talk to him—"

Victoria raised her hand, stopping Caroline mid-sentence. "Is this related to the threatening notes that Lavinia received?"

"Possibly. There is no guarantee with William, but Dane says that he has some valuable information. Nevertheless, you shouldn't feel pressured to do something you don't want."

Victoria grimaced. "And all he wants is to speak to me?"

"Just five minutes, and you don't even have to leave this room. I told him that he has to speak in front of everyone or not at all."

Victoria took a deep breath. "Then it's fine. I can pretend to listen to him for five minutes and then you get what you need."

"Are you certain?" Caroline squeezed Victoria's fingers.

She nodded. "Absolutely."

"Thank you." Caroline turned toward William, who stood a few feet away from the doorway, seeming nonchalant. "You can speak now."

William bowed theatrically, then took a step forward. "Victoria…" He cleared his throat. "Victoria. I wished to speak to you in private, but—"

"You humiliated me publicly. Or at least in front of these same people. If you've decided to apologize, you shouldn't do so in private. But if you're not here to apologize, I can't even imagine what you want to say to me." Victoria pointedly averted her face.

William smiled. "You're very direct. It's one of the things I love about you."

"William—" Roth growled.

"I was given five minutes, Bastian. You'll have your turn." With that, William stepped closer to Victoria, dismissing her uncle, dismissing everyone, his gaze concentrated on his wife. He reached for her, but she stepped away. "Fair enough." He took a step back, his face thoughtful. "When we first met," he finally said. "When I saw you for the first time in that rose garden, my aim was never to deceive you. I was so taken by your beauty that the only thing I wanted was to speak to you. And once I did, once I learned of your generous soul, your kindness and your guilelessness, once I heard you pronounce my name"—he chuckled—"well, I could not let you go."

Caroline stilled. She had not expected William to actually deliver a heartfelt apology. To be honest, she didn't know what she'd expected from his speech. Sarcastic comments? Smug attitude? Whatever it was, it was not what she was hearing now.

"You spoke of wanting—*needing* to marry a lord," William continued. "But I deceived myself into thinking that once you knew me, once you fell in love with me, that would not matter. I know that I was wrong when I didn't tell you the entire truth, but it was only because I was selfish enough to never want to let you go. It was only because I loved you too much to let you marry anyone else. And I love you still. And I shall love you forever… If you could only give me a chance to prove it to you."

There was a long pause while everyone just stood there,

silent, not certain how to feel. Not that it mattered what anyone else was feeling, just Victoria.

Nevertheless, Caroline's heart squeezed. She'd only seen Victoria and William together once in the garden of Roth's house party. That was the night when Victoria realized that William had lied to her about who he was and tricked her into marrying him.

Caroline had been certain from that point on that William had done it for his own selfish reasons. Only now she wondered if that selfish reason had simply been love.

Not that it justified his actions. Not that Caroline would advise Victoria to forgive him. Just that for once she thought she understood what drove him to behave this way. And for a selfish person, as everyone claimed William to be, it might have seemed like the only right course of action.

Caroline glanced at her husband, standing a few feet away. A man who had always been driven by honor and duty. A man who was the antithesis of selfishness, and therefore, perhaps, incapable of love. Only duty.

"I don't believe you," Victoria said softly. And Caroline could have sworn she saw pain in William's eyes. Did he truly love her this much?

At that moment, the doors burst open downstairs with such a loud bang that it was audible in the parlor. Caroline and Dane exchanged glances before rushing toward the stairs.

They were met by the butler halfway through and he extended a note. "An urgent missive from Lord and Lady Payne," he said.

Oh, God, what now?

Caroline took the note with a shaking hand and read the contents.

I am in labor. Please, collect the gossips.
Annalise.

Chapter 18

"I can't believe you invited the ladies who have never given birth before!" Annalise's mother, Lady Ardee, bristled for the dozenth time. "Oh, how the times have changed. People do not respect tradition anymore."

Annalise lay in bed with midwives busting around her, while Lavinia, Helen, Olivia, Caroline, and Victoria all collected in Annalise's bedchamber, stirring the caudle, decorating the crib, and sewing or embroidering childbed linens to keep their hands busy.

Lady Elinor was given a chamber to rest in, as she wasn't up for the activities in the birthing chamber.

Annalise's mother wasn't wrong. Caroline, for one, was terrified by what she was going to experience in this room tonight. She was not afraid of large, foul-smelling thugs, nor was she scared of organizing vast holiday feasts, but witnessing the miracle of birth had her palms perspiring.

Nevertheless, she wasn't going to leave her friend in the hands of strangers.

"Mother," Annalise said with a grimace. "You said that a gossip is a group of women who make certain that I feel comfortable during birthing. Not some women I have not seen in over a decade."

"My cousins were expecting you to call them," Lady Ardee said as she gulped her wine. "What am I going to tell them now? It isn't done. It is simply not done."

"Somehow, that's the least of my worries right now," Annalise said, shifting in bed and battling with pillows.

Lavinia rushed toward the bed. "What do you need?"

"I can't find a comfortable position," Annalise complained.

Olivia was next to come to her aid. Together with Lavinia, they started arranging pillows as Annalise shifted this way and that, not able to settle on a single position.

Her mother didn't seem to hear them or even notice what they were doing. "How are these young women supposed to help you if they don't know what to do?"

Annalise gritted through her teeth, "They'll learn."

"We are going to give birth sooner or later," Olivia chimed in. "It's better if we see it before doing it. Right?"

Lady Ardee let out a peal of laughter. "That's what you think now." She finished her glass of wine just as Annalise lay back against the pillows, looking content. "I shall go and check on our guests. I wasn't looking forward to entertaining guests today, Annalise, dear."

"You don't need to entertain them. Blake is there," Annalise said weakly.

"Right, Blake is there." Her mother rolled her eyes and stormed out of the room.

The women in the room all exchanged glances before Lavinia waved a dismissive hand. "She's always been like this."

"Oh, Lord!" Annalise scrunched up her face, getting all red and curling from pain.

Lavinia and Olivia froze by the bed as the midwife hurried toward Annalise with a wet cloth in her hands. Annalise groaned, bunching the covers beneath her fingers. Once she relaxed, the midwife wiped the sweat off her forehead.

"Perhaps your mother was right," Lavinia said. "We are useless."

"You are not," Annalise breathed. "There is nothing for you to do when I'm in pain. All you can do is keep me company in between."

"Is that true?" Caroline turned toward the midwife.

"It is," the woman answered. "And perhaps feed her some caudle for the pain."

Helen hurried to Annalise and handed her a cup. "Here, drink this."

"Is it very painful?" Victoria asked.

"It feels as though someone is squeezing my organs from the inside and my stomach is trying to turn me inside out."

Caroline grimaced.

"Is that normal?" Lavinia asked the midwife.

"It is nothing to worry about," the woman answered. "Women give birth all the time."

Women die in labor all the time, too.

Caroline didn't voice that out loud. This wasn't the time. And it wasn't like everyone didn't know that already. Annalise had told her earlier that she'd prepared a letter to her husband detailing what to do with her things if she passed away.

Payne didn't want to hear about it, but Annalise insisted on keeping the letter among his things in his study. Because yes, women gave birth all the time. But they didn't survive all the time. It was foolish to ignore that.

And once again, Caroline wondered why women risked their lives to deliver an heir to their husbands. Some went on to have multiple children, too.

Why? The labor was painful and carried a risk of death. The pregnancy was troublesome and Annalise, in particular, had suffered through some difficult months. And yet, she didn't seem to regret any of it, even now, when a sheen of sweat covered her forehead from pain.

"I truly did not think that I would give birth today," Annalise said between calming breaths. Then her face turned sad, as though she was about to weep, and her voice turned high. "I wanted to enjoy a holiday meal."

Everyone chuckled uncomfortably.

"But you'll receive the best Christmas present in the world," Lavinia soothed.

"Dear, I have to say, whether you were giving birth today or not, I have a feeling we would not be dining tonight," Caroline said.

"Why?" Annalise shifted in bed again and wiped at her eyes.

"Well, for one thing, my husband was late for his own feast. And for another, he brought William with him."

Annalise's mouth fell open. "William? What was he doing there?"

Lavinia let out a chuckle. "Oh, no. He wasn't just there. He is also here, under your roof. Right now."

Annalise's face turned so confused that everyone laughed. "What happened?"

"Well, the weather is ghastly, and he insists that he loves me," Victoria said without looking up from her embroidery.

192

"I don't understand," Helen finally said.

"Me either," Olivia said. "What does the weather have to do with him loving you?"

"What I don't understand," Helen interrupted, "is why such hostility toward William? I mean, I've heard the story of how your wedding came about, Victoria. I heard the rumors… I thought you loved him when you married him."

"I did! I do!" Victoria said emphatically.

"Then what does it matter that he is not a peer?"

"Because I can't go back to Russia, to my Regent sister, with a bastard for a husband. And not just any bastard. A criminal! Anna—my sister—wanted me to marry a powerful lord so we could build alliances with England. And I have failed her."

Lavinia took a deep breath. "Not that I like William one bit—I actually quite dislike him—but… marriage isn't always about politics. Or at least, it shouldn't be."

"It is easy for you to say when you're married to the Marquess of Roth, who is the Duke of Mecklenburg-Schwerin's *legitimate* half-brother!" Victoria pointed out.

"I understand marrying for necessity," Annalise said. "But now that you have found love by your own admission, would you ever be content with a politically driven marriage?"

Victoria paused at her embroidering and looked up. "Are you saying I should forgive William?"

"God, no!" Caroline scoffed.

Everyone turned to look at her.

"I can't believe you are pushing her to accept her marriage to a scoundrel like William! He tricked her. He lied to her. He must need something. That's what he always does. We all know this." *Just like his brother.* She swallowed and looked away.

"Do we?" Lavinia looked confused. "We hear rumors. Folktales. You know this more than anyone, Caroline. The rumors don't turn out to be true most of the time."

"I am not pushing her to accept him," Helen said. "I just want you to think about what *you* want, Victoria. Not anybody else. It's obvious he loves you. And if you love him, then what is a better alternative? You can't divorce him; you can't marry anyone else."

"Unhappy marriages aren't uncommon," Lavinia said. "People just take lovers and move on."

"Yes!" Victoria exclaimed excitedly. "Like my sister."

"But if you truly love William, will you want anyone else?" Annalise said softly.

Helen lowered her head, her brows furrowed. Annalise didn't mean to upset anyone, Caroline was sure, but with the conversation turning to lovers again, Caroline suddenly felt queasy.

"Let me ask you this," Helen said thoughtfully. "If you made an advantageous marriage—a political marriage that your sister would be happy with—would you take William as a lover?"

Everyone fell silent, all heads turned toward Victoria. She sat frozen, with an embroidery piece in her hand, her brows drawn over her eyes, her lips pursed.

"You don't have to answer, dear," Annalise murmured. "But perhaps this question will help you make a decision."

"My uncle will not let me decide for myself," Victoria breathed, grasping at the last excuse remaining.

"Let me worry about your uncle," Lavinia said with a wink.

The room dipped into silence once more, as everyone was lost in their thoughts. Only the sounds of Annalise shifting uncomfortably in bed reminded everyone why they all gathered here.

"And what about you?" Lavinia turned to Caroline. "Are you any closer to untangling the web of secrets of your marriage?"

Caroline huffed a soft laugh. "I am afraid, I am even more entangled than before."

"How do you mean?" Annalise asked from the bed.

"I mean, he disappeared for three days before Christmas. I knew he was coming home, and I knew he was conferring with servants, but he was completely ignoring me. And then he showed up late to our own Christmas feast with William in tow!"

"Do you still think he is going about his blackmailing business?"

Did she? Caroline grimaced. "I am not certain. Things have happened lately that made me question my confidence. Not the least of which was the revelation that came from St. John's investigation."

"Do you think he is just spending all this time with his mistress?" Olivia asked with a horrified grimace.

Caroline let out a chuckle. "Perhaps. You think I am wrong," she addressed Helen who was watching her with a frown on her face.

"I didn't say so." Helen gave her a weak smile.

"You don't have to. I can see the quiet disapproval on your face."

Helen smiled. "I have doubts. I have not been an active member of society for…"—she let out a laugh—"ever. I have been always sickly, which means that I am always sitting on the sidelines watching people live their lives. Which, I think, granted me an advantage. I see things that other people can't."

"For instance?"

"For instance… I see the way your husband looks at you."

Caroline glanced at the other ladies to see if they agreed with Helen's assessment. They just listened to the conversation thoughtfully. "H-how does he look at me?"

"As though you're the sun and in his eyes, the rest of the world simply spins around you."

"I don't think I take your meaning."

Helen licked her lips. "It's the same way that Jarvis used to look at Olivia before they started courting… It's the same way that William looked at Victoria today. With longing and want burning behind his eyes."

Caroline let out a laugh while Victoria shifted uncomfortably. "I am afraid you misinterpreted my husband's gazes. He looks at me as though he doesn't trust me. And he has a good reason for it."

"He looks at you like you're the woman he wants but can never have," Helen said. "I know that look. And I know that feeling enough to recognize it in others."

Caroline wanted to say something but she clamped her lips shut. Whatever Helen saw in Kensington, Caroline saw a great deal of pain in Helen herself. "Thank you," she said simply. "I shall take it under advisement."

"I know you won't," Helen said softly. "But I wish you would."

And on that, the conversation ended, because Annalise groaned from pain again, this time longer and with greater intensity.

* * *

Chapter 18

It had been hours since they came to the Payne house.

After the initial tension with William, the men now occupied a parlor, playing card games and drinking whisky, while Dane sat in the chair by the hearth reading a book.

"Gah!" Payne exclaimed as William won another hand. "How come you are always winning? I am quite certain you're cheating."

William tsked. "Careful... men have been called out for less."

"Yes, and he's going to cheat in a duel, too," Lord Roth chimed in.

William scoffed. "Oh, get off your high horse, Bastian. Decent gentlemen call out men for *not* marrying their nieces. Not the other way around."

"Most gentlemen call out other *gentlemen* and not lying bastards."

"I think the more interesting question is," St. John stepped in, as he dealt the cards, "why do you always win here, while you never do in hells?"

"Been watching me, have you?" William raised a brow, a satisfied smile on his lips.

"I pay attention."

"Well, the difference is quite simple," William said, as he studied his cards. "Gentlemen don't like to lose. If you let them win, you end up in their good graces for a long time. Here, everybody loathes me anyway—and the feeling is mutual—so, I don't care to pretend to lose."

"Pretend," Dane observed. "That's your issue, William. You always pretend. You are never just yourself."

William smirked. "Well, those are the cards life dealt me, aren't they? Being a duke's bastard, living between two worlds, belonging to none. I have to pretend to survive. Always have. Your problem, on the other hand, is being too uptight. It's Christmas, and you won't even play cards."

"Pardon, I don't think I have a problem." Dane turned the page.

"Really?" William seemed genuinely surprised. "Then perhaps I am mistaken."

"What the hell are you talking about?" Dane finally looked up from his book.

"The things between you and your wife just seemed... chilly."

Dane let out a chuckle. "You are going to lecture me on my issues with my wife when yours can't stand you."

William smiled. "Well, mine loathes me. But at least she feels some passion for me. Can't say the same about yours."

Dane pursed his lips, although William's words cut deeper than he'd anticipated.

"Why are you even still here?" St. John asked in annoyance.

"What the devil is taking so long?" Payne asked, looking at the clock. "I have to go check on my wife."

"You checked less than twenty minutes ago," Roth noted.

"And they kicked you out, anyway," William smirked. "What makes you think this time will be different?"

"She's my wife. I can't just sit here and—"

Footsteps sounded outside the door, and then Caroline appeared on the threshold. Her bearing was perfect, as always, but her eyes were wild. "Payne, she is ready to see you." And then the most beautiful smile emerged. "Congratulations, you have a son."

Payne shot off the chair so fast it toppled over. He didn't even look back. He ran past Caroline and out into the hall.

Men lifted their glasses of whisky and cheered. Dane stood and walked toward his wife, who still stood in the doorway, her eyes glassy.

"Are you tired?"

She blinked up at him, as though she hadn't noticed his approach. "No, I—I don't know. Now I understand why they prefer only to have matrons in the birthing room."

He took her hand and rubbed her knuckles. "Why?"

She let out a shaky laugh. "Well, if I had wanted children before, I wouldn't now."

"You don't want children?" What an interesting revelation.

She looked at him as though he was addled. "No. I thought it was clear from our arrangement."

"Oh." Dane thought for a moment before replying, "I thought it was me you were objecting to. Not the idea of children."

She smiled timidly, then her eyes dropped to their joined hands. She seemed startled. Like she didn't even notice he was holding her hand, rubbing soothing circles over her knuckles with his thumb. He thought she'd pull her hand away. Instead, she curled her fingers, squeezing his.

"Are you ready to go home?"

She nodded.

"I am afraid nobody is going home," Lavinia said as she appeared by Caroline's side.

Caroline immediately pulled her hand out of his hold. She cleared her throat and addressed Lavinia. "Why not?"

"Have you seen the storm outside? The roads are icy. A carriage could break an axle or a horse could break its leg. Besides, it's the middle of the night. And if anything does happen, you risk being stranded."

"Oh." Caroline frowned. "Well, if Annalise needs help organizing—"

Lavinia interrupted her with a raise of a hand. "Everything is being arranged. Annalise's mother has already asked the housekeeper to prepare a few bedchambers for us. They are being aired out as we speak. They say they have enough room... Except..."

"Except?" Dane prompted.

"Well, we'd have to share."

"Share," Caroline repeated mechanically.

"With our spouses," Lavinia confirmed.

"Pardon?" Caroline looked absolutely confused.

Dane had to purse his lips to keep from smiling. He enjoyed the idea of sharing a room with his wife. And he loved it even more that she looked absolutely flustered at the idea.

"I have no problem with that," William said from behind them.

"Not you," Lavinia said sternly. "There'll be a room for you far, far away from the family wing."

"And where will my wife sleep?" He raised a brow.

Caroline licked her lips. "I can stay with Victoria—"

"You can't," Lavinia interrupted with a slight grimace. "She'll be staying with Helen. There is no other way this can work."

"Well..." Caroline looked at Dane, her gaze troubled, before addressing Lavinia again. "Are you certain it's risky to leave now? We are not in the middle of nowhere. We're still in London. Perhaps we can—"

"I've seen horses trip and fall a few feet away from the house," Dane interrupted swiftly. "We shouldn't risk it."

Caroline looked at him wide-eyed. "Did you hear about the

rooms?"

"You look like you're about to fall off your feet," Dane observed. And she did. Both she and Lavinia looked quite tired and rather rattled.

"Yes," Lavinia said absently, then entered the room and walked toward her husband.

"You're right. We are quite tired. But I don't have my maid with me. I don't have any other clothes."

Dane pursed his lips. "I can help you."

Caroline's eyes widened further. "With my clothes?"

"With whatever you need. I shall not take advantage," he added softly for Caroline's ears only.

She looked at him strangely and opened her mouth to retort, but then closed it. Her eyes traveled somewhere behind his back. "Before any of that... Let us speak with William. I won't be able to sleep before I hear everything he has to say about my uncle."

Dane nodded. He doubted she'd be able to sleep after she heard what he had to say either. But at least, this time, they would be sharing a bedchamber and she wouldn't be able to run off into the night.

Chapter 19

Caroline settled in the chair opposite William, her husband by her side. "I am ready to listen," she said. "Well, where do you want me to start?" William asked. "After all, you've been so gracious. I had a marvelous Christmas evening."

Caroline could not return the sentiment. "Start at the beginning."

William made a show of settling into his chair. He stretched his legs and crossed them at the ankles, while he was carelessly leaning, half-lying against the back of the chair. "It was a long time ago. I was just a lad back then, eleven, maybe twelve." He shrugged as if he didn't remember, as if it didn't matter. "I had just met Hades—it doesn't matter how—and he introduced me to some... interesting people, invited me to stay with them in his gloomy mansion. But I was never much for company. I was more of a loner, you see. Still am. And by that I mean, I could always get by on my own. I have always had skills—people skills—that Hades didn't possess.

Still doesn't. He reminds me of you in that regard." He grinned at Dane. "Although, you can be silver-tongued when you need to be, while he just threatens people."

"Please, just, get to the point," Dane growled.

"Of course. Well, in my quest to strengthen my... um... public relations, I came across a group of people arranging underground auctions. They were auctioning off stolen art and forged art... at first. That's where I met your uncle."

"You're lying," Caroline said instantly. Another person trying to convince her that her uncle was a criminal.

"I have no reason to," William said with an easy smile. "Your uncle was part of the criminal society called The Brotherhood of the Crimson Fist." Dane slid her a discreet gaze, while William continued. "Very old society. Ancient. When I first met them, I thought they were just about art and forgeries but turned out that's how they initiate people into their circle."

"What are they truly about?" Caroline asked.

"Let's just say that auctioning off inanimate objects is just a front. To test one's loyalties. Doesn't make them as much money as the other things they do."

Caroline glanced between William and Dane, confused, as though she were missing something important.

"They sell people," Dane supplied.

Caroline stifled a gasp, her eyes panicked. Her husband knew this, and he still thought her uncle was part of it!

"Ah, yes. That they do," William confirmed eagerly. "You might know something about that since they sent a friend of yours on a voyage a few years back. Payne?"

"Payne?" Caroline's brows furrowed. "They were behind Annalise's husband's abduction? And you are saying that my uncle was a part of them? That's a ridiculous notion!"

"Perhaps." William shrugged. "They have a mark on a part of their body. In the form of a little red fist—crimson. Perhaps your uncle had one?"

"I never saw anything like that on him." Caroline bristled.

"You wouldn't, would you? He wouldn't parade it around. It would be hidden beneath his clothing. But that was the final part of their initiation."

"Do you have this mark on you?" Caroline asked.

"Oh, no." William waved a dismissive hand. "I didn't reach this final part, you see. I am a criminal, and I might be as bad as you'd expect. But what they dealt with, the things they did…" He tsked and shook his head. "Let's just say I didn't have the stomach for it. My morality might be gray, theirs… is pitch black."

"You're saying that my uncle was worse than you?" Caroline scoffed, but her fingers curled into the armchair cushions. "He was a marquess!"

"All of this was before he inherited. His brother had cut him off. What else was he supposed to do but turn to crime?" William raised his brow at Dane pointedly.

"If you're trying to draw parallels between his situation and yours… Don't," Dane warned.

"Oh, I wouldn't dream of it. He could've chosen honest work instead of crime. He would have easily found a place for himself in a solicitor's office, or in some other comfortable job reserved for the aristocrats. Legitimate ones." He swallowed, trying to keep the nonchalance in his expression. "If I chose work instead of crime, I would have gone to the mills to work eighteen hours a day or to a brothel."

Dane gave him a hard gaze. "I would reserve some sympathy for you, William, if I didn't know that you came by a vast amount of money—and quickly."

William scoffed. "Those riches lasted me three years."

"It's not my fault you can't manage money," Dane answered immediately, leaning in closer to William.

"Dane." Caroline placed her hand over his arm in an attempt to get his attention. It worked. He turned toward her and must have seen something in her expression that communicated her distress because he covered her hand with his and squeezed her fingers. Caroline turned back to William. "My uncle. How long was he with these people?"

William raised his eyes from Caroline and Dane's joined hands. "I don't know. I left England shortly after. When I saw him next, he was already considered a pillar of society. A marquess." He laughed. "Things the title gets people. They can get away with anything."

"Poor little William," Dane seethed.

William folded his arms across his chest as he studied Dane. "You think I deserve even less than I got. But what's my sin? Being born to a woman your father didn't deem worthy to marry? Our situations could have easily been reversed. Would you have survived the life I had? I doubt it."

"I am not going to feel sorry for your plight, William," Dane said evenly.

"Yes. But imagine for a moment if I were a duke. If I had fooled Victoria into marrying me, but instead of being a bastard, I were a legitimate duke. Would you all go against me as you have now? Or would you force poor Victoria to live with me? Would she even care? Would Roth even dare call me out on a duel? You see, you all pretend you're above me. But in reality, it is not my actions you condemn. It's my lack of a title. I may be a blackguard and a knave, but at least

I am honest about who I am." He paused, then grimaced as he must have realized the lie in his words. "Most of the time."

While Caroline agreed with some of the things William had said, she was not interested in arguing about the unfairness of fate at the moment. "Is there anything else you can tell me about my uncle? Did he leave the Brotherhood on bad terms?"

"I don't know if he left them and if so, when. All I know is that nobody leaves the Brotherhood unscathed. Or at least, that's what I hear."

"Do you know any other members of this Brotherhood?" Dane asked.

"I know that Bradshaw was." He shrugged. "I dealt with him on a few occasions before he got caught. He wasn't exactly circumspect. But many of the old guards are already dead. Most of them curiously passed away while I was on the Continent. So I can't shed any light on that."

"So you can't help us. What a surprise," Dane said coldly.

"What *can* you tell us?" Caroline chimed in.

"I know the men Bradshaw was friendly with. Young lords, all of whom rose to popularity and wealth rather quickly. Rather suspiciously."

Caroline leaned closer. "With the help of the Brotherhood?"

"Perhaps. I don't know exactly who is part of the Brotherhood and who isn't. But it's easy enough to check. Just take a peek under their clothes. I am certain you know how to entice them to take them off." William smirked at Caroline.

"Give me the names," Dane growled.

William turned toward him, looking nonchalant. "I don't know all of their names. And I don't care to. But I do know a place all of these people like to cavort in. They are not much for your high society functions. But they do like to collect every once in a while at the underground masquerades and balls held by"—he grinned—"more intriguing members of society. I happen to know where the next one will be held."

Dane stood and took a piece of paper, a quill, and an inkwell from the table. "Please, do write everything down."

* * *

Caroline stood in front of the bed in the small chamber where she was about to spend the night with the duke.

She was still preoccupied with William's words, too lost in her memories of her uncle.

Should she believe him? He had corroborated what the thief-taker had told Dane earlier. But it all felt unreal.

All of Caroline's memories of her uncle pointed to the contrary. And if he were a part of the Brotherhood of the Crimson Fist, surely Wolverstone would have known that. Surely, he wouldn't have allowed Caroline's uncle to be a part of such a terrible group.

Nothing made sense. And Caroline would rage and cry and storm off into the night if she hadn't just done that a few nights prior.

Now she was just tired. Spent.

She didn't have the strength to do anything about the revelations that kept invading the peaceful memories of her uncle.

So she just stood there at the side of the bed, staring at it. And she didn't even have the strength to be outraged by the idea that she would have to spend the night in it with her husband.

"Do you need help undressing?" Dane asked.

Caroline frowned and looked down at her clothing. "I might need help with my stays." Well, not might. She *would* need help with the stays. She just didn't quite feel comfortable disrobing before her husband.

Even with everything that had passed between them—or perhaps because of everything that had passed between them—she felt extremely shy.

Dane moved to the other side of the bed, opposite her, and started slowly disrobing. "I can help you with that," he said as he took off his coat.

He untied his cravat and placed it on a chair by the bed. Next, off went the waistcoat. He struggled with it slightly. Perhaps it was difficult for him to take off his clothing without his valet. Should she have offered assistance?

By the time the thought had crossed her mind, he was already untying his hair from the queue, and now his hair was gently lying against his shoulders.

"Are you certain you don't need help with your gown?" Dane asked with a raised brow.

Caroline colored. She had been staring, watching him disrobe, and therefore not disrobing herself. "No. I am just waiting for you to crawl into bed and face away from me," she lied.

"Then how will I help you with your stays?"

How, indeed?

Caroline turned away from him and started unpinning her gown. Her fingers were shaking, either from fatigue, the frustration of this night's additional revelations, or perhaps it was the idea of undressing before her husband that had her nervous. She couldn't tell exactly what she was feeling. Her mind was in disarray.

She was finally able to remove the gown. The stomacher went next, then the petticoats, followed by the panniers and underpetticoats.

There she was, standing in a single nightshift, stockings, and her stays, not quite certain what to do next.

And then she felt warm fingers at her back, tugging at the ties of her stays.

Caroline stilled. Dane's breath worried wisps of hair at the back of her neck, sending shivers down her spine.

"Do you think what William said is true?" she asked, trying to think about anything but his fingers innocently brushing her back.

"I don't think he has a reason to lie," came her husband's rumbling voice. "He wants to get back into Princess Victoria's good graces. So I think he would do anything to achieve his goal, even helping me."

A pause.

"Do you think he loves her?" she asked.

A light puff of air hit Caroline's nape. A scoff. "I don't know William well enough to tell you that. I do know, however, that once he sets his mind to something, he doesn't stop until he achieves it."

Caroline's stays gave way and loosened, dropping to the floor.

"All done," Dane murmured, swiping a lock of hair away from her nape.

They stood like that, her back to him, their breathing and the cracking of the fireplace the only sounds in the room.

"Can you look at me?" There was a strange note in his voice. Caroline couldn't quite identify it. But it felt almost as though he was afraid she was angry with him.

She turned slowly and raised her face to his.

"Do you want me to take down your hair?"

She blinked up at him, startled. She was about to protest—it was unheard of for a duke to deal with his wife's hairpins. And yet he reached out and started taking them out one by one and dropping them to the floor.

Caroline's eyes closed of their own volition. It felt nice, having the tips of his fingers scratch her head, combing through her hair, massaging her scalp.

After a few minutes of concentrated effort, all the pins were out, and her hair was cascading down her shoulders.

"There," he murmured. "Much better."

Caroline glanced at him, his eyes were heavy-lidded, his mouth slightly open. That image of him, half-naked, with his hair about his shoulders, his gaze fixed upon her form with great intensity, did unconscionable things to her nether regions. Her insides tightened, and an unknown warmth unfurled at her center.

Suddenly she remembered Helen's words.

I can see the way your husband looks at you. With longing and want burning behind his eyes.

Was that how he was looking at her now? Was that how he was looking at her when he thought no one was watching?

He traced her cheek lightly with his thumb, tickling her, sending shooting sensations down to her middle. Then lower. He caressed her jaw until she started rubbing her face against his fingers like a cat starved for a human touch.

And she was starved for touch.

Sure, they had touched before. But all of that was in a state of frenzy. Now they were calm and undisturbed. They were alone in a cozy, small chamber. And the air vibrated with possibilities.

"Caroline," he breathed softly, almost a whisper. "All these things we are uncovering about your uncle… They don't take away who he was to you."

Caroline huffed a bitter laugh and looked away.

"No." Dane shook his head and tipped her chin so she would look at him again. "Don't look away. Please, don't turn away from me. I don't want you to think that you need to go through this alone. I am right here. And I don't want you to think that finding out about your uncle's criminal past makes it easier for me somehow. It doesn't make me less motivated to find the blackmailer. Perhaps more so. Because I don't want to see you questioning your loyalty to your uncle's memory."

Tears appeared at the back of Caroline's eyes. "Is it wrong that I still love him?"

"No." Dane caressed her cheek with his thumb, and with this simple act of gentleness, his kindness broke down her wall, and tears sprung to her eyes.

Caroline didn't want him to see her tears and, in an attempt to hide her face, she pressed her forehead against his chest.

His arms immediately went around her, his hands drawing soothing circles on her back. And that just made her cry more.

Her shoulders shook as she cried in the arms of her husband.

She snaked her arms around him and pressed herself closer to him to keep her balance, and his arms tightened around her. They stood like that, her crying, him whispering soothing nonsense in her ear, and she completely lost track of time.

The tears had left her body, making her feel freer somehow. Better.

She stepped away, and he let her go instantly.

A kind word, a warm embrace, and the freedom to cry. That's all that was needed, apparently, for her to get rid of the weight that she had carried around her ever since her uncle had died.

And no, it didn't make his death any less tragic or her feelings toward her uncle any less complicated. But her chest didn't hurt anymore. It was as though a load had been taken off her shoulders.

"I am sorry," she said as she wiped her tears.

"Don't," he said softly. "Don't apologize."

He took her hand away from her face and wiped a stray tear away from her cheek. Then he leaned down, slowly, and Caroline tilted her head toward him.

Dane took her face between his palms and placed a warm, calming kiss on her forehead.

Caroline's eyes fell closed, and she felt the tears stream down her face again. He pressed his forehead against hers, his thumbs chasing away her tears.

"My little wife," he whispered.

And the words completely disarmed her.

With a chaste kiss and these softly whispered words, it was as though he'd finally claimed her as his.

When he'd kissed her hungrily in that alley, laying siege to her defenses with his erotic touches, he'd taken her pledge of loyalty, demanding she gave herself to him. And she did.

I'm yours, she'd cried then. And she'd meant the words.

But his words now, *My little wife,* had finally confirmed that he'd accepted her pledge and claimed her as his, too.

* * *

Something had just passed between Dane and his wife. Something unfathomable. Something he did not understand with his mind, but something he felt in his soul.

She was so fragile, his fierce duchess, so delicate.

He wanted to protect her from this world—to always keep her safely tucked beside him. He wanted to slay half the world for her and place the rest on their knees before her.

He knew that she could do it herself. She did not need a protector. And that was why he felt a special kind of trust in her allowing him to witness her tears, to wipe them away for her.

She tilted her head back, then. Her eyes searched his.

"Caroline," he whispered.

"Yes?" Her answer was breathless.

"If I kiss you now, will you slap me again?"

Caroline let out a chuckle. "I don't know. Are you willing to take that risk?"

He grabbed her chin and raised her face to his, his finger caressing her lips as her passion-filled eyes stared from beneath her heavy eyelids. "Always," he murmured, and then his face descended on hers.

Her lips tasted of her tears. They were salty, and yet there was a special kind of sweetness lying beneath.

Dane's hand went to the back of Caroline's neck, to hold it in place while he sipped on her lips. Her hands traveled up his arms, making his muscles bunch at her touch as if craving her contact. And then she grabbed his shoulders, curling her fingers into his flesh.

Dane picked her up, walked two steps to the nearby chair by the hearth, and settled her onto it. He spread her legs, so he could kneel before her, her thighs bracketing his torso, and proceeded to devour her sweet mouth.

His cock immediately sprung up and strained against the constraints of his breeches. His hands traveled down the sides of her body.

She made a little sound of protest, and Dane raised his head. "What's wrong?"

She shook her head while licking her swollen lips. "Nothing. Don't stop."

He didn't need to be told twice. With a groan, Dane resumed his ravenous kisses, plunging his tongue deeper into the corners of her mouth. Claiming her, tasting her, devouring her.

His entire body tensed, ready for the release he knew was coming. The release he had been waiting for from that night in the alley.

No, even earlier than that. From that day in Wolverstone's ballroom.

Perhaps, even before that.

His mind refused to think any further. All his energy was directed toward soaking every touch his wife bestowed upon him, every moan that ripped away from the back of her throat.

She was the woman he had been waiting for his entire life, even if he hadn't known that. She was the woman who was able to awaken every inch of his body with the mere sound of her voice, a flutter of her lashes, with a smile on her lips.

But when she kissed him back the way she was doing now, he feared he would go mad.

Except he fought to stay as sane and lucid as he could. He didn't want to miss a single moment of their shared passion.

He pulled away and moved to trail kisses down her jaw. He dropped a whisper of a kiss to her throat and heard her giggle.

Dane raised his head, a question in his eyes.

"I'm… ticklish," she explained with a gorgeous smile.

A mistake.

He lowered his head and proceeded to torture her with light kisses down her neck.

Caroline squealed with laughter, her legs flailing in the air, her fingers tugging on his hair. Dane smiled against her skin, before biting on her neck with a playful growl.

Caroline let out a shriek that quickly turned into laughter. Then she buried her face between his neck and shoulder, shaking. "Stop," she said between fits of laughter. "Someone will hear us."

He leaned away from her and raised a brow. "So what?"

She looked at him, her eyes glinting with merriment. "They'll think you are torturing me here."

Dane tsked. "Oh, my dear duchess… I haven't even begun."

Chapter 20

I haven't even begun.

The playful words should not have made her shiver with anticipation. Perhaps it was not the words at all, but rather the promise in his glinting eyes, the cadence of his gravelly voice, and the way his hands moved down her body as he said it.

As if he owned her.

And at that moment, perhaps he did.

He slid his hands down her body until they encircled her ankles. Then, as he watched her reaction with hunger in his eyes, his palms slid up her stockinged calves and up to her knees. He spread his fingers around her knees and then spread her knees wider, all the while not taking his eyes off her face.

Caroline gasped, her breathing erratic, her chest rising and falling faster and faster with her every breath. And then he moved his hands higher, grazing her thighs and hiking her nightgown up to her hips.

He still watched her with a contemplative look on his face. And when she didn't protest, he flipped the skirt of her nightgown, exposing her bare center to his gaze.

His eyes flicked down, and he caught his breath.

Caroline didn't know how to act at that moment. This was something she had never experienced before, something no one had warned her about.

Just a moment earlier, she had been vulnerable with this man emotionally, baring her soul and crying on his chest. Now, she bared her body. And the feeling of vulnerability went even deeper.

What was he thinking? Did she measure up to his expectations?

He grabbed her hips, his fingers biting into her flesh, then in one smooth motion moved her to the edge of the chair.

She squeaked, her hands immediately grabbing the armrests. He looked at her then, his eyes heavy-lidded, and licked his lips.

Caroline squirmed, her muscles tensing, and a shiver running down her body. And with that same hungry look in his eyes, still staring deep into her eyes, he took her legs and placed them on his shoulders.

Caroline caught her breath, unable to move or do anything beyond staring back at her husband's face.

He dropped his gaze to her center and slowly spread her intimate lips with his fingers, exposing her even more to his eyes. And just when she was ready to die of embarrassment, he dipped his head and kissed her.

Caroline's hips shot off the chair, and her fingertips curled into the armrest until it hurt.

"Oh, no," her husband grumbled in disapproval before

grabbing her hips to keep her in place. Then he dipped his head again and pressed another kiss to her center.

With one hand on her hip and another hand on the floor for leverage, Dane opened his mouth and licked the seam between her feminine lips. Caroline's hips bucked, but he gripped her thighs, the tips of his fingers biting into her flesh, only adding to the overall sensations shooting through her body.

If she thought she could not stand tickling before, that was because she had never imagined feeling the sensations that were now gathering between her legs. Dane's insistent strokes with his tongue sent shivers down her spine, and her body spasmed uncontrollably.

Still holding the armrest in a vice-like grip, Caroline's other hand went to cradle Dane's head. Her fingers brushed through his hair before tightening.

Dane continued his relentless licking, grunting approvingly every time she let out a moan or a whimper.

Caroline tightened her fingers in his hair and tugged him higher, toward the pulsing nub that begged to be touched. Dane chuckled hoarsely, his enormous shoulders moving and shaking her in her chair. The motion coupled with the light breath hitting against her center had Caroline squirming.

She let go of his head and gripped the back of her chair for leverage. And that's when Dane kissed her exactly where she needed it.

Caroline let out a cry, her hips attempting to shoot up again. But Dane held her tightly in his arms, his tongue already circling and lightly flicking her swollen nub.

Too lightly.

"Dane!" she cried, raising her hips, trying to communicate

to him that she needed more. But words wouldn't form on her lips, only incoherent moans and cries escaping her.

Dane licked his way lower, just under the little nub, and Caroline tensed all over. She started pulsing from within, the tension building in her burning loins.

"Yes! More!" she cried, her fingers curling into the chair painfully, her hips bucking as the pulsing sensation spread from her center.

And then pure, unadulterated bliss hit her, wave after wave, and spread throughout her limbs with every beating of her heart.

When she came to, Dane was still feasting on her, unrelenting. His tongue swept along the edges of her pleasure button, collecting every drop of moisture that left her center. His tongue, his lips, hit the nerves she didn't know she possessed, bringing her back to that place just on the verge of pleasure again.

She twisted and turned, unable to take more of it. The tickling feeling low in her belly and in her center intensified, making her squirm in frustration.

And then the flood of pleasure swallowed her whole again. And again. Until she wasn't able to move or think anymore. She just lay across that chair, limp and spent, surrounded by her husband's virile heat.

* * *

She was the sweetest of desserts, and Dane could not get enough of her. Her delicious whimpers and cries only made him want to prolong this exquisite torture. Her taste on his lips, her scent in the air, made a beast out of him.

And he would not have stopped when he did. But his need for her overpowered his desire to continue feasting upon her.

His cock felt heavy and rubbed uncomfortably against his breeches, demanding to be let out, demanding to be let into her warm center. And at this point, Dane could no longer deny his hunger.

He looked at his spent wife, lying haphazardly on the chair, a sheen of sweat covering her face and neck. Her hair was sticking to her face, and her breathing was ragged. He could stare at this vision of her his entire life and never be tired of it.

He sat up on his knees and pressed a lingering kiss to her inner thigh before lowering her legs to the floor. Then he wiped her trickling juices off his jaw and collected the remaining moisture off his lips.

"Mm." A soft rumble left his lips. "Delicious."

A full-bodied blush covered his wife's skin. She attempted to sit up, but it seemed like she had no strength left in her.

Good.

Perfect.

That's just the way he liked her. Absolutely spent.

She tugged on the skirt of her shift in an attempt of covering her lovely quim, but Dane covered her hand with his and tsked. "Oh, no, dear," he said, shaking his head. "I am not done with you yet."

Her eyes widened. "No?"

A hoarse chuckle left his lips. "Oh, you thought that was it?" He let out a laugh. "No, no, my darling wife. I promised you torture. This was just the beginning."

He took his shirt by the collar and tugged it over his head. His skin was damp from sweat and sensitive to the touch.

Chapter 20

Oh, yes, her touch. That's what he wanted to experience next.

Her eyes were running along his arms, shoulders, and chest as though she had the same idea.

Dane tugged on her hands at the same time sitting back on his bottom so that she straddled him just as she slid from her chair. Her hands immediately went to his shoulders, her fingertips skimming along his skin. His muscles bunched beneath her touch, a shiver passing through his body.

"Touch me," he whispered. "Scratch me. Bite me."

She bit her lip, her gaze running down his face. Then she spread her fingers and circled his shoulders with her palms.

Dane's eyes fell closed from pleasure, his head falling back. He felt her nose nudging his chin, and then a timid bite against his neck.

His arms went around her, holding her tightly against him. She opened her mouth wider and sucked on his skin. And that's all it took to tip over his restraint.

He squeezed her tighter, and with a growl turned them both until she lay on her back against the plush Turkish carpet, and he was on top of her, his pelvis pressing against her center.

He undid the falls of his breeches and tugged them down, before rubbing his hard, aching cock against her wet quim.

He lathered his length in her juices, and she moaned, her fingers curling into his shoulders.

"Wrap your legs around me, darling," he whispered before planting a demanding kiss on her lips. She kissed him back with wild abandon, her legs wrapping around his hips and holding him close to her.

"Oh, yes, my duchess," he breathed against her cheek, his cock rubbing against her center. "Bathe me with your juices.

Envelope me in your tight embrace."

"Please!" she cried, holding him closer to her. "More! I need more of you."

Dane pointed his cock at her entrance, his breathing rugged. His face was hot and sweaty, and his hands shaking. If he didn't enter her now, he would die.

So he pushed into her warmth only to be met with tight resistance.

Caroline whimpered, her face a grimace of pain.

Dane scowled, his need overpowering his brain. "Relax, darling," he whispered and peppered kisses on her face. "Please, just relax."

She nodded, but her muscles didn't soften.

Dane let out a breath, something between a sigh and a chuckle. He was too eager. Yes, he had pleasured her earlier, but he'd waited too long, and she'd tensed up again.

He needed to make her relax. So he worked his thumb between them and pressed it against her little hill of pleasure. He circled it and played with it as gently as he could while being wound up tight.

As Caroline's moans started leaving her lips, her passage gave way, and Dane thrust himself into her core.

Caroline cried out and he paused, her inner muscles working around him, struggling to accept his length.

Sweat trickled down his face, his arms shaking as he hovered above her, waiting for her to relax. When he felt her inner muscles give way, he withdrew a little only to thrust again.

Caroline let out a moan, her fingers fighting for a tight grip, scratching at his back.

"Yes, darling, hold on to me," he croaked and started

his rhythmic movements, thrusting into her burning core, rubbing his pelvis against hers, stimulating her lovely nub, urging her to come again.

Caroline started meeting his thrusts enthusiastically, gasps and whimpers leaving her body with each movement. Her fingers tightened on his back, sliding down his skin and scratching him as she fought for her release.

"Yes, just like that," he urged her, on the precipice of his own release.

She screamed his name, her fingers biting into his flesh, her head falling back, her entire body convulsing from the power of her climax. And that's when Dane lost all control of his faculties.

The blinding power of his orgasm shook him to the core. His hips continued moving, plunging his cock into her core, but his soul was flying among the clouds, entangled with the soul of his beloved duchess.

When he returned to the mortal plain, he was lying on top of his wife, no doubt crushing her with his weight. His breathing was back to normal, and his body was no longer burning.

He took Caroline by the buttocks and rolled onto his back, their bodies still joined.

And that's when he realized what had happened.

"Damn," he whispered.

"What?" Caroline placed her hands beneath her chin so she could look at him.

"Um." Dane caressed her hair. "I didn't use armor."

"Armor?"

"And I didn't withdraw on time." *On time?* He was still inside her, his length half-erect.

"Oh." She lowered her gaze.

"I got carried away and completely forgot. You said you didn't want children—"

She looked at him timidly as she bit her lip. "I wasn't thinking about that at all."

"God," Dane breathed, his fingers tracing her cheek. "I forgot my own name."

She let out a chuckle.

"You are not mad? I mean… we could have a child from this."

She seemed to contemplate it for a moment, then crinkled her nose. "I don't know how I feel yet."

She moved her pelvis, freeing his cock, and then wiggled out from his hold. Dane let go of her and she sat up, letting her shift cover her naked form. Then she pushed off his chest and stood. "I need to—" She didn't finish her sentence and disappeared inside the dressing room.

Dane frowned and sat up. He made a muck of things that's for certain.

He looked down. His breeches were still around his legs. He groaned and shook them off. But there was something… He stood and walked closer to the fire to notice that he had spots of blood on his cock and pelvis.

Damn.

She was a virgin.

Chapter 21

Caroline rushed into the dressing room and closed the door, leaning her back against the door and breathing heavily.

What in the world just happened?

That was the most incredible and embarrassing encounter in her entire life. She felt tender between her legs, and something was dripping down her leg.

Oh, no!

She wasn't a virgin anymore. And if that thought wasn't staggering enough, on top of that, she could be with child soon!

Oh, no, oh, no, oh, no!

She had been a virgin a few moments ago, but she wasn't clueless. She knew what an encounter like this entailed but she just wasn't thinking.

Her breath had been stolen by her husband's passionate kisses and apparently her mind, too. She knew there were ways to prevent a babe.

She took off her stockings, then walked to the wash basin, took a piece of cloth, and dipped it in. She needed to scrub herself clean before returning to the bedroom.

Then, once they returned home, she'd ask Rea to fix her a brew against getting with child. She'd read all about them.

Caroline paused in the process of scrubbing her skin. Would she?

For some reason, the idea of having Dane's babe in her belly wasn't as frightening as she'd thought it would be.

Certainly, she never wanted a babe… But then she'd never had a man whom she wanted as much as she wanted her husband. Perhaps, keeping a part of him for herself wasn't such a bad thing.

Then she remembered Annalise's cries and screams as she gave birth and grimaced. Next came the image of Annalise holding her squirming babe in her arms, happy.

Ugh! She was too confused to think clearly now.

She couldn't do anything about it now anyway. All she could do was clean herself as best as she was able. And then she would go back into the room and face her husband.

Or else, she would go back into the room, hide her face, and burrow under the covers.

Caroline slipped inside the room to find her husband standing in the middle in all his naked glory.

Naked, he looked bigger somehow. More imposing. She had seen his naked chest a few times now. But every time she saw it, she became mesmerized by the muscles knotting under his skin.

Then her gaze fell lower to his half-erect length. It stirred.

Caroline's entire body heated.

"I better… um… I need to clean up," he said, then walked

up to her and planted a kiss on her lips before stalking into the dressing room.

Caroline jumped onto the bed and scrambled to hide under the covers before he came back out again.

She didn't know why she cared if he saw her in her semi-transparent shift again. He had already seen her in all manner of undress and had not only seen her but touched her, kissed her, and licked her.

She shivered. And yet she felt a strange kind of vulnerability now.

Dane walked into the room a few moments later. He blew out the candle by the bedside and crawled under the covers.

He didn't touch her or kiss her again as she hoped he would. Instead, he just lay on his side of the bed facing her. "You were a virgin," he stated evenly.

Caroline was startled by his chosen topic. "Um... Of course."

"Of course?" he repeated. "We were married for five months and you loathed me. You could have taken a lover."

Caroline lowered her gaze.

Why hadn't she taken a lover during the time since they married? She was certain she could find opportunities if she wanted. But that was the answer, wasn't it? She didn't want to.

She'd never had the kind of craving that she had for her husband. She'd never wanted anyone else.

But of course, he would be surprised by her abstinence. He'd had a mistress this entire time. Did he still have this mistress? Was he planning to stop seeing her?

Surely not after what had happened! Unless, of course, he wanted children and she didn't... What if he already had children?

If the act of conceiving a child was this incredibly fulfilling and wonderful, she no longer wondered why some women kept birthing child after child.

His fingers touched her lightly beneath her chin, bringing her back to the present. "Where did your mind take you?" he asked gently.

She looked into his deep, gray eyes and she struggled to reconcile with the idea that he lay like this, naked, in bed with other women. "Is it always like this?" she asked, her voice small.

"What?" He furrowed his brows.

"What we did… does it always feel this…" She paused, her cheeks burning again.

"Wonderful?" he asked with a teasing smile. "If you weren't going to say wonderful, I don't think I want to hear the rest of that question."

Caroline let out a chuckle, suddenly not feeling as self-conscious anymore. "Yes, wonderful."

"Come here." He opened his arms, and Caroline eagerly moved toward him, until her head was pressed against his chest, her body snuggled to his side. "No. It doesn't *always* feel like this. I don't recall it ever being this good." Caroline's cheeks burned even harder. "And that's why. I forgot about everything else. Are you certain you're not angry at me for forgetting myself and… well, coming inside you?"

"I am not angry," she said. "I am just confused and uncertain."

He tipped her face toward him and looked into her eyes. "What do you feel uncertain about? Tell me."

Caroline watched him carefully, trying to put her fears into words. It was a difficult endeavor. She had never tried to do that before. She just thought she'd never have children and that's that. "When I was a little girl," she started thoughtfully, "after my parents died, I had nightmares that I was the only person left in this world. Then, when my uncle took me in, I would wake up in the middle of the night and run to his room to see that he was indeed there, that he was breathing. These fears were irrational, but I suppose it's the same with having a babe. I am not afraid to die in labor, although, perhaps that would be an understandable fear. I am afraid of leaving the child behind alone and passing along all my fears and anxieties. I don't know. It's not rational, but that's how I feel."

"I don't think the fears you have are irrational. You care too much, and you think it is easier not to care at all." He took a deep breath. "I understand. But if we find out that you are indeed with child, I will not let you die in labor, I promise."

He looked so fierce and serious as he said so that it immediately prompted a burst of laughter. "You can't promise me that! You're not even going to be present at the birthing!"

"Oh, I shall be." His voice was grave.

"No!" She squirmed in his arms, just imagining him watching her like they were watching Annalise during her most intimate and trying time of her life. "That's disturbing. You should be nowhere near the birthing chamber."

He chuckled and cuddled her close. "And yet, I shall be. I hope you can trust me enough so we can deal with your fears together."

Caroline breathed in deeply. His words did have a calming effect. "Thank you," she whispered.

He smiled. "But you were about to tell me about the lack of lovers in your bed. A fact about which I am incredibly happy, but I am curious. Is that because you never wanted to have children?"

Caroline shrugged. "Perhaps. I just… I don't know. I never met anyone I wanted to be this intimate with."

A slow smile stretched his lips. "Until you met me. I am quite honored."

She swatted at him. "Don't be smug."

"Why not? I am the only man in the world who's touched you this intimately. Lucky for them."

"Lucky for them?" Caroline frowned.

"Well, yes. If someone had touched you, I'd be compelled to kill them," he said in a matter-of-fact tone as if he were discussing what to have for dinner.

"You are not serious," she said with a chuckle.

He rolled her to her back then, covering her body with his as his hand grabbed the nape of her neck. "I am utterly serious," he whispered, then kissed her lips. "You're mine. No one else gets to touch you. Ever."

"What about you?" she whispered back. "Does anyone else get to touch you?"

He let out a hoarse chuckle. "No, my love. You are the only one."

My love. The words warmed her, but his reassurance wasn't enough. "You mean from now on."

He watched her strangely for a moment, before saying, "If you are asking if I had lovers before you, then yes. I did. But I have not had one for a while. And definitely not anymore. Other than you, that is." The last sentence he said with a grin and kissed her again.

Not anymore? What about the actress whose townhouse St. John had investigated? Was she his lover no more? Caroline's mind got distracted as he swept his tongue inside her. But she wasn't done asking questions. When they finished kissing, she would ask him... He kissed her deeper, his tongue sliding against hers, mimicking the act of love.

What were they speaking of? Ah, yes, the lovers. She pushed at him lightly until he let go of her lips.

He moved to kiss her cheek, her jaw.

"And..." She swallowed, feeling flustered. "Do you have children with any of your past lovers?"

Dane met her gaze again, his brow raised, a question in his eyes.

"Since what we did results in a babe... and you had lovers before—"

"No," he immediately cut her off. He took her hand and pressed a kiss to her fingers. "I am not the man to leave behind bastards. If you believe one thing about me, I'd rather you believe this. I've always used armor with other women. There's a sheath one can wear over one's cock, it prevents anything transferring from me to the lady, or a lady to me. I've never been with a woman without it." He grimaced lightly, then pressed another kiss to her hand. "With you I just... I forgot about everything. And to be completely honest, I never want anything to be between us. No barriers. I just want the feel of my skin against yours." He crimped the fabric of her night shift with his fingers. "But if you still think you don't want children, then I shall respect that and will use all the means of armor from now on."

"But don't you need an heir?" she asked, turning onto her side, so she could see him better.

Dane let out a sigh. "I have young brothers. They can take on the title. I don't much care."

"You don't? But most peers want their own children to take the title."

"Yes, I know. My father was like that." He took her hand again and rubbed it against his stubbly cheek as he spoke. "He tortured my mother with his attentions until she gave birth to me. And then he tortured her more for a spare. She died trying to give him another child." He kissed her fingers and held them against his lips as he spoke, lost in thought. "And to what end? He never cared about me. Neither did he care about the two boys he sired with his next wife or anyone he sired on the side. I would never do that to you." He kissed her fingers one more time before pressing her hand against his chest. Caroline could feel the steady beating of his heart and it soothed her.

There could be a babe growing inside her and she should have felt panicked, but she didn't. Perhaps the panic would come later. If she'd missed her monthly courses. If the doctor confirmed her fears.

Or perhaps the steady presence of the man beside her gave her enough confidence to not panic. Because at some point throughout their marriage, she'd started to trust him. And she couldn't even pinpoint the moment that had happened.

"My father only cared about his legacy, his name, his reputation," Dane continued his story. "Perhaps someone out there thinks he was a good man. But none of them are people who truly knew him. Some people want to be like their parents. I strive to be the opposite."

"You are the opposite," she said softly.

He raised a brow. "How do you mean?"

"You don't care what people think about you. You only care about doing what's right. You looked out for Lavinia when she

232

lived with her abusive father. You offered to marry Annalise when her situation got dire. You were forced to marry me, and yet you cared for me the best you could and never forced me to do anything I didn't want."

A slow smile blessed his lips. "Does this mean you don't think I am the blackmailer anymore?"

She chuckled and rolled onto her back. "I am not quite convinced yet."

He laughed and then rolled on top of her. He swept the locks of her hair away from her face before kissing her on the nose, then slowly moving to her lips. "I can definitely do a better job of convincing in that case." His hands went to roam her body.

"No," Caroline whispered. "Not just now."

He frowned before giving her a chaste peck on her lips. "Are you feeling sore, then?"

She nodded. "A little."

"Hm, then I'm afraid I'll have to try and convince you some other time." He chuckled as he rolled onto his back, but he took her with him, holding her close to his body.

She pressed her hand against his mighty chest, and he cradled her head against the crook of his shoulder.

"I might have been too rough with you today," he said, his voice rumbling through his chest and vibrating through her entire body. "I should have been gentler."

"No," she replied immediately. "You were perfect. It was… magnificent."

"Was it?" he asked with a smile in his voice. "I am glad to hear that. Still, if I knew this was your first time… " He paused sharply and the next time he spoke, his voice turned concerned. "Have your bruises healed from the fall?"

233

She was wearing a shift and her stockings during their most intimate encounters, so most of her body was shielded from his gaze. Most of her bruises now carried a yellowish tint and that image would not be very arousing, she imagined. "Most of them," she assured him after a moment of thought. "The wrist still aches at times."

"Hmm…" came a pleasant rumbling sound from the area of his chest. "Good thing I didn't attempt to tie you up then."

Caroline threw him a startled glance and saw merriment dancing in his eyes. He was jesting. But the idea of being tied up and open for him to do whatever he pleased sent desire shooting through her body.

She lowered her eyes and cuddled closer to him.

Dane played with her hair, his soothing motions, and the steady rise and fall of his chest lulling her. Caroline's eyes drooped, and she was in a place somewhere between dreamworld and reality when Dane spoke next.

"I am sorry if I ruined Christmas dinner today," he said.

"If?" Caroline chuckled, coming back to a pleasant reality.

"Well, I can't take credit for the entire evening, I am afraid. At the very least, we should share responsibility with Annalise's babe."

Caroline giggled and slapped him playfully on the chest. His hand descended on hers and held her trapped between his palm and his body.

"I just wanted to solve this damn riddle as soon as I could, so you would not put yourself in danger anymore. I didn't think William would demand to come with me."

Caroline shrugged. "That's fine. Everyone was late and… I suppose it's my own fault for setting high expectations for the feast. I was so preoccupied with making it grand so that I wouldn't feel lonely."

The bed creaked as Dane shifted to look at her. She could feel his gaze on her. "You felt lonely?"

Caroline let out a huff of laughter. "I was not exactly surrounded by my loving family. And it's not your fault; we have an arrangement."

"Had an arrangement."

"Had an arrangement," she repeated with a smile. "It's just that when my parents were alive, we always celebrated together. I remember opening hundreds of presents on the day after Christmas... Or at least it seemed that way. And then when I moved to live with my uncle, he just wanted to live up to my memories of them."

"And now you have a husband who leaves you the first thing in the morning on Christmas and ruins the dinner."

Caroline chuckled. "I suppose I should get used to that. If you're not the blackmailer—"

"If?" He let out an indignant huff.

"—then I have no legitimate way of divorcing you."

There was a beat of silence. "Do you still want to?"

Caroline freed her hand from under his and started drawing tiny circles on his chest. "As you can see, I am slowly reconsidering."

"Too slowly," he grumbled.

He shifted from beneath her and turned them both so he could see her face. "Since the day when you rescued me at that factory, I've had these nagging thoughts in my mind. And even though I think I figured out the answer, I'd be a fool not to ask this question out loud."

Caroline blinked at him. "What is the question?"

"You are not Erebus, are you?"

Caroline let out a burst of laughter. "No, I am not. Why did you think I was?"

He shrugged. "I didn't truly think you were, but a few things led me to doubt myself. Your name is not on the roster, and you seem to trust him implicitly."

"My name is not on the roster, because I am not truly a part of society," she said honestly. "I am a woman. There are different rules for me, I gather. I was trained by my father before he died and then continued training by myself. My uncle taught me fencing and archery. I was initiated when I was thirteen, like everyone else. And I do receive the most important notes, but I am not a true member. And I don't think my father would have wanted me to be." She narrowed her eyes as another thought crossed her mind. "My father died when I was five! Did you think I was Erebus this entire time? You know we inherit our mantles from our parents."

He grinned. "Maybe you inherited it from your uncle."

One side of her mouth kicked up in a smile. "My uncle who was a criminal? Hmm… Erebus and a bandit. Now that is the kind of power I aspire to have."

"You do?" He raised a brow, and Caroline just chuckled in answer.

They resumed their positions, Dane lay on his back, Caroline placed her head on his chest as different thoughts passed through her mind. She was still not telling her husband the full truth. And she wasn't certain that she should have.

She cleared her throat. "Tell me, how did you usually spend Christmas?"

He let out a deep sigh, his chest moving from under her body. "I didn't. I was raised as an heir for the dukedom, my father's progeny. As I said, my father wasn't exactly a loving man and my mother had always been sickly. So I worked and studied, and well, I wasn't treated as a child. Which meant, no gifts."

"No gifts?" Caroline raised her brow, not that he could see.

"No, but I can't complain. I was privileged. I always had food on the table, the best education money could buy."

"And yet you inherited the title without a penny to your name. I saw that."

"When you went through my papers?" He chuckled.

"Yes." There was no need to deny it. He already knew that she'd gone through his things. "So what happened? If your father was all about his title and his legacy, how come he squandered his fortune away?"

"He didn't." Dane's voice turned grave.

Caroline razed her gaze, watching as he squared his jaw. Giving him time to say more if he wished so. And he did.

"It's William."

Caroline scrunched up her nose. "William squandered it all away?"

"No, there was no squandering. Not at first, anyway. My father always lived for show. He needed everyone to see that he was the best. That he had the most expensive houses and the most expensive horses. But in the same way, he needed to have the best heir. He needed to be the perfect duke. The best Shadow. How he was any good at this based upon who he was, I do not know. But it was all about status to him. And he went on and on about how grand his social standing was and how I was his one and only progeny." He swallowed. "And then William appeared. Out of nowhere. He is only one year younger than me, you know. He was… scrawny, dirty, with bruises all over his body. It was around the same time when he first met Hades.

"I was thirteen at the time. I was horrified by the image. He insisted he was my father's son. My father denied it, of course. But William wanted our father to legitimize him. If kings can do it why not dukes, right?" He scoffed.

"Your father refused," Caroline guessed.

"Of course, he did. A whore's son would never be a legitimate son to a duke, he said. Then William asked him to at least acknowledge him." There was a burst of hoarse laughter. "My father refused again. And he threw him out of the house like an unwanted puppy."

"But he did acknowledge him in the end," Caroline said. "Everybody knows that William is your brother."

"As I said"—Dane heaved a sigh—"William always gets what he wants."

"How did he do it?"

"What my father didn't know at the time was that William had made some powerful friends. Within a week, rumors spread about William, about my father's associations with numerous women. Rumors about more illegitimate children—which might be true, but it was never proven. Or at least, I never saw any of them.

"My father was furious. So he made a deal with William. He sent him off to school in France and paid for everything. And gave him the money only so that William would stop spreading the rumors. That's where most of the money went. Taking the rest, my father tried to rebuild his fortune. Not with honest work, of course, but by gambling. In the end, he lost it all. So I got the title and the estates, but none of the wealth."

"But the rumors didn't stop," Caroline said softly.

Dane let out a laugh. "People don't forget a thing like that. When my father died, everything seemingly quieted down. But as soon as William returned, looking sharp and crisp, but still as sly and wily, rumors resurfaced. Nobody questioned his parentage anymore. I mean, look at him." He scoffed. "He is exactly like my father."

Caroline was silent for a few moments before asking, "Is that why you and William are hostile toward each other? Because he took the fortune while you took the title?"

He let out a sniff, his hand playing with her hair. "You're the only child so you won't understand this, but having siblings is… complicated. Having a bastard sibling… Well, they haven't invented a word for what it's like yet."

Chapter 22

The fire cheerfully cracked in the hearth, spreading the warmth and scent of winter throughout the chamber. Caroline let out a sigh of contentment. The morning after Christmas was her favorite day of the year. It was the day when the entire family gathered in the morning to open presents and spend time together with no duties or expectations.

Of course, this year was different. But she was still among family, with the newest member welcomed to the world just the night before.

Caroline stretched in bed only to bump against something hard and hot behind her.

For a moment she froze, not quite certain what to do.

She was in bed with her husband!

And not only that, she'd acted like a complete wanton last night!

Caroline remembered their last night's 'interactions' and her cheeks started burning. She looked at the chair she'd sat in last night while Dane feasted on her center and her entire body tensed. She closed her eyes from embarrassment.

She needed to get out of this room before her husband awakened. She didn't know how she would face him otherwise.

She tried to wriggle out of the bed as quietly as possible when Dane's arm snaked around her and pressed her back against his hard, hot body. His nose burrowed in the crook of her neck and he inhaled, then rubbed her neck with his nose, sending shivers down her spine.

"Dane?" she asked carefully.

"Mm?" came his sleepy reply. He caressed her belly with his hand, and then that shameless hand traveled up and cupped her breast!

"Dane!" she shrieked, and he laughed hoarsely, his entire body shaking.

"Good morning," he croaked in a hoarse, morning voice.

"Good morning."

"Apologies if I did something inappropriate." Interestingly, he didn't move to correct that mistake. He still lay there with his hand now rubbing her breast, his nose against her neck, his breath tickling her skin.

"Inappropriate?" Caroline's voice was strangely high-pitched. "No."

"No?" He grunted. "Then may I continue?" He ran his thumb against her nipple, and she squirmed.

"Now?"

He kissed her shoulder. "Mhm... now."

"But it's morning."

He chuckled again, his body shaking, vibrating through hers. Then his other arm snaked its way around her and cupped her between her legs. Caroline's hips moved to rub her center against his hand.

"Mm, so?" he murmured against her skin.

"It's daylight," she whispered as he started rubbing circles through the shift.

"Mm, yes, it is," he said and then trailed kisses down her neck.

Caroline was about to give in, but the sounds of doors opening and closing and people talking outside their door took Caroline out of the amorous mood.

"I need to"—she wriggled out of his embrace—"go."

Dane groaned and fell back onto his back.

Caroline sat up and covered herself with the sheet. Her hand self-consciously went to her hair, because of course, it was all tangled and probably looked like a bird's nest. She grimaced and moved to slide out of the bed. At that moment, Dane looked at her and froze as if transfixed.

"What's wrong?" Caroline asked.

"Nothing." He shook his head.

"Then why are you staring at me like this?"

A soft smile blessed his lips. "It's just…"

"Just what?" Her hand again crept to her tangled hair.

"You're too beautiful," he said. "I can't seem to take my eyes off you."

Caroline couldn't find an appropriate response.

She looked beautiful? Usually, yes. But not right now.

Dane crawled out of bed and stretched. "You are always so buttoned up, so proper. Nary a hair out of place."

"Not right now," Caroline said under her breath.

"Yes, exactly. Right now, you're just… you." He turned toward her with a grin. "And I find you incredibly beautiful this way."

Was he jesting? He must have been. Because nobody looked beautiful first thing in the morning. Well, except for him. He seemed fresh and rejuvenated. His hair lay perfectly against his bare shoulders in soft waves. His skin, unburdened of the powder or rouge he usually wore to Parliament, had a healthy tint of golden glow and his sharp cheeks had a natural pink blush. His square jaw was covered with morning stubble, emphasizing his full lips.

Then her eyes dropped lower, down his chiseled chest adorned with tiny black hairs. Her gaze traveled lower still and settled on his raging erect length.

Caroline blinked, her mouth opening slightly. It had been dark last night, and she had been drunk on passion. She hadn't truly seen this part of him clearly. Now it seemed… huge!

No wonder she was sore this morning.

His cock stood tall and proud among the curly intimate hairs. It was red and covered with veins. Rather beautiful. She wondered how it would feel between her fingers…

His length jumped as though also curious to find out the answer to her silent question.

Dane cleared his throat.

Caroline blinked and met his gaze. He raised his brow, his lips pursed in an attempt not to laugh.

She was staring, Caroline realized in horror. And he saw it!

Heat flooded her cheeks and spread along her body. "I need to—" She didn't finish the sentence as she fled into the dressing room.

Caroline dressed with the help of the maid while her husband performed his morning ablutions and then quickly left the room. She was too anxious and uncertain to speak to him this morning, and she also wanted to check on Annalise

243

and the new little babe as soon as she could.

The labor had seemed like a horrifying experience to Caroline. And she was worried for her friend's well-being.

Caroline entered the room only to find all the women already gathered by Annalise's side.

"How are you feeling?" Caroline asked when all the greetings were over.

"Very tired," Annalise said. "And extremely happy."

"Are you hurting?"

Annalise pursed her lips. "A little, yes. I feel some aches and soreness, but nothing that would keep me in bed for long. Certainly, nothing that requires me to stay in bed for forty days," she said the last sentence with a grudging look toward her mother.

"Tradition requires it," her mother said without looking up from her embroidery.

"It doesn't require you to actually stay in bed," Olivia said. "My mother says that—"

"Tut-tut," Mrs. Ardee interrupted. "It's called a lying-in chamber for a reason. Not 'dancing around and doing chores chamber.'"

The women exchanged quick laughing glances. It wasn't like ladies had laborious chores to perform. The most that was required of Annalise was to pour tea, write letters, and embroider. All of which could be done without getting out of bed. But Caroline imagined it would get dull sitting in one chamber for forty days. And she imagined Annalise would not be sticking to that part of tradition either.

Satisfied that her friend was not indeed dying and was in good spirits, Caroline moved toward the crib. The babe was wrapped in childbed linen that Caroline had acquired from a local draper. He was sleeping peacefully, one little arm waving in the air as he twitched in his sleep.

He was so tiny.

How could anything so tiny ever be terrifying?

* * *

The snow fell noiselessly on the ground outside the frozen glass windows. There was no wind, no noise of carriages moving across the street. This was the perfect place and the perfect weather for the morning after Christmas.

Dane was enjoying his coffee in the morning room while the entire house seemed to be sleeping. The side tables were laden with leftover Christmas food and drinks, but no servant was in sight. This seemed more like the Christmas mornings he remembered. Not that it snowed every year. That was just a gift of nature this time. But the quiet mornings when it seemed like he was all alone in the world were exactly how he remembered the holidays.

Then there was a swish of silky fabric and his wife entered the room.

And this was how he wanted to celebrate Christmas every year from now on. He didn't want to be alone anymore. He wanted to wake up every morning with his wife in his arms and then enjoy a quiet breakfast together.

Her mahogany hair was now tightly collected in a bun. Her dress was ironed out and tightly fitted to her body. She was the perfect duchess once more, not the woman from this morning, rosy-cheeked and all disheveled. Not the woman from last night, half-naked, moaning in his arms.

A few days ago, he would have said that he'd preferred her

the other way—disheveled, out of sorts.

He had to concede that he enjoyed the sight of her in either appearance.

"Annalise is ready to take guests," she said. "Would you like to see her and the babe?"

Dane stood, feeling rather nervous. "I would, very much."

Annalise was a long-time friend of his. He was very excited about her good fortune. He cared for her very much. When she was in dire straits, when her husband was presumed dead, he had even offered his hand in marriage to help her.

Oh, how different life would have turned out if her husband hadn't returned from the brink of death the night of Annalise and Dane's betrothal ball. Dane would have married Annalise. Perhaps she would be holding his babe now in her hands. He would have never married Caroline...

Dane offered his arm, and Caroline placed her hand on his sleeve. No longer tentative, her touch was firm, her fingers curling into his coat, her heat warming him from the inside the way the morning coffee hadn't done.

He looked down at her, wondering what she was thinking at the moment. She stole a glance his way.

He smiled. "Merry Christmas, Caroline."

Her smile was timid as she replied, "Merry Christmas, Dane."

They walked the rest of the way in silence until they entered Annalise's lying-in chamber and were greeted by female chatter.

Ladies were talking and laughing, adding to the warm feeling of a family gathering. Annalise lay in bed, looking tired but happy. A cheerful glow emanated from her eyes. Her husband, Payne, sat by the bed holding her hand.

Caroline pulled away from his side and joined the ladies sitting by the crib. Dane awkwardly walked toward Annalise and paused. "Merry Christmas," he said with a smile.

"Merry Christmas." Annalise smiled back. "Please, sit."

Dane pulled up a chair and sat next to Payne. "How do you feel?"

Annalise let out a sigh. "Tired, but happy."

Payne squeezed his wife's fingers.

"And now I will have to sit in this bed for forty days. Let's hope I won't go mad."

"Oh, please, do not be overdramatic," Lady Ardee said from behind Dane. "You are not the first woman to do this, and you won't be the last."

Annalise rolled her eyes.

"I apologize we don't have a gift," Dane said.

"Oh, no." Annalise perked up. "Your wife took care of it. She brought the entire crate of clothing and childbed linen."

"Did she?" Dane turned to look at his wife just as Lavinia handed her the babe. The child was bundled into some sort of white cloth decorated with lace, and his wife looked completely flabbergasted at the responsibility that was quite literally in her hands. He smiled. "She always thinks of everything, doesn't she?"

"It wouldn't be Caroline if she didn't," Annalise answered.

Caroline looked at him then, with such a terrified expression on his face that he chuckled. She wasn't afraid of him even though she'd thought him to be a monster. She wasn't afraid of the thugs she'd faced in the alley. And yet she was afraid of the tiny babe in her arms. And Dane could not quite take his eyes off her.

She didn't want children. And until this moment when

Dane saw his terrified wife holding a babe in his arms, neither had Dane. But now, the idea of a little girl with his wife's mahogany red hair, her expressive green eyes, her sharp wit, and her brazen attitude made his chest warm. The vision of his wife swelling and growing round with his babe completely disarmed him and filled him with pleasure.

"What's his name?" Dane asked, without turning to face Annalise.

"Noel."

Dane smiled. "How fitting."

Annalise let out a laugh. "He was my ultimate Christmas gift."

Dane stood and walked toward his wife. She smiled at him, then as he got close, whispered so that nobody would hear, "I am afraid to move."

"Don't worry," Dane whispered back. Then he leaned in and wrapped his arms around the babe. Before lifting him away from his wife's terrified embrace, he pressed a kiss to her cheek.

She looked up at him gratefully. "Thank you."

He looked down at the squirming babe in his arms and then at his blushing wife. "You don't have to be afraid of anything. I will always be here to lend a hand."

* * *

Everyone left Annalise's chamber a few minutes later. She needed the rest, and so did the babe. Payne stayed with his wife while Annalise's mother shepherded everyone out of the room.

"I think it's time for us to leave," Caroline said as they all filed into the corridor. "My coachmen are the only ones who haven't left for their hard-earned day off, and that's because they're waiting to drive us all home."

Dane nodded. "I will go and let them know to prepare the carriages." His gaze lingered on Caroline before he left, and Caroline found herself staring after him.

"I take it things are going better?" Helen asked with a wide smile as she passed Caroline.

How do you know? Caroline followed after Helen. "Why do you say that?"

Helen shrugged. "As I said, I am adept at watching people and noticing little nuances."

Caroline chuckled. "You must be magic."

Helen laughed outright. "Actually, I just saw him kissing you in Annalise's room. That was difficult to miss."

Caroline's cheeks burned. That kiss had felt so natural that she didn't even think to feel embarrassed about that at the time. She hadn't paid it any heed. Did everyone notice? Did it even matter?

"But I see your hesitation," Helen added. "And I just wanted to tell you. Don't. Don't hesitate to be happy. You never know how much time you have with a person." She gave her a small smile and slipped into her room.

Caroline paused by Helen's door, thinking about her words. Despite her newly found trust in her husband, she still had doubts and concerns. She was used to relying only on herself, and after the revelations about her uncle, perhaps that was a good thing. She didn't want to be disappointed in people again. She didn't want to feel only to lose again.

But then there was Helen, whose husband had been openly unfaithful to her. She had loved her husband nonetheless.

And she didn't seem to regret any of it. Only the time she hadn't spent with her husband. The things she hadn't told him.

Perhaps Caroline was taking the cowardly way out by not giving herself fully to her husband.

Or perhaps the comparison was unfair because Helen's life wasn't as entangled in secrets and lies.

Caroline had started to trust her husband. And perhaps that trust would grow over time. But there was still this nagging feeling in the back of her mind whispering to her to not give in completely.

As Caroline entered the chamber, the memories of last night hit her hard. The chair, the plush carpet, the bed. All the wicked things she'd let her husband do to her flashed before her eyes. And then the fear set in. She could be with child.

Caroline squeezed her eyes shut and tried to dispel the memories from her mind. She went to the dressing room and splashed some water onto her face. Then she stood there, thinking of the night before and if she was going to allow her husband more access to her before the mystery of the blackmailer was solved.

It was so nice to be wanted... craved. She felt so safe in his arms.

With a groan, Caroline left the room and hurried toward the hall. She needed more time. She wasn't ready to deal with her conflicting emotions.

As she was making her way down the stairs, she stumbled onto Dane who was taking the stairs with ground-eating strides. He grabbed her by the hand as they met in the middle, his eyes panicked. "Where's Victoria?"

Caroline's pulse started drumming in her head. She had

never seen her husband so out of sorts. "I don't know. Why?"

"She is in the drawing room," Lavinia said from the steps above. "Talking to William."

"Alone?" Dane frowned.

"No, Sebastian is with them. Why? Is something amiss?"

"I'd say so, yes." Dane raised a gazette in his hand. "Have any of you read this?"

Caroline reached for it, and he let go of the paper, letting her take it.

"No," Lavinia said, coming closer to them. "What's wrong?"

Dane swallowed. "Victoria's sister… She's been imprisoned."

"What?"

Caroline read the words in the paper, disbelieving her eyes. It said that Victoria's nephew, the young czar, was overthrown by his cousin, Princess Elizabeth, in a coup that happened early in December. He and his family, including his mother—Victoria's sister—were now imprisoned in an undisclosed location.

"There was a coup," Caroline said, then passed the paper to a worried Lavinia. "Oh my God."

"We have to tell her," Dane asserted.

Caroline looked up at him with a pleading gaze. How? How did one tell a person that their home had been overtaken and their family was imprisoned? Dane took her hand and squeezed her fingers. "Come, my duchess. We have to do it. Now."

They walked toward the drawing room with a partly closed door. Caroline peeked inside while gathering her strength to tell Victoria the terrible news.

Cousin Sebastian stood in the corner, watching the couple

conversing in the middle of the room.

Victoria and William stood about six feet apart, but they were gazing into each other's eyes with such a longing that Caroline's heart squeezed. Was this what Helen had been talking about?

Was this how Dane looked at her?

Caroline peeked at her husband, who was also watching the young couple. He glanced down at her as he noticed her regard and gave her a reassuring smile.

They walked in then, and Victoria turned to look at them with a soft smile. "Is it time to go then?"

Caroline threw a glance at her husband once more. *I can't do this,* she pleaded with him.

He nodded and stepped forward. "Victoria, there's something you need to read first." He extended the paper.

Victoria looked from Dane to Caroline, then her gaze shifted to Lavinia, who stepped into the room. She looked panicked and uncertain.

This wasn't an ideal way to handle this situation. Caroline felt it. But she didn't feel it was appropriate to delay imparting the news of this magnitude just because the timing was not ideal.

Victoria took the paper into her slack fingers, the paper shaking in her hands. Cousin Sebastian strode to Victoria and read over her shoulder, while Dane walked toward William and whispered something to him that made him blanch.

Victoria froze with her eyes wide, the gazette held tightly between her fingers. "Did I read it right? Tell me I read it wrong."

"I am afraid you didn't," Caroline said.

"Victoria." William stepped toward her, and she instinctively stepped back.

"No," she said, shaking her head. "Don't come close to me."

"I want to help." He reached for her, his voice cracking on the last word.

"Help?" Her voice was sharp. "How can you help? It's all your fault!"

"How is it my fault?" he asked, aghast.

She crumpled the paper and threw it at him. "Because I should have been with them when this happened! I could have prevented this if I'd married advantageously!"

"You don't know that," William protested, shaking his head.

"All I know is you ruined everything," she spat. Then she turned on her heel and fled.

Lavinia threw a worried glance at the room before following after her.

William stepped to follow them, but Dane blocked his path. "Not now."

"Let me through," William growled.

"I said not now!"

William took another step, standing toe to toe with Dane, his features dark.

Caroline was afraid another duel was about to get called. She stepped forward and placed a calming hand on Dane's arm as she looked at William. "She needs time. She won't listen. There's nothing you can do now."

"She is right," Cousin Sebastian said as he picked up the crumpled gazette and straightened it, reading through the article again.

William squared his jaw and stepped away. "How is this my fault?" he asked no one in particular. "I might have saved her. She could've been in Russia when that happened if we hadn't married."

Caroline swallowed. "You will never be able to convince her of that."

He scoffed. "I can try."

"To what end? She's grieving. If she is ever to come back to you, she needs to do it on her own. If she is to realize that you're not to blame, she has to come to it on her own time. You won't be able to convince her."

Dane threw her a strange glance at her words. Caroline looked at him and raised a questioning brow. He simply shook his head.

"Listen to my wife," he addressed William. "You need to leave. If you truly love her, you will stop being selfish and will let her figure out the truth on her own. Whatever the truth is. Now let's go. I shall take you home."

William scoffed but didn't argue. Instead, he turned on his heel and left the room.

"I'll watch him," Dane said and tipped his head. "We'll be waiting for you by the carriage. It's ready."

Caroline nodded. "Thank you." Then she turned to her cousin, standing silently in the room, his features dark. "Please, send me a note when Victoria is ready to take visitors. We should... I don't even know what to do in a case like this. But I am certain that there is something we can do, right?"

Sebastian swallowed and nodded. "I will send you a missive."

Caroline gave him a small smile and left the room.

Chapter 23

D ane knocked on the door of their adjoining chambers for the third time since their marriage.

"Please, come in," Caroline answered.

Dane walked into the room to find his lovely wife sitting at her vanity in her shift, brushing out her hair.

He leaned his shoulder against the wall and just watched her silently. Her dark red hair glinted in the firelight, her thick locks cascading down her shoulders like a waterfall.

She looked up at him then and raised her brow. "Did you want something?"

Dane just smiled. "No."

She paused at brushing her hair, her features confused. "No?"

"I suppose I just wanted to see you. Watch you. Bathe in the vision of you."

She smiled and looked away. Dane could see the confusion and uncertainty in her eyes. She wasn't ready to trust him yet. Perhaps even less so after the revelations of the night before.

If her doting uncle could have tricked her for so long, anyone else could, too.

She cleared her throat before speaking. "I wonder if we can help Victoria in some way."

The change of subject was abrupt, but not unexpected. She had probably been thinking about it before he entered her room. He had been too. "I was wondering the same."

"As a duke, you might have some ways to negotiate with Russia, perhaps ask them to release her family to us."

Dane grimaced. It wouldn't be easy, he knew. Russia was not known for having great relations with England in the first place. That was one of the reasons Victoria's sister was pushing her to marry an English lord. She wanted to strengthen the relationship between her empire and the Western countries. But now that there was a new ruler, who knew what she would do?

"I think our first course of action is to reach out to the Duke of Mecklenburg-Schwerin and devise a plan together. He probably got the news earlier than us, and I hope something has already been done."

Caroline placed her brush on the vanity and turned to look at him, her eyes vulnerable. "You do not sound hopeful."

"It's been twenty days since the coup. Who knows what has happened in those twenty days."

Caroline nodded. "I never thought I'd say this, but I am grateful for William in this instance. I know that Victoria blames him for all the world's sins at the moment. But if he hadn't married her, she would have already returned to Russia and been there at the time of the coup. And I don't know if her presence there would have helped or hurt her sister. But I am just grateful she is here with us. Safe."

Dane pushed off the wall, his shoulder giving a dull ache. He grimaced. It must have been the weather or the vigorous activity of last night that had brought the ache back into his muscles. If it was the latter, he wasn't bemoaning it one bit.

Her gaze dropped to his shoulder, always perceptive. "Are you hurting?"

He waved the issue away. "It's not a big deal. There's actually something else I wanted to talk to you about."

"Oh?" She stood and walked toward him, meeting him in the middle. She placed her hands around his shoulder and pulled it back gently. "It's stiff."

"Yes. It's just the result of it being dislocated a few weeks ago. Do not worry."

"What did you want to talk to me about?" she asked as she walked back to her vanity table and started looking through some jars.

"That night when you ran off all by yourself to the docks, it made me determined to find the blackmailer myself. That was why I went to William by myself. And I wouldn't have told you about seeing him at all if he didn't insist upon speaking with Victoria. I would have just gotten the answers I needed and continued the search for the blackmailer on my own."

She turned to him, a frown between her brows. "I thought we agreed to act together."

"My duty is to protect you. No matter how capable you think you are. People with more experience had been hurt. And I didn't even know what your experience was."

"I saved you, didn't I?" She raised her eyebrow.

"Yes, well, and then I saved you."

"So we are even." She went back to looking through her jars.

257

"Not in my mind, Caroline. I don't care what happens to me, but I can't let anything else happen to you. So I was planning… I was thinking of keeping you away from the search further. I was determined to not let you go to the function William told us about."

She straightened, her eyes icy. "Pardon me?"

"It is my job to keep you safe," Dane said with no remorse.

"So you were going to go behind my back. Again." Her words were sharp.

"Yes."

She threw up her hands. "And now you're telling me this to get me mad at you again?"

"No." He let out a breath. "I am telling you this to let you know that I have changed my mind."

He pulled out a piece of paper with the information William had written down earlier from the pocket of his breeches and placed it on the vanity right before his wife. "I want to keep you safe, Caroline. I want you to have a burden-free life. But most of all, I want you to trust me. And after what you said to William about Victoria earlier today, about how Victoria would not be able to trust him until he let her figure it out on her own… I suppose you weren't talking just about her."

She took the note in her fingers and played with the paper, watching it with a glassy stare. "Thank you for realizing that."

He stepped closer to her and took her hand in his. She raised her head, bringing their faces so close they were almost touching.

He dipped his head, closing the gap. And then their lips touched, and it was as though the entire world lit up with joy.

A single kiss, a touch, was all it took for him to forget all the troubles of the world. She leaned away and gave him a timid smile. "Take off your shirt. And go lie on the bed."

Dane raised his brow. "I like when you take charge and tell me what to do."

She smiled slyly. "I shall be certain to remember that."

Dane didn't even think. His shirt was off in a moment, although his shoulder protested against the violent action. Then he plopped onto the bed, one hand under his head, watching his duchess with heavy-lidded eyes.

His wife took a jar from the vanity and moved toward him. "On your belly, please."

Dane raised a brow. "I know you haven't had much experience... but that would be a very difficult position for me to perform to your satisfaction."

Caroline let out a beautiful peal of laughter. "Turn on your stomach," she said, still laughing. "I am going to make your shoulder feel better."

He frowned. "How?"

"Turn around." She raised a brow.

"You do like telling me what to do." Dane turned slowly, lying prone on the bed, his arms stretched by the sides of his body, his head turned.

Caroline hitched up her skirts and saddled his rear. His cock twitched and swelled inside his breeches, his skin tightening uncomfortably.

"See," Dane said thoughtfully. "I still maintain that I should be facing the other way."

Caroline chuckled. "Lie still." She opened the jar and the smell of lavender penetrated his senses. She dipped her fingers inside and then touched her oily fingers to his aching shoulder. She then proceeded to knead his muscles, her fingers effortlessly but firmly sliding around his back and shoulder.

"Hmm," Dane drawled. "I actually quite enjoy it."

There was a smile in Caroline's voice when she replied, "This should make your shoulder feel better."

"I have to assure you, my shoulder is not the only body part that's aching."

Caroline let out a laugh. "If you behave, perhaps I could help you in those areas too."

"You tease me, Duchess," he croaked.

He was very relaxed now under the ministrations of his duchess and uncomfortably erect. How those two things could be true at the same time, he didn't know. And yet they were.

"Where did you learn to do this?" he asked, his voice slightly slurred.

"Rea taught me."

"Your lady's maid taught you?"

"Well, she did this to me many times, I think I can imitate her actions quite well."

"She did this. To you." Dane tried to imagine the delicate maid massaging his wife, and once he did, the image couldn't quite leave his mind.

"Yes." She sounded nonplussed. "Who do you think took care of my injuries from hopping from roof to roof at night?"

"She kneaded your back. Your bare back," he reiterated.

"Yes." Now she sounded annoyed.

"I think I'd like to see that. Does she sit on you the way you're sitting on me? Wait…" He paused and turned to look at her, just as she took her breath to answer. "Is she naked too when she does this? Because that I'd pay to see!"

Caroline sat up straight and slapped him on his arm.

Dane laughed and turned, tumbling her onto her back. Then he leaned in close until their lips were a hair's breadth away. "You know the only woman I crave to see naked is you."

"I wasn't done," she whispered back.

"Oh, I think you're done, my duchess. My shoulder is not stiff anymore, although something else is."

Caroline let out a giggle. "You're a terrible flirt. I never knew that about you."

"Well," Dane breathed, running his fingers down her cheek. "You bring out the worst in me." He kissed her deeply, and she returned his kiss enthusiastically, without any reservations. She met his kiss stroke for stroke, bite for bite. Her fingers sank into his hair, holding his head close to her.

Dane tore his mouth away, breathing deeply.

"No," she whimpered and bracketed his face with her palms, pulling him down for another kiss.

He kissed her hungrily one more time before pulling away again. "No, no." He tsked. "You're done commanding me."

She licked her lips seductively. God, she was too enticing. "But you said you liked it."

"And I am going to like torturing you, too." His eyes roamed down her body. "Let's see what's under this nightgown."

With that, he took her nightshift by the neckline and tore it down the middle.

Caroline let out a little squeak, then looked at him, laughter on her lips. "I could have just taken it off."

Dane gave her a grin. "I couldn't wait."

His eyes devoured the freshly revealed naked skin as he contemplated all the things he wanted to do to her. First, he ripped a strip of cloth out of her ruined nightshift.

"Did you have to—" She didn't finish her protest as Dane

descended on her, kissing her again. As his tongue plunged in between her lips, he took her wrists and held them together over her head.

He raised his head and licked the remaining taste of her off his lips. "Yes, I had to," he said hoarsely, then sat up and tied her hands to the headboard. "It's time for my revenge."

Then he stood and left the room.

* * *

Caroline's shift was torn right down the middle, which meant that the corners slid down, baring her entirely. Her hands were tied to the bedpost, which meant she couldn't cover herself up. And the most horrifying thing of all was that her husband just left her lying like this.

Seconds felt like hours in her position, and she started to wonder if this was the torture he had planned for her.

Just when she was about to cry out for him, Dane returned to the room, completely naked.

Caroline had started to get used to his bare form. And if he planned to just stand there while she lay tied up on the bed, she couldn't quite call it torture. She found him rather gorgeous, and she doubted she would ever tire of looking at him.

"Hm, what am I going to do with you?" he asked as he slowly moved closer to her. He placed something on the bedside table, but it was too dark to see what it was, and then crawled onto the bed.

Caroline wiggled her fingers. "You have me tied up. You can do whatever you want to me."

"Hmmm…" His voice was a pleasant rumble. "I like the

sound of that."

He moved closer to her, then ran a finger up her calf, sending tickling sensations up her body. Caroline bent her knees, drawing her legs closer to her torso.

Dane growled in disapproval. "Do you want me to tie your legs, too?"

"It tickles," Caroline complained and watched a wolfish smile appear on her husband's face.

"Does it?" He spread her knees apart, his gaze studying her body inch by inch. Then he lowered his head and kissed the inside of her knee. Then he moved up her thigh, kissing, licking, nibbling.

Caroline tensed, her fingers curling around her restraints. When he reached the apex of her sex, he watched her carefully, licking his lips, looking like a cat ready for his bowl of milk, and then he blew right into her center. Shivers crawled up her body, and she shifted again.

Dane took her by the hips, and she prepared to receive the same treatment as the night before, her fingers and toes curling in anticipation. He moved his head closer to her body, and then kissed her just above her center, about an inch over the line of her intimate hair.

Caroline let out a gasp. "Dane," she rebuked.

Dane let out a hoarse chuckle, his breath hitting against her skin and making her squirm. "Oh, did you think I was going to be easy on you like the last time? No, my dear. I promised you torture, and torture you shall receive."

Then he proceeded to kiss and nibble on her skin just around every place where she needed his touch. She was getting heated and frustrated as she squirmed beneath him. The lack of ability to pull his head to right where she needed his mouth made her whimper.

"Dane!" she cried in frustration.

"What, my dear?" he asked as he kissed between her breasts.

"I want your touch," she breathed, arching her back.

He rose above her, his face a few inches away from hers, his body not touching hers anywhere.

"Where?" His eyes were dark, his gaze heavy.

"Anywhere. Everywhere."

He shook his head, then kissed her on the nose. "Tell me where."

She arched her body again, wanting to graze his skin against hers, but he pulled away. "Tell me."

Caroline swallowed her pride, shame, and any feeling other than need. "My breasts," she breathed out. "Touch them."

A wicked grin appeared on his lips. Then he slowly, carefully cupped her breasts with his hands, intentionally avoiding touching her nipples.

"Is this better?" he asked in a low, gravelly voice.

"No." She whimpered, ready to cry from frustration.

He chuckled. "No? Should I stop?"

"Dane!" she cried again, twisting beneath his fingers, trying to get him to touch her where she wanted. "Stop torturing me."

He chuckled low as he lowered his head and kissed her below her jawline. "My poor little duchess," he whispered against her skin, then moved his hands down the sides of her body.

It wasn't what she needed. Her body burned with desire and in particular, a few places pulsed aching for his touch. But it did bring slight relief to her senses. He lowered his head and kissed her neck.

A little better.

Then moved down to her clavicles.

Carolin let out a sigh. "Lower, please," she breathed.

Dane kissed the top of her breast.

"Lower," she said, throwing her head back.

He moved his lips a bit lower.

"Lower," she whispered through her heated frenzy.

Then he finally placed his mouth over her nipple. Caroline moaned, her hips rising as her body arched, stuffing more of her breast into his mouth. Dane wrapped his arm around her, holding her close as his other hand closed around her other breast, rubbing his palm over her nipple. Hot liquid seeped from between her legs, and her body hummed with arousal.

Dane sucked on her beaded peak as he pinched the other nipple between his fingers.

Caroline wrapped her legs around his hips and rubbed her center against his body. Her fingers closed around the restraints that had her tied to the bedpost as she moved her hips, mimicking the motions of the salacious act.

She bit her lip, her mouth feeling empty as he switched attention from one breast to the other, kissing, licking, biting.

"Kiss me, Dane," she moaned, unable to stay quiet.

He raised his head and licked his swollen lips.

"I want to taste you."

Dane moved lithely against her body and took her mouth in a scorching kiss. The strokes of his tongue against hers soothed her and burned her at the same time. The slow movements of his body against her drove her wild. Then his hand moved lower and touched her center.

He growled and tore his mouth away. "You're so wet," he whispered, his eyes burning with desire. He collected

265

her moisture and slid his fingers up to circle her swollen nub. Then he dipped two fingers inside her while his thumb continued drawing magical circles over her tiny hill.

A primal cry ripped from her lungs at the fiery sensation. She felt as though her soul had been ripped from her body in sensual bliss. He continued moving his fingers as his tongue plunged in and out of her mouth, lighting up all her senses. She twisted and squirmed beneath him, unable to silence her cries of pleasure.

Thousands of white sparks lit behind her eyelids as she came, her body shooting off the bed. She opened her eyes as Dane sat back on his knees. He withdrew his hand from her center and brought it to his lips. And then he sucked her juices off his fingers.

Just like that, with one simple action, he lit up the desire within her again. Caroline's muscles spasmed, closing over the emptiness. Her gaze ran down his body. His muscles were bunched as if he was taut with desire, too.

His cock rose proudly from the patch of intimate hair, hard and large. And her fingers curled in an urge to squeeze him.

"Untie me," she whispered breathlessly. "I want to touch you."

"Not yet," he croaked. Then he moved toward the bedside table and picked something up.

He slowly covered his length with a sheath and tied it with a bow at the base.

Caroline raised a brow. "Is that my Christmas gift?"

He chuckled low. "But you don't get to unwrap it."

"As long as I get to touch it." She shrugged.

Dane untied her hands carefully, then rubbed and massaged her wrists. "Do they hurt?"

"No. It bit a little into my skin, but I liked it."

Dane let out a chuckle before covering her mouth with his and kissing her hungrily. "You are a constant revelation," he said as he pulled away.

Then he picked up a jar of oil that she rubbed his shoulder with and raised a brow. "Now if you'd like to ease the ache from the other stiff part of my body…"

Caroline bit her lips. She dipped her fingers into the jar and then slowly, carefully wrapped her hand around his aroused length.

They both gasped at the contact. Her muscles tensed, and she had to take a moment to rein in her desires. She met his burning gaze and squeezed his length as she moved her fingers up and down.

He grabbed her by the nape of her neck and covered her mouth with his.

He plunged his tongue inside and matched the rhythm of her strokes. And then his fingers found her center and entered her core, bringing her to the heights of bliss once again.

"Hold on to my shoulders," he croaked. And when she did, he took her by the hips and picked her up. She immediately wrapped her legs around his torso as he lowered her gently onto his cock.

She slid down his length almost effortlessly, the friction adding to their mutual pleasurable sensations. Dane groaned, his face a grimace of pain.

"You're so tight," he whispered. "And so wonderfully hot."

And then he moved, driving more of him into her core. Caroline let out a cry and then she was lost in ecstasy again. Their moans and whimpers blended into one sensual song, their bodies moving in unison, feeding off each other's desires, and giving each other comfort and fulfillment.

They moved like that for what seemed like an eternity until their blissful act was punctuated by an earth-shattering release.

Chapter 24

"I don't like this idea at all," Dane grumbled as they entered Lady Carlyle's ballroom.

"Yes, and you've said so before," Caroline said through a fake smile.

This was the first outing for Caroline and Dane since Christmas. They had spent a few blissful days and nights in bed, and they would not have left their house this night, either, except that this was the ball William had informed them about.

Lady Carlyle was a young and wealthy widow, who enjoyed a more relaxed company than starched and proper aristocrats. So she often arranged balls and invited people of all ilk, including but not limited to people of artistic professions and businessmen.

Such a melting pot of individuals always contained a few rogue aristocrats, but overall, the atmosphere was less formal and a lot more relaxed.

"Well, I still don't like it."

"Do you have any better ideas?" She raised her brow, and he let out a sigh.

"No."

"Then I bid you good evening." Caroline flashed him a radiant smile and disengaged from him with a flourish.

She walked along the edge of the ballroom, searching for familiar faces.

They knew a few things about the blackmailer at this point. This person likely knew about her uncle's involvement with the Brotherhood, which meant it was equally as likely that he was part of the Brotherhood himself. He was old enough to have been part of the Brotherhood over fifteen years ago but young enough to carry out the elaborate blackmailing scheme. And he was present at Roth's house party a few weeks ago, as he managed to send notes to Roth about Lavinia's plight while at the house.

Caroline had taken the list of all the guests from Lavinia earlier this week and had circled everyone who matched the correct age range. Now it was the time to find them and flush them out.

Not everyone from Roth's house party was at this party. But other members of the Brotherhood might be present. And catching just one of those people would be enough for Caroline's plan to bring merit.

Ah, there was Lord Hexley! And he fit the description perfectly.

Caroline walked toward him, a spring in her step. "Good evening, my lord. Are you enjoying the night?"

"I wasn't until now," he said, turning toward her and looking quite taken aback. "Now my night seems brighter."

She laughed. "Truly, my lord? I did not think my shine

could brighten the night."

One side of his mouth kicked up in a smile. "Would you like to dance?"

"I would love that immensely," Caroline answered enthusiastically. "But do you know what I would like even more?" She leaned in conspiratorially.

His eyes glinted with curiosity and intrigue. "What?"

"Perhaps a more clandestine meeting." She blinked up at him coquettishly.

"You would?" He seemed absolutely flabbergasted. And not without reason. Until now, Caroline had spoken to him perhaps twice and always without much interest. But she didn't have time to flirt and dance around the subject.

"Of course, if you're not interested—" she started with a pout, and the man immediately got all flustered.

"I am, of course. How can you think that? I—" He faltered, his gaze scanning her figure.

Caroline shivered unpleasantly but stretched her smile wider.

"Then let us leave." She weaved her hand through his arm, and before the man realized what was going on, she was leading him away from the ballroom.

They made their way down the corridor, and Caroline stopped by the door to the library. "Oh, I forgot one important thing," she said with a grimace.

"I shall go fetch it for you," Lord Hexley said solicitously.

"Oh, no." She placed a hand against his chest. "No need for that. It's a little embarrassing, actually. I shall get it myself. How about you… um… get undressed?" She bit her lip.

"N-now?" He blinked up at her innocently. Poor chap.

"Yes. You go in and get ready. When I come back, I

would love to see you in all your"—she lowered her eyes suggestively—"manly glory."

Hexley nodded like an eager pup and disappeared behind the doors to the library. Caroline leaned against the wall and let out a deep sigh. She had never had an issue talking and flirting with gentlemen. But luring them for a tryst was a new and nerve-wracking experience. She only hoped it wasn't for nothing.

Fast-approaching steps sounded from the direction of the ballroom, and Caroline pushed off the wall. Dane reached her quickly, seeming out of breath.

"Are you all right?" His brows were furrowed as his gaze ran along her length.

"Yes." She instinctively reached for his hand, and Dane squeezed her fingers.

"Are you certain? Did he—"

"Nothing happened. I am unscathed. I promise."

Dane nodded and pressed a kiss to her forehead. "Go back inside then," he whispered against her skin and let go of her hand.

Caroline threw him a smile before returning to the ballroom and getting a glass of wine. She stood there, nervously tapping her foot and looking for someone else who fit their general description.

A few minutes later, Dane returned to the ballroom and immediately stalked toward Caroline.

"Well?" she asked as he reached her side.

"He has no mark that I could see. And not much else to look at, to be honest."

Caroline sputtered a laugh. "I didn't miss anything by leaving him to you, then."

Dane raised a brow. Caroline mirrored his action.

Lord Hexley appeared back in the ballroom, looking just as red as the mark Caroline and Dane were looking for.

Caroline shook her head. "After tonight, the word will get out that the Duke of Kensington is the biggest cuckold, who incidentally is the most jealous man in the world."

Dane let out a deep sigh. "Well, they'll be half right."

She gave him an innocent grin. "Let me find another suspect."

"I'll be watching you closely," Dane promised.

What followed was the most fun and yet the most embarrassing hour of Caroline's life. She had sent two more unsuspecting men into a trap and then watched them return into the ballroom a few moments later, shamed and unable to meet her eyes.

She didn't even want to think about what gossip would come out of this night and if men would continue to seek her out, or on the contrary, would stay far, far away.

None of the men so far had any marks on their bodies, at least, not that Dane could see. Caroline had already started to wonder if William had just come up with the lie to entertain himself with their clumsy attempts at unmasking a member of the Brotherhood.

Dane entered the ballroom once again and shook his head. *Blast!*

Well, there were a few more men who fit their criteria that she hadn't approached yet. She needed to do it fast, before all the rumors set in about the duchess's unsuccessful attempts at seduction.

Just at that moment, Ian McAllistair appeared at her elbow, eliminating her need to choose from her list. He was one of the men she was looking for. She turned toward him with a beguiling smile. "Good evening, my lord. How are you enjoying this evening?"

"Your Grace," he said with his slurred, gravelly voice. "What a pleasure."

"You look quite… charming tonight," she said with a flirtatious lilt in her voice.

"Why, thank you," he slurred. "You are even more so. I would invite you to dance, Your Grace. But I am afraid my legs are not holding me so well after a few glasses of whisky. I'd hate to tread all over your slippers." His eyes glinted with merriment, and his crooked smile was boyishly innocent.

Lord Ian McAllistair was quite handsome if one was willing to look beyond his constant state of inebriation, and therefore his complete lack of concern about the state of his attire.

"Perhaps we should step out of the ballroom instead?" she offered. "The fresh air does wonders to unsteady legs."

He chuckled. "I am afraid, at this point, nothing will do my legs any good. Or any part of me for that matter."

Caroline bit her lip, thinking how else she could entice the rogue to go with her to the library. Her gaze immediately searched for Dane, hoping that seeing him could help her mind.

She found him rather quickly, but when she did, she was rather surprised at what she saw. A beautiful, dark-haired woman with lush curves and a scandalously revealing gown was standing before him, much too close for Caroline's liking.

And she was leaning toward him much in the same way as Caroline had been doing to other men this entire evening.

Lord McAllistair followed Caroline's gaze, before glancing at her. And for a moment, she thought she saw sympathy in his eyes... or perhaps pity. "It's Miss Nicolette Burke. Quite a popular actress."

Miss Nicolette Burke. Caroline's heart stilled. She knew that name. Not only that, she had researched that name. When St. John first sent her the note saying that she lived at the address that was paid for and sustained by Dane, Caroline had looked into her to make certain she had no criminal ties.

She didn't. What she did have, however, was a round bosom and a hand on Caroline's husband's chest.

"I see," Lord McAllistair said softly.

"You see what?" Caroline turned toward him sharply.

"That you're trying to drown your sorrows with the first poor chap who happens by," he almost sang. "Apologies." He bowed his head. "It can't be me." He raised his glass and sauntered away, swaying lightly on his feet. For a drunken fool, he sure noticed a lot.

Caroline turned toward Dane once again only to find him gone.

* * *

Dane looked around in search of his wife. He circled the ballroom, looked for her outside, and went to the library where they were supposed to trap the unsuspecting suspects, and yet she was nowhere to be found.

Where had she gone?

Had she taken a man to another room? And what? Stayed for a tryst?

Dane wasn't willing to even entertain that idea.

So where was she?

He'd only been gone five minutes. Five blasted minutes!

Where had she disappeared to in that amount of time?

Dane scrubbed his face in agitation. How could he leave her alone even for a short time? Damn Nicolette for distracting him, leading him away.

"Looking for your wife?" a booming voice said from behind him. Dane turned and beheld the Duke of Wolverstone.

"Yes," he said, stepping closer. "Have you seen her?"

"Yes." He nodded.

"Well, where is she?"

"First, I need to speak to you about something."

Dane looked around, getting agitated. "I'd really like to find my wife."

"Fine." Wolverstone let out a sigh. "Come with me."

He proceeded to walk slowly toward the exit. Dane matched his steps.

"I know what you were doing tonight," Wolverstone said with a straight face.

Dane raised a brow. "Do you?"

"Yes. And I am here to tell you that you're looking in the wrong direction."

"What are you talking about?"

"I am talking about you stirring trouble, looking for marks on people's bodies," the duke said between his teeth.

Dane looked at him, not hiding the surprise in his eyes.

"Only an idiot would not figure out what you were doing," Wolverstone grumbled. "I told Caroline to leave it alone, and she wouldn't listen. Maybe she'll listen to you."

They exited the ballroom and walked down the corridor.

"You knew," Dane accused. "All this time, you knew that her uncle was part of the Brotherhood of the Crimson Fist."

"Of course, I knew!" Wolverstone cried. "But Caroline

didn't."

Dane scoffed. "She needs to know the truth. She deserves to know what happened to her uncle."

"What good will it do?" Wolverstone hissed as he led Dane into the library and closed the door behind him.

Dane looked around. "If you brought me here for a tryst, I am flattered, but not interested," he said dryly.

Wolverstone just watched him stonily, unimpressed. "I brought you here to tell you to cease looking into the Brotherhood. Caroline worshiped her uncle. She loved him beyond measure. Why muddy his memory?"

"The truth about him doesn't change how she felt about him," Dane exclaimed.

"No, but it taints the memories. I tried to keep her from it all, to protect her. Now it is your job. And you've blundered it already."

"You're wrong," Dane bristled. How could this man justify hiding something this enormous from a person he claimed to love?

Wolverstone shook his head. "You're looking for a black-mailer, which is a noble cause. But dredging up the past simply won't help. It will only put Caroline in danger."

Dane pursed his lips. "You seem to know everything."

Wolverstone shrugged. "I do."

Dane let out a bitter chuckle as understanding finally dawned on him. "It's you. Isn't it? You are Erebus. I was a blind idiot for not seeing it earlier, but it had to be you. Or Caroline's uncle, but we both know that isn't true."

This explained Caroline's name being absent from the roster. It wasn't because she was a lady, or at least, that wasn't the only reason. Wolverstone didn't want anyone to know that she was ever part of the Shadows. He had tried to protect her. And that explained the blind faith Caroline had in the man. Because, of course, she knew.

"Caroline's uncle was my friend," the duke said. "He came to me when he realized how grave a mistake he'd made. He didn't know the depth to which the Brotherhood went. And as his friend, I took care of it."

"How?" Dane raised a brow.

Wolverstone cleared his throat. "Let's just say I thinned their ranks a little. I erased all information about him being in the Brotherhood with the help of the Shadows. I made sure they wouldn't bother him or Caroline. And all was well until you started dredging it up again. You're putting her in danger."

"She won't stop looking into this," Dane hissed. "Her friend—our friend—is in danger."

"Whoever the blackmailer is, they are not a part of the Brotherhood," Wolverstone assured him. "They can't be. It probably doesn't even have anything to do with them. You don't want to fight both of those evils, Kensington. You have to let it go."

"I won't. I can't let them get away with all the atrocities. And how can you?" Dane felt rather offended by the notion.

"Do you think I will let anyone get away with impersonating Erebus? Those blackmailers are using my name," Wolverstone barked. "The Shadows are my legacy, and I will kill anyone who tries to besmirch it. But I won't let it kill more of the people I care about. That would just make me angry. And I promise you. You don't want to see me angry."

Dane watched Wolverstone carefully, calculating his next move. This was the leader of the Shadows. Probably the most powerful man in England next to the King. And yet, he was telling him to give up the search for the blackmailer.

"You were Roth's friend," he said carefully. "Do you know why he insisted upon my marriage to his niece?" Dane stepped closer, but Wolverstone just shrugged.

"I don't know. Perhaps he thought that you were an upstanding man, one who does not deal with criminals."

"Is that truly the reason?" Dane narrowed his eyes.

"I don't know who the blackmailer is if that's what you're asking."

Dane could see the truth in the old man's eyes. "But her uncle knew," Dane guessed.

Wolverstone looked away for a moment before meeting his gaze again. "He had his suspicions. He never shared them with me, however. But if I were you, I would concentrate on the most important task at hand."

"Which is?"

"Keeping Caroline safe. And making her happy. Because now you know who I am and what I am capable of. I don't care if you are one of my best men. If you fail, I'll take care of you. And it won't be pleasant. "

Chapter 25

Caroline stood on the balcony, looking out. She had a flower in her hand, and she picked the petals one by one, throwing them into the air. The petals floated prettily before the wind carried them away.

She was so beautiful, his wife. But her features were thoughtful if not sad. What had happened in those five minutes he was away from the ballroom? Dane was almost too afraid to ask.

He stepped onto the balcony and cleared his throat softly, so as not to spook her. "It's rather cold for a lady to stand outside on the balcony, wouldn't you say?"

She didn't turn around as she replied, "I don't feel the cold."

He stepped even closer, feeling more worried than before. "Can you look at me?" He reached out for her, but she stepped back, and then a light shiver passed through her.

"You *are* cold!" He shook his head. "Come. Let's go inside."

"I don't want to," she said and stepped away again.

"Did something happen?" His voice was harsher than he

intended. "Did someone touch you?"

"No." Caroline finally looked at him, and there was pain in her eyes. "Where have you been?"

He took a deep breath. This conversation was not going to be easy. "I just spoke to Wolverstone."

She raised her brows. "Wolverstone?"

"Yes. And he told me to cease what we are doing."

"Pardon? What are we doing?"

"He said to stop looking into the Brotherhood. He said that it's too dangerous."

Caroline waved a dismissive hand. "He is being overprotective of me. He has always kept me safe, and he thinks that by making me stop looking into the blackmailer I will be safer."

Dane lowered his gaze for a brief moment, knowing what was to come. "I think he is right."

Caroline's head snapped up. "What?"

"It is too dangerous. If he figured out what we were trying to do tonight, so did the Brotherhood. And they don't care if you're a duchess, they will hurt you all the same. And I can't let that happen."

"I am not some damsel in need of saving. I can take care of myself," she said angrily, white puffs of air leaving her mouth.

"Maybe you can. Maybe you can't. But I cannot afford to find out."

"So what? You're going to forbid me from investigating this?"

"Yes, I am."

Her mouth opened, and her eyes rounded. Now not only pain shone in those expressive eyes of hers but also disbelief. "We've been on this track for weeks. You promised to help me find the person responsible for my uncle's untimely demise and now when we are finally getting close, you're going to tell me to stop? What changed tonight?"

Dane tried to rein in his patience. "I've found out that you were keeping things from me, that's what. And your secret could cost us dearly."

"*I* was keeping things from you?" Caroline bristled. "You are the one always going behind my back. You are the one lying to me! Even now!"

"I am not!" he barked.

"Then tell me the truth. For once. Why did you suddenly change your mind?"

"Because I found out who your *friend* the Duke of Wolverstone truly is!"

Caroline froze for a moment. "What does that have to do with anything?"

"You didn't find it fit to tell me?"

She turned away. "This wasn't my secret to keep."

"Don't you find it odd," Dane said, moving closer to her, "that he has tried to stop you from looking into blackmail from the start?"

Caroline's brows lowered over her eyes. "You're accusing *him* of blackmail now? You're mad!"

"Caroline—" He stepped toward her, and she leaped away. He froze, blinking in confusion. "Darling, I am trying to be logical."

Darling, she mouthed as tears sprung to her eyes. Then she added in a mere whisper, "Don't touch me."

He curled his fingers into a fist, his brows furrowed. "Caroline, I have my reasons for saying this. You don't have to believe me. But the least you can do is hear me out."

"Fine, talk." Caroline rubbed her arms. She was getting cold, damn it. And she stubbornly refused to accept his warmth, his touch, and she wouldn't leave this damn balcony.

"He is your uncle's friend," Dane said, irritated. "He has been your uncle's friend for as long as you've known him. Which means he knows everything there is to know about your uncle. He *is* Erebus. And yet he is trying to dissuade us from looking into the blackmailer, the person we think is impersonating him! Unless, of course, there's no one to impersonate and it's just him. He is powerful. He is in a position to blackmail not only people close to him but anyone he sets his eyes upon."

"Why do you wish to turn everyone I trust against me?" Caroline said in a small voice.

"And why do you trust him implicitly?"

"I trust him because he kept me safe all this time! He cared for me when no one else did. He supported my uncle during the most difficult years of his life. He is the closest thing I have left to a family—"

"I am your family, Caroline!" Dane snapped. "Why do you believe everyone but me? You're too blinded by your loyalty to him, just like you were too blinded by your loyalty to your uncle to see that he used to be a criminal."

"Don't talk to me about criminals and loyalty! Your brother is the biggest criminal of all, and I don't see you accusing him of anything!" Caroline let out a puff of air. "If you truly believe that Wolverstone is behind the blackmail, then why did you try to make me stop looking into it?"

"How is that not apparent to you?" Dane threw up his hands. "He is the most powerful person in London. He commands the Shadows. There is nothing he can't get away with."

"You're afraid," she said scathingly.

"Of course, I am afraid! I am afraid that you're not even a

little frightened. I am afraid that your fearless attitude and your lack of trust in me will get you killed! I am afraid that you will run into danger again, and I will be too late to stop you."

"So you want to keep me locked in the house?" she spat angrily.

"If that's what it takes!"

"Because you don't think I can do this."

"Because I fucking love you!" he finally exploded.

This was the wrong time. Wrong place. Wrong everything. And she was not in a receptive mood to hear the truth from him. But he was tired of fighting her. Tired of her stubbornness. So tired that she could not see the truth.

And just as he expected—although he'd hoped his expectations were wrong—she said, "I don't believe you."

* * *

How could he do that? How could he confess his love for her in the same breath as lying to her and forcing her into giving up her search? How could she ever believe his words again?

Her heart ached, and her soul felt tired.

"You will never trust me, will you?" His voice was resigned.

Caroline swallowed a large lump in her throat. "Have you ever given me a reason to?"

"I proved to you time and time again—"

"You proved nothing! You lied to me from the start. You told me that you loved me on the same night as you met with your mistress!"

He blinked. "My what?"

"Don't even try to lie to me again, Dane. Do not insult my

intelligence in the same conversation where you accuse the only person who always stood by me, who never lied to me. You, on the other hand—" She swallowed, unable to continue.

"I don't have a mistress," he insisted. "I—"

"No? Then who is Miss Nicolette Burke to you?"

He froze, his eyes wide. Caught in a lie. Then he slowly raised a staying hand. "She used to be, I admit. But not anymore. I haven't been with her since the beginning of our marriage."

"Truly? Not even today?" she asked seethingly.

"I spoke with her, yes… I shouldn't have and for that, the mistake is mine. But I owed her an explanation. I had to tell her to her face that I will not be visiting her again."

Caroline scoffed. He ran a hand through his hair and tugged on his cravat. "It's been months since we've seen each other. I disappeared without a trace. I needed to tell her it was over."

"Tonight? After six months of our marriage?"

"I know," he said, his breathing labored. "I should have done that a long time ago. But I never intended to resume relations with her. Certainly not since the day you found me on the factory floor."

"Then why did you not tell me about her?" Her voice broke a little, tears burning at the back of her eyes.

"Because in my mind that relationship was over. She cornered me tonight wanting explanations, perhaps another tryst, and I had to lead her away to not cause a scene. I handled it poorly, I admit, but I never lied to you."

He stepped closer to her. Slowly. As if trying not to spook an injured animal. "Truth be told, I was too busy to visit her since our marriage. Later, when I started developing the urge, she wasn't the woman I wanted. She hasn't even entered my mind. Why would I go to her when I have you? Why would I ever seek her out when the passion I found with you is something people only dream about?"

Everything inside Caroline tightened. She felt confused and vulnerable and weak, feelings she had never felt before. Caroline licked her lips. "She is beautiful."

He let out a chuckle. "If beauty was all that I sought, then I would have married you the first time I saw you."

She blinked up at him. "What?"

"You are the most beautiful woman I've ever laid my eyes upon. I realized that even before we got to know each other better. Before I even liked you."

Caroline didn't know whether to laugh or to cry. "You disliked me?"

Dane scoffed. "Absolutely. When I met you for the first time, I thought you were cold and shrewish. You were not a young debutante anymore, but still, you were always surrounded by suitors and yet, unmarried. I thought that was because you would not accept anyone less than a duke. I thought that's why your uncle forced me to marry you. I thought you were a pretty thing with no substance. Boring, predictable."

"Um… Thank you. I feel better now." Caroline threw up her hand.

Dane took her hands in his and tugged her closer. "No, I did not like you then at all. But I didn't know you either. Those were all my assumptions. I had only your exterior to judge you by, and we both know that I am a terrible judge. The first time I saw who you really were… When I saw you at the factory—"

"When you fainted," she said with a low chuckle, humor her only defense.

"I did." He smiled. "I fainted from the feelings overwhelming me because for the first time, I saw the real you. And you struck me unconscious. Quite literally. I knew then that I wanted to have a real marriage with you."

"Even then?" She raised her brow in disbelief.

"Even then. And I still do."

"But why?" Her voice was small.

"Because I saw the spark in you. Your wit, intelligence, and adventurous spirit. What I see in you goes beyond just looks. What I feel for you transcends all the mortal definitions of beauty. I crave your presence all the damn time. I miss you even in my dreams. And it's not because of how you look—although your beauty is quite addicting. But because my soul is attached to yours by an unbreakable thread. And whenever you're far away, it tugs me to you. I have never felt that toward another human being. No... nobody has ever felt that toward anyone."

He stepped even closer and enveloped her in a warm embrace. Caroline shivered pleasantly.

"I would never do anything to jeopardize what we have," he whispered against her hair. "Not for the world. And especially not for a quick romp with someone else."

Caroline closed her eyes and burrowed into his coat. And then she admitted something she had never admitted to anyone else. "I am afraid, Dane. I don't want to hurt anymore. And you're the one person who can make me bleed."

Dane leaned his cheek against the top of her head. "I know exactly how you feel."

Chapter 26

Caroline and Dane half-sat, half-lay on the floor of his study, looking through all the evidence they had collected about the blackmailer.

Caroline kicked off her slippers as she moved to lie on her stomach, propping herself on her elbow, her stockinged feet in the air. Her gown was rumpled, and her hair was falling out of her coiffure, and yet she didn't seem to care.

She was incredibly beautiful. And he would rather spend the night tickling her until she shrieked from laughter and then making love to her until she cried from pleasure. But his relentless wife didn't want to give up the search for her uncle's blackmailer even if none of the evidence made any sense.

For Dane, there were only two possibilities in his mind. Either Wolverstone was wrong, or he was lying.

If Wolverstone was wrong, Dane could see the Brotherhood's motive to blackmail every person close to power: the late Lord Roth, a powerful marquess, and Lavinia, a lady who was about to marry the Earl of Pembroke and the heir to the Wolverstone dukedom.

Perhaps they even knew that Wolverstone was Erebus after his not-so-subtle attempt at thinning their ranks but couldn't get close to him.

Or they were afraid of him, so they blackmailed everyone in his vicinity.

Caroline was the closest thing he had to a daughter, and both Roth and Lavinia had connections to her.

Perhaps these blackmail attempts had everything to do with Caroline herself.

There were too many 'ifs' and 'perhaps' in this scenario. But too many motives meant too many possibilities that he was indeed right and that the blackmailer was part of the Brotherhood.

But if Wolverstone was lying, and *he* was the actual blackmailer, then what motive did he have to blackmail anyone?

He definitely had the opportunity. During his years as Erebus, he'd probably unearthed a plethora of secrets.

But as the man seemed to have cared about Caroline enough to hide her name from the Shadows' roster, the closeness of his targets to Caroline seemed incidental.

And why would he try and blackmail the bride of his own heir?

Dane had to agree that Wolverstone didn't seem to have any motives. Unless, of course, he just failed to see them.

Then, of course, there was the third possibility, the possibility which his wife was more inclined to pursue. That the blackmailer was neither Erebus nor part of the Brotherhood and was simply aiming at powerful people.

But for what purpose? It couldn't have been random. Surely

they wanted something.

"Ugh, I am seeing double," Caroline complained as she looked at the notes before her. She had drawn a map with all the parties involved and tried to draw bridges between them to figure out who had the biggest motive and opportunity. "And my neck is stiff."

Dane rolled next to her on the floor and started rubbing her neck. "Perhaps you need a little kneading... Should I bring the oils?"

Caroline turned to him, her brow raised. "Are you trying to seduce me, Your Grace?"

"Am I that obvious?" Dane grinned.

Caroline chuckled and leaned into him for a kiss.

A knock sounded at that moment, and Caroline pulled away before Dane could kiss her.

Damn.

She chuckled before getting up and dusting off her gown. "Come in."

Dane stood just as the butler opened the door. "The Duke of Wolverstone for you," he said.

Dane and Caroline exchanged a glance.

"Invite him here. And ask the housekeeper to bring us some tea," Caroline said before kneeling down and picking up all the papers. Dane helped her collect all their evidence and hide it behind his work ledgers.

Wolverstone entered just as they put the finishing touches to Dane's rather busy desk. "Caroline," he said fondly and went to squeeze her hands. He bowed shortly to Dane. "Kensington."

Dane reciprocated and invited the duke to sit.

Once they were all seated before the hearth, with a steaming cup of tea in their hands, Wolverstone looked around the room. "I knew you wouldn't take my advice."

"Pardon me?" Dane raised a brow.

"You haven't stopped looking for the blackmailer."

Caroline pursed her lips. "It was not my husband's decision. It was mine. I have the right to know who drove my uncle to madness, and I have the right to revenge."

"I don't think you realize the gravity of what you're doing. You're stirring people who need not be stirred."

"Do you mean you?" Dane asked evenly.

Wolverstone scoffed. "People far more dangerous than I. But as I said, I knew you wouldn't leave it alone, so I brought you something." He took out a journal and leafed through it. In the middle, there were a few notes. He extended them toward Caroline.

She took the notes and looked through them one by one.

"These are some of the first threatening notes that your uncle received."

"When was this?" Dane asked.

"Only a few years ago. Two, three, perhaps? When Roth still trusted me. "

"Two years ago." Caroline frowned. "So, he wasn't black-mailed his entire life."

"I am afraid this isn't the first miscalculation you've made. And that is why I urge you to leave it alone."

"These notes," Caroline said, still reading through them, "they ask him to vote a specific way, to side with some people's agendas. This blackmailing scheme is political."

"Then it could be the Brotherhood of the Crimson Fist," Dane said. "They definitely have political agendas. Perhaps the newer members of the Brotherhood found out about his early alliance with them and decided to use it against him."

Wolverstone shook his head. "Everyone who knew of his alliance was"—he cleared his throat—"taken care of."

Almost everyone. Dane frowned.

"And everyone, down to a lowly criminal, has political agendas now," Wolverstone continued. "You think that I am urging you to stop looking into them because it is in my best interest. But you're wrong. I've been looking into this myself since the beginning. These blackmailers have besmirched my name. You've all heard the whispers and rumors about the Shadows and our criminal ways. They all started the moment these threatening notes appeared. Whoever this blackmailer is, he is not only threatening people but is ruining the Shadows. The legacy I worked hard to build. I am not inclined to let them get away with this."

"Then why haven't you asked the Shadows to take care of this?" Dane asked.

"Because it is not as easy as it seems." Wolverstone cleared his throat. "These notes are signed with my name. Which leads me to believe that it's one of the Shadows. That we have a traitor in our midst."

"Not necessarily," Caroline said. "The whispers about the Shadows have prevailed in the last few years. As you said, people assume we are criminals. Someone could have just used the name to cover their deeds."

Wolverstone shook his head. "Who else would know the name Erebus other than a Shadow? And blackmail is not their only sin. It's like they want to bring down the Shadows. Just as these notes started surfacing, I started hearing the talk about a man who called himself Erebus. And apparently, what this fake Erebus claims to do is to take care of people's problems—people who have been wronged by aristocrats. He claims to punish the guilty in my name. But his targets are only the rich and the powerful."

"Except for Lavinia," Dane grumbled.

"I have tried to fish him out. I have hired people to look into this false Erebus, but all my leads came up dry. I have even tried to hire this person, claiming I was a poor soul needing to exact revenge against a powerful duke. But he always sends thugs for the initial meeting and then he researches the claims until he is ready to either accept the offer or reject. And if you're rejected, you never hear from him again.

"I've failed twice to recruit him. And the thugs from the initial meetings led back to Hades' hell. But you all know that if something leads to Hades' hell, there is no hope of getting any information out of them. Those people are loyal."

"So you think that this blackmailer is Hades."

"It is possible," Wolverstone agreed. "It is not his modus operandi, but there is no way to know for certain. His fortress is highly secured."

"Not highly," Dane said. "You managed to burn it to the ground once."

"That's the only time we had evidence of his wrong-doings."

"When he abducted Helen," Caroline murmured to herself.

"And I am determined to teach a lesson to everyone who angers the Shadows. We are not to be trifled with. But now that Hades is the thief-taker's brother-in-law, he is twice as powerful and therefore less attainable. Still, if we can prove that it was he who forged my name onto these blackmailing notes and cost me a friend in the process... I will no longer hold back. Whoever is tainting the Shadows' name is going to die. No other options. And that is one of the reasons why

I wanted to keep you away from this," Wolverstone said as he looked at Caroline. "I want to keep you away from this darkness."

"You can do that. Or you can let me help. For instance, these notes"—Caroline scrunched up her nose thoughtfully—"the handwriting in them is slightly different." She walked toward the desk and picked out the latest notes to compare. Then she came back and showed it to everyone. "See? The letters S and W can be easily differentiated. Whoever this is, they haven't perfected their forging skills yet."

"Can I take a look?" Dane asked.

"Of course," Caroline handed the notes to him, and he studied them carefully.

The handwriting still highly resembled his. But Caroline was right. Some sweeping strokes in the letters W and S had a different, yet familiar pattern. Too familiar.

Suspicions started invading his mind, but he couldn't say them out loud. Not in front of Wolverstone. Yet he needed to be certain. "Would you excuse me for a moment?"

"Is anything amiss?" Caroline asked.

Dane took her hand in his and kissed her knuckles. "No. I just need to check something. I'll be right back."

Caroline nodded with a smile and immediately turned toward Wolverstone. She trusted Dane completely, he realized. And he didn't want to break that trust. But at the same time, if his suspicions turned out to be true, he would have to test the strength of their marriage once more.

Dane left the study and hurried toward Caroline's room. He strode to her bedside table and lit the candle. He sifted through the few things occupying the table and almost immediately found what he was looking for. The note William had written with the details about Lady Carlyle's ball.

Dane let out a deep breath and brought the note closer to his eyes. The sweeping strokes to these letters were unmistakable. Still, he took the blackmailing note Wolverstone had brought with him today and compared the handwriting side-by-side.

It wasn't an exact match. The notes still looked more like Dane's handwriting than William's... Except for the letters S and W.

* * *

"But you agree that my uncle knew the person who was blackmailing him," Caroline said to Wolverstone as she sipped on her cup of tea.

"I believe so. But he wouldn't tell me."

"I don't understand why he would do that unless he thought it was you. I do not mean to sound as if I am accusing you. I am just very confused."

Wolverstone shifted in his seat. "Your uncle was ill. You know that. It is hard to understand the exact nature of his illness, but he was getting forgetful and his mind had weakened. That only prompted him to get more and more paranoid. Sometimes he would forget the things he told me and then be rather surprised that I knew them." He swallowed. "At some point, he stopped trusting me. I don't know exactly how that happened, but it just did. And I think trying to coax the truth out of him made him even more suspicious."

"He never told me anything either," Caroline agreed. "And he was very suspicious of anyone who came into our home. I can't imagine how it must be to live with this fear. I am just surprised that he trusted Kensington enough to insist on our marriage."

Wolverstone's face softened in a fond smile. "He was afraid for you. For him, you were the only thing worth living for. He was afraid you would be vulnerable without him. And I suppose he married you off to the most powerful bachelor in the country. The only man, who in this mind, was capable of keeping you safe... and happy. I can't say that he made the wrong decision." He paused. "Did he?"

Caroline looked up, startled. "Pardon me?"

"I suppose I am trying to ask if you're indeed happy with Kensington."

Caroline's lips split into an easy smile. "I am. Very. It wasn't easy... I suppose it still isn't easy. I miss my uncle very much. And with all the secrets that my uncle kept from me, I became almost as paranoid as him. I was suspecting everyone, acting irrationally. And that isn't me at all. I always managed to keep my head. But..." She shook her head. "I suspected and blamed everyone for my uncle's demise. At one point, I even suspected you." She let out a chuckle.

Wolverstone pressed his lips into a thin line. "I can't say I blame you. Your uncle had no reason not to trust me. I was the one to pull him out of the Brotherhood. I was the one who always stood by him. I promised to take care of you, and I did that to the best of my ability."

"You taught me everything about being a Shadow." Caroline smiled. "And even so, you then kept my name out of any official Shadows' records."

He shrugged. "I made certain that you didn't have to lead the life that your father had led. But to your uncle, it wasn't enough. His illness made him distrustful of everyone. And since you trusted him, I can understand you being suspicious of me."

Caroline bit her lip. "My suspicions weren't the result of my uncle's distrust… Rather, I think I started trusting my husband."

She expected the duke to get annoyed or exasperated, but he smiled instead. "I am glad to hear that. I am also glad that he cares enough about you to be suspicious of me. I can respect that. I am not going to be here forever, dear Caroline. And I am glad that your uncle's last desperate act is paying off."

"Dane was the first man on my list of suspicions," she said with a smile. "It took me a while to start trusting him. I think it was the hardest thing I had to do because he is in a position to hurt me the most."

Wolverstone reached out and covered her hand in his before squeezing it tightly. "Because you love him," he finished for her.

Caroline let out a breath and nodded. "I do." Her eyes filled with tears. These weren't sad tears, but they weren't happy either. The emotions overfilled her and the only outlet for them was her tears.

Her gaze dropped to the seat next to her, the seat that her husband had occupied a few minutes earlier. And then her emotional expression turned into a frown. "He has been gone a while, hasn't he?"

Wolverstone cocked his head to the side and matched Caroline's frown. "He has."

Caroline stood and dusted her skirts. "I'll go check where he went. Please," she added when the duke made to stand as well, "enjoy your tea. I shall be right back."

Caroline left the study and realized that she had no idea

where to look for her husband. She thought to check his room first, but he wasn't there. The adjoining doors to her room were open and she walked through them, thinking he might be in her chamber.

Wrong again.

Caroline let out a breath. Something felt wrong about this entire situation. Why would Dane just slip away like this?

Caroline made her way downstairs and approached the butler. "Did you happen to see where the duke went?"

He nodded. "Yes, Your Grace. And he asked me to pass these notes on to you if you were to ask about him."

Caroline frowned. "Why didn't you give me these right away?"

The butler raised his chin. "His Grace's instructions were clear. To give them to you *only* if you asked about him."

Caroline took the notes irritably and studied them.

These were the blackmailing notes that Wolverstone had brought with him today. One of them was missing, and in its place was another old, rumpled note and a freshly written one.

The older one was the note William had written with the directions to Lady Carlyle's ball. And the other was a new note written in Dane's hand.

> *I am sorry, darling. I had to leave. I couldn't do it any other way. Not with Wolverstone sitting right next to you.*
>
> *D*

Caroline frowned at the note. "That's all?"

Wolverstone appeared by her side at that exact moment.

"Is something amiss?" he asked, coming closer.

Caroline couldn't quite answer the question yet. She flipped the note from her husband this way and that, searching for some hidden meaning. Then she flipped through the other notes, rereading them. He wouldn't leave these for her if he didn't think she'd understand their meaning.

She squinted at the notes and compared them side by side.

"Oh, my God," she exclaimed as she finally realized what Dane saw. "It's William."

* * *

Dane jumped off the horse before she had a chance to come to a stop. This time, a groom ran up to him and caught Midnight's reins.

"Don't take her far," Dane barked as he made his way to the front door. "I won't be long."

He banged on the door like a madman and was soon greeted by a man he assumed to be William's butler.

"Is your master home?" Dane asked without preamble, pushing his way inside. "William!" he shouted at the top of his lungs.

He rushed toward the room where William had led him the last time and just as he was about to enter, the door opened and William appeared, with his hair tousled, just as before, in his single banyan, a drink hanging between his fingers.

"Twice in the same week. That has to be—"

"There is no time for your smug attitude," Dane barked. He pulled out the blackmailing note addressed to Caroline's uncle and slapped it against William's chest. "I know you did this."

William took it slowly and scanned the note with his eyes. "I have no idea what you're talking about."

"There is no time for your lying, William. You were careful, and you were very misleading but the older notes don't lie. You tried to forge my handwriting, and you used Erebus's name to hide behind, but it was you all along."

William shrugged. "Maybe it was. So what?" He took a sip of his whisky, visibly unperturbed.

"So what? Are you mad? People suffered because of what you did. They died! Do you not care at all?"

William just stood there, watching Dane.

"Why in the devil did you do it? Explain to me now. Because some powerful people are looking for you, and they'll be here soon."

William let out a laugh, then pushed his way past Dane. Dane followed in his tracks.

"You know my motives. You always have," William said without looking at him. "That's why you never cared to toss me into the gaol."

Dane scoffed. "I understood your motives when you recklessly aligned yourself with Hades and his group of criminals. But these are innocent people we are talking about!"

"Innocent?" William finally turned on him. They stood in the main hall, now. Just before the grand staircase. "There is no such thing as an innocent aristocrat."

"Your hatred blinds you."

William scoffed. "You're one to talk."

"I stood aside when you joined Hades and his ilk because even though he isn't without sin, at least, he has honor. But what you're doing now is madness!" Dane cried.

Chapter 26

"That's not the first time I've been accused of that."

"What is your excuse, William? Tell me why you stooped so low to do the bidding of lowly creatures with vendettas. For that is what you're doing, is it not? You're blackmailing people, trying to get them to do another's bidding."

"Perhaps."

Dane scoffed. "My wife's uncle killed himself because of you!"

"*Not* because of me!" William growled. "He killed himself because of guilt. Because he couldn't live with himself and with the atrocities that he'd done while being a part of the Brotherhood. He is the farthest man from innocence you could find."

"And therefore he deserved to die?"

William pursed his lips. "No one forced him to do it."

"You did!" Dane shouted. He ran a hand through his hair. "And what about Lavinia? What did she do?"

"She was a means to an end. But she wasn't innocent either. She murdered her father."

"In self-defense! And that man was a scoundrel. That man deserved to be punished, not her."

"Everything worked out for her benefit, anyway." William shrugged and took another sip. "Now if you could leave—"

"I am not going anywhere. I've tolerated your behavior, I've made excuses for how you were brought up—"

"Brought up?" William let out a laugh. "I was sold to a brothel by my father. Is that how I was brought up?"

Dane swallowed. "It does not justify what you're doing now! Blackmailing people for personal gain?"

"I only blackmail those who deserve it. And perhaps I have my selfish reasons for that. But you know as well as I do that it's impossible to blackmail the innocent."

Dane shook his head in disbelief. "You wrecked people's lives."

"And you are mistaking me for someone who cares," William spat.

"Oh, you will care very much because there is a very powerful and very angry man coming for you. The one you impersonated. That was a very foolish thing to do, by the way."

William shrugged. "Was it? I wasn't caught for years. And even now, can you truly prove it was me?"

"I hardly think the proof is necessary," Dane said through his teeth.

At that moment, the door to the house was thrown open and Wolverstone appeared on the doorstep.

Chapter 27

Wolverstone, an elegant old man, stood on the threshold of William's house with a sword in his hands.

He stood straight and proud, his eyes lit with a desire to kill. Dane was not certain if he could indeed kill William, a much younger opponent. But he wasn't willing to test that theory.

He took a step forward, blocking his idiot little brother. "I can't let you do this. He did not mean any harm."

"Did I not?" William said from behind. "I feel like I did."

"William, do shut up!" Dane barked at him. "And leave. He is going to kill you."

William shrugged. "I already lost Victoria. I have nothing else to lose."

"Oh, yes, you do. Your life perhaps?"

"I don't care about that."

"You heard him," Wolverstone growled. "Now step aside. He has to answer for his crimes."

"Fine," Dane conceded. "Let's arrange a duel. I shall stand

as his second."

Wolverstone shook his head. "I am afraid this requires immediate action." His gaze shifted to William. "You disgraced my name. You drove my friend to insanity. You blackmailed innocent people. And you're going to pay."

"And you speak too much, old man," William said with a sniff and then finished his drink with one last gulp.

Wolverstone lunged at him at that moment, forcing both William and Dane to jump out of the way.

Wolverstone attacked William with one cut after another, but William was spry and managed to avoid them all. Even his glass was still in his hand, unscathed.

"Wolverstone, stop!" Dane yelled and charged toward him.

He knocked the duke off his feet, and they both ended up lying tangled on the floor.

Dane turned to William and waved a hand at him. "Leave! Now! Soon this house will be crawling with Shadows. They will kill you."

"Oh, I don't need Shadows," Wolverstone growled as he picked up his sword again. "I will take care of him myself."

Dane stood, blocking the duke's way to William. "You'll have to kill me first."

"That will not be a problem," Wolverstone said and thrust his sword at Dane.

Dane jumped to the side and then again, and again, evading the attack, cursing himself for not taking his sword with him in his great haste. Only his trusty little dagger was strapped to the inside of his boot. And even that was currently out of reach.

Wolverstone continued relentlessly swinging his sword, and as he missed Dane once again, he hit the wall candelabra, causing the candles to fall to the floor and immediately catch fire.

Now the carpet was burning, and the fire was slowly but steadily climbing up the walls.

"Dane!" William called from the side and tossed him a sword.

Dane ducked under Wolverstone's attack and rolled to get to the weapon. He caught it just in time to block another of Wolverstone's cuts.

William rushed away and a moment later, noise started rising in the house as the servants ran out of their rooms with buckets of water. But the fire was spreading too fast.

"What in the devil are you doing?" Dane asked through his teeth, their swords crossed in front of their faces.

"What in the devil are you? Do you think Caroline will forgive you this?"

"I can't let you kill my brother. No matter who he is."

"Your loyalties are skewed," Wolverstone seethed and pushed at the sword, thrusting Dane against the wall. He rushed at William, who was organizing his servants to try and douse the fire.

Fire had quickly spread along the carpet and it was now overtaking the stairs. Sweat trickled down Dane's face and his back.

Dane ran after Wolverstone and tackled him again.

"Damn it, William!" he yelled. "It's no use. You have to get out of here! And take the servants with you!"

At that moment, the door opened, the wind blowing the fire around the house, the flames consuming everything in sight. Wolverstone, not caring for everything burning around them, charged at Dane.

Dane blocked his attack, before kicking him hard in the chest. Wolverstone flew past the burning carpet and ended up on the other side of fire with a burning coat.

Dane rushed toward him, but the fire rose high, blocking his path. And that's when he saw Caroline, standing on the threshold wide-eyed.

She immediately ran toward Wolverstone and kneeled before him, her eyes panicked.

Dane stepped closer to her, but the fire spread between them, not letting him pass.

"Dane, we have to go!" William yelled from the top of the stairs. "There is an exit this way."

Caroline helped put out Wolverstone's coat and then helped him up. The duke seemed more or less unscathed.

Then she looked at Dane, through the wall of fire, her eyes filled with betrayal and sorrow.

"Caroline!" he yelled, but he doubted she'd hear him through the noise surrounding them.

Then she just shook her head and turned away.

* * *

Caroline wished a few things had gone differently.

She wished she had realized that the contents of the note from her husband were meant just for her and not Wolverstone. She wished she hadn't said out loud that it was William who was responsible for the blackmail. She wished she hadn't had to run and change into her riding habit, because her evening gown wasn't appropriate for riding.

But she wished even more that her husband had taken the time to explain everything that was going on before racing off into the night.

If all these things had happened the way she wished, she would not be standing at the threshold of a burning building watching her husband fight the man who had taken care of her since the death of her parents.

Or at least, this was another thing Caroline wished had gone differently.

Just at that moment, Dane kicked Wolverstone in his chest, and he flew through the wall of fire and landed a few feet away from Caroline. And that's when Dane noticed her.

She could see the panic in his eyes.

Perhaps it was because the building was on fire. Or possibly it was because he had been caught betraying her once more. Caroline didn't have time to analyze her feelings or opinions. She rushed toward Wolverstone and helped him out of his burning coat. She patted down the little embers of the fire that burned through his clothing. He was definitely hurt. And he could have been killed.

Perhaps he would have been if she hadn't arrived on time.

How could you, Dane?

The silent question nagged at her brain.

Wolverstone got up and pushed her away. "What the devil are you doing here?" he yelled through the sounds of the roaring fire.

"I am trying to save your life!" she screamed back, her eyes tearing up from the smoke and the heat.

"This is my fight!" he yelled. "That bastard ruined my legacy and drove my friend to madness. And it's no place for you."

The floor crumbled a few feet away and turned into a pit. Caroline took Wolverstone by his arm and tugged him away. They rushed out of the burning house, coughing and gasping for air.

"You shouldn't have come!" Wolverstone said once he regained his voice.

"Then you would have died!" Caroline screamed. "Is that what you wanted? To die?"

"I wanted to kill the bastard who ruined my legacy," he hissed, then whispered furiously, "The Shadows were an elite force, silent warriors who helped people—*not* ruined them! Now we are regarded as criminals, and it's all because of his schemes. My friend is dead—"

"He was my uncle!" Caroline stomped her foot in irritation as tears sprang to her eyes. "You—all of you men are selfish idiots! Yes! All of you! You don't care about anyone but yourself and your damn legacy! If my uncle truly cared about me, he would have confessed it all. He wouldn't have kept it all to himself and let it drive him to madness! If you cared about the people around you, you would have asked for help. And if Dane—if Dane—" Tears rolled down her cheeks freely now. "Ugh!" She turned away and wiped her tears as she took a deep breath.

Men started appearing from the surrounding houses to help fight the fire. Fire engines were brought in a bit later.

Since the house was quite solitary in its location from others, there was a chance the fire would not spread to other buildings in the vicinity. But William's house would not survive the damages.

Caroline wiped at her cheeks as she watched the house burn to the ground, and she fought not to compare it to the trust she had in the men around her.

Her uncle was a criminal who'd hidden it for many years. Then he'd betrothed her to a stranger and killed himself. The family friend she'd trusted her entire life had been willing to die for the damn legacy that was already ruined. And her husband had been willing to kill that friend for his bastard brother who'd driven her uncle to suicide.

It was a vicious cycle of violence and betrayal, and Caroline was tired of it all. And just like her trust, the house gave a final shake and crumpled to the ground.

* * *

"I brought you some tea," Lavinia said as she peeked inside Caroline's room a few hours later—or at least the room that was allocated to Caroline while she was staying at the Roth house. It wasn't the same room where she'd lived when this house was her uncle's, but it was home nonetheless.

She came here right after leaving Wolverstone at his townhouse. She didn't feel like going home, and she didn't want to be alone. So she went to a place where she knew she'd be welcomed no matter the hour.

"Me too," Victoria said as she followed behind Lavinia. "Well, not really. I didn't bring you tea. But I just wanted to be here for you."

"Thank you, my dear friends," Caroline said with a weak smile.

"I suppose we have both been fooled by the sons of Kensington," Victoria said softly. Then she turned to Lavinia. "I can't believe William was the one who blackmailed you. And I can't believe that I can't believe it. Was I truly this blind?"

Caroline let out a breath, looking at a point somewhere beyond Victoria's shoulder, not quite able to meet either of her friends' gazes. "You were in love."

"Why did he do it?" Lavinia asked.

Caroline shrugged. "I don't know. Wolverstone says that he was only acting as a third party. People paid him money to blackmail people and he did it. Making it seem like this was an organized machine. As if Erebus was behind it."

"Who paid him to blackmail me?" Lavinia asked.

Caroline shrugged. "I don't know. And I don't know if we'll ever get to ask him."

Lavinia bristled. "Well, I will certainly ask Dane. How could he stand up for William after what he did?"

Victoria crinkled her nose. "He is his brother. No matter what he did…"

"Please, do not excuse Dane's actions!" Caroline said. "He betrayed me. Again!"

"Well, I for one, am done defending him!" Lavinia said emphatically.

"Thank you!" Caroline took her hand and squeezed.

"I didn't say I defend him!" Victoria exclaimed. "I just understand why he did it. I still think he is wrong."

Caroline took Victoria's hand in her free one and squeezed. "Thank you, dear."

Lavinia nodded. "And if he decides to come anywhere near this house, Sebastian is going to throw him out!"

"Good!" Caroline smiled at her riled-up friend.

And that's when they heard the noise downstairs.

* * *

Dane was greeted with a nice, hard punch in the face.

Well, not truly. First, the butler invited him in and directed him toward Roth's study. Roth made a great show of

310

welcoming him with a warm smile. And then he hit him without warning right in the face.

Not that Dane didn't see the punch coming. Of course, he did. He had great reflexes. And he wasn't exactly expecting a warm welcome. But he refused to duck or block the punch because he knew that he deserved it. And perhaps even more.

Dane staggered, and his hands immediately went to cover his nose, while Roth shook out his punching hand.

"I came here to see my wife," Dane said between his teeth. Tears sprung to his eyes, blurring the view in front of him. He wiped them away and pinched his nose from hurting.

"Well, your wife doesn't want to see you."

Dane straightened, regaining his composure. "I would like to hear that from her."

Roth frowned. "How is she going to say that without seeing you since she refuses to see you?"

Dane let out a breath. "I need to explain to her what happened."

Roth crossed his arms over his chest and leaned his hips against the desk. "Explain to me. And then I shall pass on your message. Because I am beyond curious to find out how you could defend and side with a man who blackmailed my wife!"

"I didn't side with him!" Dane barked, then let out a breath to calm himself. "I didn't side with him. But Wolverstone was going to kill him. You understand that, don't you? I couldn't let him do that. As it was, he burned his house down to the ground."

Roth's nose twitched. "Somehow, I can't muster pity for the man who *blackmailed* my wife!"

Dane scrubbed his face. "I understand why you are angry

311

with him. I am not trying to justify his actions... I simply don't believe he deserves to die."

"And my uncle did?" Caroline's voice sounded from behind, and Dane whirled on her, his breathing labored.

She stood like a vision, wrapped in a dressing gown that was a bit too big for her, her hair haphazardly laying against her shoulders and covering her breasts. Her eyes were lit with fury, her lips pursed in a disapproving pinch. She was magnificent. God, how he missed her already.

"I am not trying to make excuses for William," he said when he was able to catch his breath. "I am not. What he did was wrong. But he *is* my brother. My younger brother has suffered a lot. I have a responsibility to him. And he might not do things in the ways I approve of... He is selfish and always looks for a benefit for himself, but in his heart, he is not a bad man."

"Right." Caroline scoffed. "He is a benevolent blackmailer who has wrecked many lives."

"He thought he was in the right... He thought the world owed him that much for the way he grew up."

"That is preposterous!"

"It is! And I am not saying it isn't. I am just saying that I can't in good conscience leave my little brother to die. No matter who he is or what he did."

Caroline turned away.

"He is not just one thing, Caroline. Just like your uncle wasn't."

Her eyes met his again, lit with anger. "Do not compare them!"

"He won't be blackmailing anyone anymore," Dane hastened to add. "In fact, he is leaving the country. He has nothing left here. That should be punishment enough."

"And yet it isn't," Caroline said coldly.

Dane licked his lips and stepped toward her. She stepped back. "What do you want me to do? Do you want me to tie him up so you can hit him and make him pay? Do you want to hit me?" He spread his arms. "Go ahead. I will stand here as long as you require."

"What if I require you to leave?" came her immediate answer.

He clenched his jaw. "You are my wife."

"And therefore I should listen to what you have to say?" She scoffed. "You are a lot like William. I wonder why I never saw that."

Dane swallowed. He had nothing to say to that.

"But he was wrong," she said thoughtfully. "That night he made a grand speech about how if he were a duke, we would forgive him easily, but he was wrong. The fact that you're a duke does not matter."

"Caroline…" Her name was a prayer, a benediction.

"Just tell me who had Lavinia blackmailed," she said and raised her chin.

Dane rummaged through his pockets and took out a piece of paper. He extended it toward her but she stepped back. "Give it to Cousin Bastian."

Dane let out a breath but did as she asked. "It was her guardian. I suppose he wanted to marry her off to Pembroke and then demand all the riches that he'd lost to him. But once Lavinia married Roth"—Dane threw his gaze toward the marquess, who was scanning the list with his gaze—"William refused to continue blackmailing her. The last note he sent to you during the house party was just him… out of anger after your duel over his marriage to Victoria. But he isn't going to bother you anymore. He won't bother anyone anymore. As I said. He is leaving the country tomorrow."

Caroline swallowed visibly. "What about my uncle? Who blackmailed him?"

Dane grimaced. "That was all William."

"Why?" Caroline's chest rose with heaving breaths.

"That he wouldn't tell me."

Caroline turned on her heel and prepared to storm away.

"Caroline!" Dane called after her and she stopped.

She threw a gaze over her shoulder, but without saying anything, she walked away.

Chapter 28

Caroline returned to her room just in time for her stomach to feel queasy. She knew that feeling and just as she thought it, a warm liquid seeped out of her. She ran to the dressing room and fashioned a linen padding for herself.

Her courses had arrived. Just on time.

She let out a breath, not quite understanding the overwhelming feelings inside her. What was she feeling? Was it sadness for a child that would not be?

And if it were sadness, then why? She'd never wanted a babe. The idea of a babe frightened her; the responsibility terrified her as did the physical trials that childbirth entailed. And now she felt rather upset.

Perhaps she was just feeling emotional. She always felt that way during her courses. It shouldn't have been a surprise.

Or perhaps during her days and weeks with her husband, she had started reconsidering the idea. Because as frightening the prospect of having a babe was to her, it was just as exciting now.

She had experienced so many new things with her husband, pleasures that she never thought existed, and she was looking forward to experiencing more.

Had been looking forward to experiencing more…

Now, she wasn't certain what she wanted. She wasn't certain that excitement and pleasure were worth the heartbreak.

She slowly waddled toward the bed and burrowed inside the covers.

Or perhaps she was afraid she would be all alone again. Those few days with her husband by her side felt almost magical. She felt as though she belonged somewhere, and she was loath to lose that feeling.

Caroline shook herself from the maudlin thoughts. She still had her family by her side. And perhaps it wasn't the same, but she was grateful for cousin Sebastian's help. She was grateful and beyond relieved to have her friends. She wasn't completely alone in this world and that was comforting.

Her body relaxed as she felt the slow but pleasant pull of sleep.

There was a rap on the window.

Caroline sat up immediately.

It was night. It was freezing cold outside.

But there was an unmistakable and undeniable rap at her bedroom window.

There it was again.

Caroline looked at her window and saw a looming shadow staring in. She was startled but just for a moment. Because although that shadow might have seemed terrifying to some, she recognized it immediately.

So she got out of bed and stomped to the window.

"Why are you here?" she asked irritably as she cracked the window open.

Dane peered into the crack, looking quite comical in this rather strange situation. "I thought it was obvious. I came to beg for forgiveness and understanding."

"Well, you're not getting either." Caroline moved to close the window, but he blocked her attempt as he put his hand on the windowpane.

"I understand why you are angry with me. Just let me explain to you—"

"You don't need to explain anything," Caroline said. "I understand quite well. William is your family, although you can't stand him. And I mean nothing to you because I am merely your wife. So you went behind my back—again!—and almost killed the closest person I have to my family."

"Wolverstone is quite capable of surviving. I hope you know that I had no intention of hurting him."

"Your intention of hurting him is exactly what I saw." She raised her chin.

"Caroline, please don't make this into something it isn't. All I was trying to do was save my brother. And I didn't mean to do it behind your back. I would have told you my plans on the spot if Wolverstone hadn't been there. But he was. And if I had pulled you aside to tell you, he would have known that something was wrong. The man is Erebus, Caroline. He can doom a person with his single word. And I know that you probably think that William doesn't deserve to live after all that he's done. But I have a responsibility to him."

"Why?" she asked weakly. "Why do you feel you have to save him after everything that he's done?"

Dane let out a breath, the white cloud entering the room

through the window. It was freezing out, the frost drawing ornaments on the window glass. And yet Dane didn't push the window open, didn't ask her to, either. Didn't ask to be let in.

He just leaned his head against the window. God only knew what he was propped against while sitting on the wall.

"I told you that my father was a harsh and wicked man. He was cold and cruel to me and my mother. He was brutal and unforgiving. He was convinced he was making a man out of me. He trained me to be resilient and strong and for that, if for nothing else, I suppose, I should be grateful. But he was a terrible father to live with. And as much as it was difficult for me, it was worse for William. A lot worse.

"I told you a little about how he came to our doorstep when I was thirteen… But I haven't told you that he came once before when he was younger."

Caroline stepped closer and sat on the floor by the window, engrossed in his story.

"His mother had told him about his parentage when he was very young. And when she fell ill—dying—he came to ask for help from our father. He was a tiny little thing… six or seven? He crawled inside the house somehow and surprised my father enough that he had to hear him out. William didn't ask anything for himself. He asked the late duke to shelter his mother so she could get better… It was cold and dirty where they lived. He thought that if she were warm that maybe—" Dane looked away.

Tears sprung to Caroline's eyes and her throat constricted. "Your father refused and she died," Caroline guessed.

"Yes." Dane's voice was hoarse. "But he also did something worse. He didn't want to risk William coming back… So he sold him—or gave him, I don't know—to a brothel."

Caroline reared in horror. "No!"

"I shouldn't be telling you this," Dane croaked out the words. "But my father told it to me proudly, as if it was an accomplishment to let a woman die. To let a little child suffer. He told me that so I would know how to deal with bastards." He swallowed hard.

"How old were you when he told you about it?"

Dane shrugged. "I don't know. Young. Too young to do anything about it. But old enough to realize I never wanted to be like my father. The rest of the story is even worse. I won't horrify you with details, but that's how William met Hades a few years later. A man with a similar fate and a drive for vengeance against aristocrats. And the rest I've already told you."

Caroline sat in horrified silence, trying to process her husband's words. She'd heard about the cruelty of Lavinia's father. She'd heard the stories of other entitled, abusive men. But this was something out of Greek mythologies. Dane's father might not have eaten his children alive, but he may as well have.

"That's why the rumors about William's parentage persisted, isn't it?" she finally asked. "You never bothered to squash them. You wanted everyone to know he was your father's son. In your own way, you acknowledged that he is your brother."

Dane's silhouette moved, probably in a shrug. "He *is* my brother. That's just a fact. And not only do I not give up on my family, but I had a life more privileged than his. I owe it to him to give back at least a little of the life that my father stole from him. I can't right all the wrongs my father committed. But I can save William."

319

Caroline licked her lips. "That guilt you carry should never have been your burden. And it's terrible what William went through. But just because he suffered greatly doesn't mean he has the right to pass on that suffering to others."

Dane shifted closer to the window. "But do you think he should die for that? Because that's the question, isn't it? I didn't side with him against you, I simply couldn't let him die."

"Wolverstone would not have killed him," she said unconvincingly. He had been angry enough to try.

Dane let out a chuckle. "Do you truly believe that?"

Caroline pursed her lips. "I understand not willing to let him die. I even understand that you have some misguided sense of responsibility to him. But what you have to understand is that my husband, the man who claimed to love me, stood against the man who had cared for me greatly after I lost my family, and then aided the man who hurt a lot of people I love! When it came to me or him, you chose him."

"That's not how it was at all!"

"Perhaps not. But that's how I see it. And I don't see how I can ever trust you again. And without trust"—she shook her head—"I don't know what else there can be between us."

"Caroline—"

"You weave elaborate tales about family, Dane. But *I* am supposed to be your family. And no matter your logical points... right now it just hurts."

"Then let me ease your pain," he said, his voice hoarse. "Tell me what I can do. Do you want me to stay here out in the cold until you forgive me? I will. I might freeze to this roof, but I will stay here as long as you require."

Caroline sat up on her knees and moved closer to him.

Dane was staring back at her through the window, his lashes, stubble, and his eyebrows covered with frost. His look would have been quite comical if it wasn't tragic. "I think at this point, you can just leave me alone."

"No, I can't leave you alone. I can't—"

"You asked me what I need, Dane. And that's what I need. I need time away from you."

There was a pause. "For how long?"

"I don't know." She moved to close the window, but he put his fingers on the window pane.

"Fine," he said with a nod. "If you say you need time, then you shall get time. But I am not giving up on us. I love you. And I hope you will come to believe it. And you can be mad at me for saving my brother, but I know you. You will come to understand the logic behind my actions and you *will* forgive me."

She scoffed. "That's rather self-assured of you to assume."

"Perhaps. But contrary to what you might think, I know you quite well. You say you cannot trust me, but I think that you already do. Because yes, I went behind your back yet again. But every time I did so, I had a good reason. I do not go behind your back to visit a mistress. I do not go behind your back to torture innocents, gamble, or do anything else that might be detrimental to our relationship or the lives of other people. And I won't promise to not do it again.

"Perhaps, I will go behind your back yet again. But it will always be in service of you. To protect you. To keep you safe and sheltered. So, be mad at me. Keep me away from you for as long as you like. I shall give you time and space. But when you're ready, I shall be waiting for you. At home."

Then he let go of the window and disappeared out of sight.

Caroline opened the window wider and stuck her torso out, looking for a sign of him. But he was nowhere to be found.

* * *

Caroline sat embroidering the next morning in the drawing room with Lavinia. Victoria had secluded herself in her room after everything that had happened, feeling rather hopeless about her life and future.

Victoria's sister did manage to send her a letter saying that she was under house arrest and asked Victoria not to worry. But Victoria wasn't daft. She knew that any correspondence from her sister was checked by the guards. So those assurances didn't alleviate the fear in her heart.

Victoria wrote back to her sister and pleaded with the new Tsaritsa to let them go, but so far, her pleas had gone unanswered.

Victoria was now without support from her sister and estranged from the only man she'd ever loved.

In comparison, Caroline's life was perfect.

And then there was William.

After what Dane had told Caroline the night before, she couldn't keep her mind off of him.

She didn't feel pity for the man. She felt pity for the little boy who'd suffered greatly. And she imagined that's exactly how Dane still saw William, as a hurt little boy in need of a family.

Caroline had lost her parents when she was young. But she'd had a home, an uncle who loved her, and all the privileges the money could buy. It didn't buy the feeling of security. It didn't stop the irrational fears of being alone. But for William, the situation must have been thousands of times worse.

And yet, she struggled to forgive his atrocious actions. And she would never advise Victoria to forgive him either.

Some people believed that the love of a woman could save the worst of scoundrels. Caroline was not one of those people. She hoped she would see William save himself. Because as much as she hated him, she truly wished he could be saved.

The butler appeared on the threshold. "Your Grace, My Lady." He bowed low. "There is a package for Her Grace."

"Oh." Caroline put down her embroidery and walked to meet the butler. He handed her a rectangular box, bowed, and walked away.

"What is it?" Lavinia asked as she walked toward Caroline.

"I don't know."

They both sat on a settee next to the window as Caroline opened the box. It contained the most beautiful set of rubies she had ever seen: a radiant pair of earrings and a matching necklace.

Beneath lay the note:

Christmas gift number one.

Caroline smiled as she took the note and stroked it between her fingers. There wasn't a signature, but there was no one else this present could have been from. And she also knew his handwriting well enough not to doubt it.

"It's beautiful!" Lavinia exclaimed.

"Isn't it?" Caroline grinned and placed the necklace against her neck.

"Is Dane trying to buy your forgiveness?" Lavinia asked with a raised brow.

Caroline put the necklace back into the box and shook her

head. "I don't think so. He just knows that I love Christmas presents."

Lavinia raised a brow. "It's past twelfth night."

"I know." Caroline smiled. "I just told him once that my parents used to gift me hundreds of presents for Christmas. I suppose he just wanted to let me know that he remembers. And that he cares."

"Do I hear forgiveness in your tone?"

Caroline let out a sigh. "He is not the one I am mad at. And yes, I still feel that he should have told me about William before rushing over there and that he should have handled things differently. But in his heart, he is a man who always does the right thing. And I suppose I should just learn to trust him."

Lavinia grimaced a little. "He is a man you can rely on. I know I did for many years."

Caroline swallowed. "I don't know if I apologized for stealing him away from you—"

"That is not necessary at all," Lavinia interrupted instantly. "If you hadn't, I wouldn't have married Sebastian. And let's be honest, I'd be miserable." She chuckled and placed a hand atop Caroline's. "And you wouldn't have fallen in love with Dane. Everything worked out for the best."

Caroline nodded. "And I definitely didn't apologize for not trusting you about him. I mean, when I suspected him to be the blackmailer."

Lavinia waved a hand with a smile, but then she immediately turned toward Caroline with wide eyes. "Did you apologize to him?"

Caroline crinkled her nose. "No?"

Lavinia laughed merrily. "Perhaps you should try that."

"Perhaps I should." She paused, twirling the box of rubies in her hands. "Do you know that Dane never got presents as a child?"

Lavinia looked at Caroline strangely, then simply shook her head. "No, I did not."

Caroline stood resolutely. "I think it's time for me to go back home."

Lavinia grinned as she got up. "I really hope that you will find buckets of happiness with Dane. But know that you will always have a home here."

Chapter 29

Caroline didn't go home straight away. First, she went to the shops looking for a present for her husband. But therein lay a problem. What does one buy a man who has everything?

After walking around for a few hours, she was finally able to pick something she thought he would love and then made her way back home.

She was happy, and she was glad to be returning home. Whatever issues she had with her husband, they would resolve them together.

And she wasn't even trying to hide the fact that she was looking forward to seeing him.

Caroline entered the house with a smile on her face.

She ascended the stairs with a skip in her step. She wanted to see her husband right away so she rushed into his bedroom only to find it empty.

With slightly duller spirits, she went into his study, but he wasn't there either. She should have asked the butler if he was home before running around the entire townhouse she realized a little too late. But she was so excited about seeing him that she hadn't even considered that he might be away.

Caroline made her way downstairs and approached the butler. "I can't find the duke anywhere. Is he not home?"

"No, Your Grace."

Caroline frowned. "When did he leave?"

"Last night, Your Grace."

Caroline faltered. "Last night?"

The butler nodded.

"But he sent me a gift today," she mumbled to herself.

"He ordered the gift to be sent to you last night before he left," the butler answered.

Caroline threw him a sharp gaze. "So the duke left last night to see me and hasn't returned."

"Yes, Your Grace."

Caroline's heart drummed loudly in her chest. He didn't come home last night. He had come to see her, sat on her roof telling her stories, and then he'd left never to be seen again.

A buzzing noise arose in her head, making it difficult to think.

Where did he go?

Certainly, he wouldn't just disappear. He wouldn't go off and spend the night somewhere else, either.

I shall be waiting for you. At home.

These were the last words he'd said to her.

Panic started bubbling from within Caroline.

Something had happened to him. He was gone! And it was all Caroline's fault.

If she had just gone home with him… If she hadn't left in the first place—

She rubbed her temples. Now wasn't the time to give in to panic. Wherever Dane was, she needed to find him.

But how? And where did she even start?

Wolverstone would not help her after what had happened the night before. But luckily, she had other friends who would.

* * *

Dane woke up shivering from the cold.

He was completely naked—which wasn't surprising at all because he often slept without a stitch on—but never had he experienced this bone-chilling cold.

Was Caroline hogging all the covers again? He smiled at the thought.

And it felt as though the fire had died down in the hearth. Perhaps the window was open, too. He looked forward to snuggling close to his wife.

First, he needed to close the damn window.

Dane tried to move only to realize his hands were bound behind his back. Had Caroline forgotten to untie him after a sizzling night?

But the ache in his body and the freezing chilliness signaled to him that something was very wrong.

A warm hand settled on his arm, and Dane shivered again. "Caroline," he croaked, his voice quite hoarse.

"If you call me Caroline one more time, I am leaving you here to die," a familiar voice said from behind him.

Startled, Dane jolted to a seated position. And immediately flinched from pain.

He looked around only to realize that he was not at home

at all. He was sitting on a bare wooden floor, completely and utterly naked. Only there were also bruises all over his body.

What the devil happened last night?

And where the devil am I?

He felt a sawing motion behind his back as someone tried to remove his ropes.

Right! Someone was here with him. Dane turned his head toward the person working on untying the ropes.

William.

"Stay still," he said. "I don't know how much time we have before they come back."

"Who?" Dane looked around in horror. He was in an empty building with scraped-up walls and bare windows.

William narrowed his eyes. "Don't you remember anything?"

Dane thought hard, but only random flashes came to his mind. "I really don't."

"Well," William said as he finally freed his hands. "You were caught by some miscreants working for the Brotherhood. I don't think they appreciated you looking into them."

"Because of you," Dane growled.

"And they left you a souvenir." William pointed to Dane's left thigh.

Dane squinted at the mark of a black fist. "Oh, Lord."

"Now, get up. We need to go." William helped Dane to his feet. He wrinkled his nose at Dane's naked form before taking off his coat. "Here, cover yourself up, would you?"

Dane put on the coat and groaned from the pleasure he gained from the warmth. "What are you doing here?" he asked hoarsely.

"Well, I was passing through… Can we walk as I explain? I

don't know if they are planning to come back and in case they are, I really don't fancy being stranded here with you naked."

Dane looked down at his bare feet. "Give me your shoes."

"I am not going to give you my shoes," William said in an offended manner.

"I can't walk barefoot." He curled his toes, or at least he tried to. They had stiffened from the cold.

William muttered something under his breath. "The best I can do is give you my stockings, but you'll owe me." He immediately knelt down to comply.

"Really? I will owe you?"

William shrugged as he handed Dane his stockings. "You saved me, I saved you. This makes us even. But I don't ever remember you giving me your stockings, so yes. Now you owe me."

Dane shook his head. "I am not going to address your faulty logic, William. At least not before you get me out of here."

"What? Are you going to lecture me on my chosen way of life again?"

Dane took a step and faltered, his knees protesting the motion. William rolled his eyes and then threw Dane's arm over his shoulders and helped bear his weight.

"The way I grew up it's a wonder I turned out as well as I did," William continued as they slowly made their way.

"At some point, that excuse stops working," Dane said. "I brushed it off when you were younger, when you had no other choices. But you've lived a life of privilege for a few years now. You don't have to do the things you did to survive."

"And now I can be a noble knight," William quipped.

"You have to own up to your actions, brother. And decide what kind of man you're going to be."

William threw him a strange look but didn't answer. Dane shook his head. He was wasting his breath. "How did you find me here, anyway? And what happened?"

"As I said, I was passing through Mayfair—"

"You were passing through?"

William let out a breath. "Fine. I wanted to see Victoria and talk to her one more time before I left. I am still determined to leave as you advised." Dane rolled his eyes. *Advised.* More like threatened. "But before I could walk up to the door, I saw a few men accosting you and dragging you to their carriage."

Dane threw him a suspicious look. "I was at the back of the house. If you were standing by the main entrance, you wouldn't have seen it."

William raised his eyes heavenward. "Very well, perhaps I was going to climb the window to Victoria's chamber. What does it matter?"

"You were going to sneak up to your wife's window like some burglar?"

William threw him a surprised glance. "You're one to talk."

They slowly walked through long, empty corridors.

"Either way, I saw them take you. And I could have wasted time alerting everyone to your disappearance, but I knew if I did that, we'd never find you. So I followed them instead."

"Why didn't you interfere earlier?" Dane growled.

"And get us both killed? No, thank you. Besides, they didn't want to kill you. They were just sending you and your friends a message to not look into the Brotherhood anymore. Hence the mark. A black one is a warning," he clarified in a patronizing tone of voice.

Dane grunted something non-committal as they made their way out of the building. "Where are we?"

"At the docks. Come. My horse is a few streets over."

Dane looked down at himself. "I dare say it will be extremely uncomfortable for me to ride the horse bare-arsed. Are we going to double on it?"

William's face contorted in a grimace. "I shall happily lend you my mount. And you can keep the saddle."

A low whistle sounded from somewhere nearby.

"Damn it!" William disengaged from Dane and bared his sword. Then he took out a dagger and handed it to Dane. "I know you can barely walk. But I'm afraid you'll have to fight."

Dane clutched the dagger in his cold fingers. Fight? He could barely stand. He surmised that he'd only been lying naked in the abandoned building for a few hours, otherwise he'd have died from cold. But those hours were enough for him to barely be able to feel his toes and fingers.

He was getting warmed up, and he only hoped that the thrill of the fight would get the blood pumping in his veins again.

William stood, vigilant with his back to Dane. And Dane would never admit it out loud, but it felt nice having his brother guarding his back.

They looked around silently, their backs to each other.

The wind blew some debris past them, and the trees rustled nearby. But there was no one else about. Only silence.

And then two Shadows fell from the sky—or rather descended from the roof of a nearby building.

For a moment, Dane tensed, thinking that Wolverstone had sent his men after him, but he quickly relaxed. Because he recognized the gait and the athletic but unmistakably feminine figure of one of the Shadows.

She tore the mask away as she ran toward him.

"Interesting," William mused.

Dane didn't know if William said anything further. He didn't notice anything else that happened except that his wife crashed against his chest.

Her arms wrapped around his body as she muttered something under her breath. Dane held her tightly to his chest, his heart beating loudly and his body warming instantly.

"You're alive," she breathed as she disengaged from him and looked up into his face. Her eyes were teary, and her breath was ragged.

Dane smiled at her and for a moment, they were lost in each other's gazes.

Then she turned to William and slapped him on his chest. "What did you do to him?"

"Ow!" William rubbed his chest, then glanced at Dane. "She is very strong."

The second Shadow finally moved closer to them. St. John took off the mask and handkerchief, revealing himself.

"Don't you try to weasel your way out of this!" Caroline attacked William. "I am not—"

"Caroline, dear, look at me," Dane cajoled his wife. He took her by the chin and turned her toward him. "He saved me."

"Saved you?" Caroline's gaze ran down his body, and she squinted at him. "You're naked!"

"Yes, but they didn't hurt me—"

Caroline patted his body, troubling his bruises. Dane winced.

"—much."

"Who are *they*? What happened?"

"I would advise that we shouldn't stand in the middle of the street discussing this," William said.

"I have to agree with the bastard," St. John said.

William threw him a distasteful grimace.

"Cousin Sebastian is waiting for us a few streets over with a carriage," Caroline told Dane. She was still looking at him strangely as if she didn't believe he was indeed alive.

"We should move," St. John said. Then he turned to William. "But I would advise you to leave. Far, far away. Erebus is not happy. There's a price on your head."

William shrugged. "I didn't expect anything less. Well, now that you're safe, I suppose nothing is holding me here," he said and turned away.

"William." Dane stopped him in his tracks.

William turned back and gave him a charming smile. "You owe me a pair of stockings, brother. At least, I got to keep my saddle." And with a wink, he disappeared behind a corner of the alley.

Caroline pressed herself close to him again, and Dane's attention turned back to his wife. He cuddled her close and kissed the top of her head.

"We have to go," St. John said before he walked toward them and offered his shoulder.

Dane leaned on St. John with his wife plastered tightly to his side. And together, they quickly made their way toward Roth's carriage.

"Thank you," Dane said as he disengaged from St. John and moved toward the vehicle. "And I don't just mean lending me a shoulder just now. But for coming to save me."

St. John grinned. "Just repaying the favor." He put on his mask and a handkerchief, then gave a brief nod before disappearing into the shadows.

"I'll be riding outside," Roth said and patted Dane on his shoulder.

Dane happily settled into the carriage and was immediately embraced by his wife. She seemed distraught and rather out of sorts.

"Are you feeling fine?" Dane asked inanely.

She burrowed her face deeper into his—William's—coat.

"Darling," Dane said softly. "Look at me."

Caroline shook her head. The carriage jolted to a start, and Caroline only burrowed even deeper into his coat.

Dane took her face between his palms and raised it to his. Caroline had tears running down her cheeks.

"Why are you crying?" He chased her tears away with his thumbs.

"I was so afraid," she whispered. "I was afraid I lost you."

Dane couldn't help it. He smiled.

"Why are you smiling?" She crinkled her brows.

"I am sorry that I caused you distress," Dane said, still smiling. "Actually, I am not."

"What?" She blinked up at him, startled. But at least she was no longer crying.

"I mean... I am alive, and I wish I hadn't caused you stress... But I am happy that I did."

"What?" she repeated louder.

Dane let out a chuckle. "I am saying it wrong. I am not glad I caused you distress... Well, I am but..." He took her hands in his. "Please, excuse my mumbling, my brain is still thawing. I just mean... I am happy to know that you care this much."

Caroline's face turned thunderous. "Of course, I care!" She took his face between her palms and kissed him hard on the lips. "I love you, you idiot!"

Dane let out a chuckle. "I am glad." Then he lowered his head and kissed her deeply.

* * *

Soft, warm hands ran over his chest, then up to his shoulder, touching him gently. Dane moaned in pleasure.

Then he froze. "It's not William, is it?"

His wife gave a beautiful laugh. "I am sorry to disappoint."

Dane opened his eyes and tugged his wife until she lay down against his chest.

He was lying snugly in his bed, the pleasant smell of oils Caroline had been rubbing him with calming his mind.

"I didn't mean to wake you," she said. "But Rea told me to rub this oil on you every four hours. It's supposed to make your bruises heal quicker."

"I am glad you woke me up," he said and pressed a kiss to the top of her head.

"You are?" She pressed her hands against his chest and propped her chin so she could look at him.

"If there's a choice between sleep and being awake next to you, just know that I will always choose to be awake next to you."

Caroline smiled. "I feel the same way."

Dane's heart constricted in his chest... in hope. "Do you mean that? Because when we last spoke—"

"I know. And I am not taking back my words. I am still unhappy about the way you leave me behind and do things on your own but... I understand." She sat up. "What I realized recently is that ever since my parents' death, I have been trying to control everything. I was doing everything myself, relying only on myself. That way I was never disappointed. I was never unpleasantly surprised. And then my uncle died and turned my world upside-down again. And that made me fight for control even more." She let out a breath. "But that's not how the world works. I can't control everything and, I suppose, I need to learn to live with that. And I need to learn to appreciate the good and the bad surprises that come my way and just trust that things will work themselves out. I need to trust that we can handle anything as long as we're together."

Dane took her hands in his. "We *can* handle anything as long as we're together."

She nodded. "Before marrying you, I was convinced that this marriage would ruin my life. But I was too focused on revenge to let my fears stop me. If I had let my fears stop me, I would have never experienced the greatest love of my life. And similarly, if the fear of trusting you completely will hold me back, I will miss out on some grand adventures."

Dane smiled. "I love you."

"I love you, too." She smiled back. "And I am ready to embark on some grand adventures together."

Dane tugged on her hands until she leaned in for a lingering kiss.

"Mm, I like that," he said as she sat up again. "I was just thinking about taking a few months off to travel."

"You were?" Her smile widened.

"Yes. We stirred the pot a bit with our little search for the members of the Brotherhood. And Erebus is angry with me. So I think it's a perfect time for us to leave for a bit."

Caroline chuckled. "I love that idea." She swallowed and licked her lips. "But um… when I was talking about grand adventures, traveling wasn't what I had in mind."

Dane raised a brow. "It wasn't?" He tried to sit up, and Caroline moved to help him lean against the pillows.

"I… um… my courses started yesterday," Caroline said quietly.

The change in the subject completely disarmed him. "Oh." He couldn't think of anything else to say.

"And it made me… sad somehow."

"Sad?" He took her hands and squeezed her fingers.

"Yes. I know I've been reluctant."

"Reluctant?" He let out a chuckle. "You were adamant against having children."

"Yes, I know. But perhaps I am ready to change my mind. As I said… I am working on conquering my fears and embarking on some grand adventures."

He brought her hand to his lips and kissed her knuckles. "Whatever you want."

Her smile turned gentle, but the next minute, she tugged her hand away and jumped up. "I completely forgot."

She rushed into her room through the adjoining room door. Dane blinked, uncertain of what just happened.

She reappeared with an onyx sculpture of a horse in her hands. She grinned as she brought it to him. "Merry Christmas," she said, barely holding on to her laughter. "It's gift number one."

* * *

In the meantime...

There was a strange noise downstairs. Or at least a noise Helen didn't expect to hear. A baby's crying.

For a moment, Helen thought she was still dreaming. After

all, what would a babe be doing in this house?

Had Annalise broken free from her house for a visit? Had the forty days passed already? Helen didn't think so.

But the child's crying noises were unmistakable. And then there were stomping footsteps in the corridor. Something was going on.

Helen sat up in bed. She didn't feel nauseous, and her headache wasn't bothering her too much. Good.

She threw a dressing gown over her nightgown and wrapped it tightly around her willowy form. Then she put on her slippers and slowly made her way to the door.

The servants were rushing from one side of the corridor to another, bringing linen, water, and some other items.

Helen started to get more worried. Was someone hurt? She hurried downstairs and saw Jarvis standing in the hall, holding a basket with a crying babe. He looked completely lost, uncertain of what to do with the poor thing.

Olivia was nowhere to be found.

"Jarvis? What is it?" Helen asked and rushed toward him.

Jarvis tried for a smile. "There's a little guest in the house," he said as he raised the basket slightly. "Olivia went to write a note to Annalise asking for a few things for the babe."

"Where did it come from?" Helen peered at the little angel inside the basket.

Mrs. Lenard, the housekeeper, appeared by their side with a young woman in tow. "Althea has recently given birth. She'll try to feed the poor thing if you relinquish him... her to us."

"Of course," Jarvis handed the basket to the women and they hurried away. Then he turned toward Helen with a slight grimace. "There was a note inside the basket." He handed her a note.

Helen took it with a shaking hand. Somehow she felt that the contents of that note would change her life forever. Blood rushed to her head, drowning out all other sounds as she read.

Mrs. Helen St. John. This child is your husband's. Do with it as you please.

Epilogue

Ten months later...

D ane prowled the room like a caged beast.

Sweat was trickling down his forehead, his coat was nowhere in sight, and his cravat was hanging by a thread around his red and veiny neck.

They'd been stuck in this room for nine hours, and this probably wasn't the most time they'd ever spent together in one day, but to Caroline, it seemed like it was.

"Do you want some more caudle, dear?" Caroline asked weakly.

He turned sharply toward her. "Are you in pain again?"

She shook her head. "No, but it seems like you are."

He tried for a weak smile. "It's been forever. I don't know how you can do this. And I am worried that I am not doing all that I could." He threw a glance at the midwives huddled at the foot of the bed.

Caroline swallowed a smile. "Darling, come here."

Dane came toward her and knelt by her side. He took her hand in his and squeezed.

"I saw Annalise go through this. There is nothing you can do."

She grimaced as an excruciating pain twisted her from the inside. For the next few seconds, she didn't feel anything aside from pain, and then Dane's hand in hers, his reassuring presence, and his soothing words.

The midwives rushed toward her, wiping sweat off her forehead, bringing her more caudle, but Caroline just waved them away. The poor women were frightened to death by her imposing husband and fussed about her more than necessary.

This—Caroline realized—was the exact reason why men were not allowed in the birthing chamber. Yet she was glad to have her husband beside her nonetheless.

She'd asked her friends not to come because she didn't want them to see her like this, all disheveled and in pain. But her husband had seen her in every state of distress, and he insisted on being in her room even if she had resisted at first.

And that's the last thing Caroline thought before the harrowing pain rendered her mind blank. What happened next was like in a daze.

The pain, the blood, her husband's horrified expressions. Caroline would have laughed—would laugh later—but not just yet.

And then the babe was out, and the world stilled.

The midwife wiped her out, wrapped her in a linen sheet, and placed her on Caroline's chest.

Dane's eyes were wide as he watched the little babe lying on his wife. "She is... so tiny," he said.

Tears trickled down Caroline's cheeks, and she let them. She was too afraid to move.

She let out a deep breath and raised her eyes to her husband's. He was teary-eyed, too.

"That's gift number 305," she said with a chuckle.

The end

Loved the book? Sign-up to get a free novelette:
https://sendfox.com/sadiebosque
By signing-up you'll also get new release alerts, bonus content such as extra epilogues, deleted scenes and other writing updates!

Read more from *The Shadows* series!
Seducing Her Wicked Rogue is the next book in series.

Keep Reading for a Deleted Scene.

Deleted Scene

Dane came down the next morning to see his wife sitting at the foot of their sixteen-foot-long table. She glanced at him when he entered and smiled. "Good morning." A warm welcome if he'd ever had one.

"Good morning," he said as she turned back to her food.

Dane looked at the head of the table where he was supposed to sit and felt a strange aversion to that place. He didn't want to sit there all alone, watching his wife from six feet away, with candles and table pieces sitting in the way.

He must have stood there thinking for quite some time because Caroline looked at him again and raised her brow.

"Don't you find it odd," he said conversationally, "that we are the only people eating at this table, and yet we are forced to eat in different corners of the room?"

Caroline looked at his place on the other side of the table and frowned. "I never thought about it."

"Well, would you like to break the tradition and meet in the middle?"

She chewed thoughtfully, and he was afraid she might decline. Then she finally nodded. "Very well."

Dane smiled and asked the footmen to move their place settings to the middle of the room. And once they did that, he asked them to leave.

Caroline looked at him curiously. "Why did you ask them to leave?"

Dane sat next to his wife and looked at her beautiful features. He realized that he'd never truly noticed how deeply green her eyes were. This was probably the reason why emeralds suited her so well.

Her lips were plump and juicy, he just wanted to suck on them all day long. Forget breakfast, or any other meal, or any other activity for that matter. He would happily spend his days sucking on his wife's lips.

"Dane?"

Dane blinked, coming back to the real world, realizing that he hadn't answered her previous question. Right. He cleared his throat. "I wanted to talk with you. Privately."

"Oh." She blinked up at him. "What about?"

Dane let out a breath. "Everything. Starting with last night."

"Last night?" She seemed confused as to what he might be referring to, so he decided to clear it up.

"Yes… Particularly what happened after I saved you from the thug."

Caroline cleared her throat. "W-what happened?"

"I kissed you," he said simply.

"Uh-huh." She pursed her lips to hold on to her smile.

"You didn't seem to like it and so I stopped."

Another uh-huh from his wife.

"But then you kissed me. And I got slightly… overwrought."

"Really?" She pursed her lips again.

"Caroline… Firstly, I'd like to apologize for the way I forced myself on you last night."

"You didn't force yourself," she said immediately, and he smiled.

"I am glad that you think so, but what I did was still wrong. You were upset and tired and confused. And my actions couldn't have helped. I took advantage of you during a very delicate situation, and I shouldn't have."

She chased her food with her fork; her features thoughtful. "Oh. So you wish it didn't happen."

"God, no!" Dane clamped his lips shut, but it was too late. The words were out.

Caroline burst out in laughter.

Dane chuckled, too. "I don't regret it for my sake. But you…" He took her hand in his. "You deserve a lot more."

"What do I deserve?" She looked at him as though transfixed.

"A warm bed. Gentle touches. Slow seduction," he said, running his thumb over her hand. Her mouth fell partly open, her eyes darkening. "You deserve tender kisses and long conversations. Not a huge brute of a husband humping you in the back of an alley."

Caroline burst out in laughter. "Humping?"

Dane couldn't help it, he laughed, too. Her laughter was infectious. "Perhaps you deserve a husband who would use gentler language, too. But you have me."

Caroline's smile turned tender. "Your apology was not necessary, but it is accepted nonetheless."

"So, you don't mind what we did?"

She licked her lips, then shook her head.

"And you wouldn't mind doing it again?"

"Doing what? Humping?" She let out a burst of laughter

346

again.

Dane brought her hand to his lips and kissed her fingers. "Yes, humping. And kissing. And perhaps a lot more."

"Dane…" She averted her gaze.

"I won't insist on it now," he said. "Not even tonight. I can wait for you. But last night proved to me that we both feel something more toward each other than animosity, dislike, indifference, or whatever it is you felt toward me when we just married. Things changed, don't you think?"

"Perhaps."

"My darling wife," he said, and she looked up at him again. "We didn't have the best start to our marriage. And to be honest, I never wished for a real marriage. My parents didn't exactly set a perfect example. And I always just assumed that this is how it is supposed to be. But with you… now… I feel it could be different."

She didn't say anything, so Dane lowered his head and pressed his lips against hers. Caroline's hand went to caress his cheek, and he leaned into her touch, rubbing his cheek against her palm.

"So sweet," he murmured against her lips.

"I… um…" She leaned away from his touch. "I don't regret what happened last night, either. But I am not certain I am ready for what you're offering."

Dane's spirits plummeted. "Oh?"

She tried for a smile before turning back to her food. "I need some time to understand what I am feeling."

Dane gave a sharp nod. "You have all the time in the world."

Thank you for reading a deleted scene from *"Taming His Wicked Duchess."* I hope you enjoyed it!

Be sure to read more from *The Shadows* series.

Ingram Content Group UK Ltd.
Milton Keynes UK
UKHW011014300323
419408UK00001B/231